D1784473

By the same author

The Glass Tower
Open Season

DAVID OSBORN

The French Decision

GRANADA

London Toronto Sydney New York

Published by Granada Publishing Limited in 1981
Reprinted 1982

ISBN 0 586 05175 9

First published in Great Britain by
Granada Publishing Limited 1980
Copyright © David Osborn 1980

Granada Publishing Limited
Frogmore, St Albans, Herts AL2 2NF
and
36 Golden Square, London W1R 4AH
866 United Nations Plaza, New York, NY 10017, USA
117 York Street, Sydney, NSW 2000, Australia
100 Skyway Avenue, Rexdale, Ontario, M9W 3A6, Canada
61 Beach Road, Auckland, New Zealand

Set, printed and bound in Great Britain by
Cox & Wyman Ltd, Reading
Set in Intertype Times

Granada ®
Granada Publishing ®

For Sir Robert and Lady Ropner
and all those good times shared.

... whatsoever a man soweth, that shall he also reap ...

Galatians, 6 : 7

Prologue

Fifty miles out of Washington they swung north away from the Shenandoah and the soft Virginia countryside turned raggedly poor and lonely.

In a little while they drove through a heavily rebutted underpass which traversed Interstate Highway 81 and then, just past the West Virginia border, turned down a washboarded dirt road which disappeared into the back-country through sumac and cat briar. Although crowded between two young men in the back seat, it was his first sense of being truly a prisoner since they'd picked him up two hours earlier at his apartment in North Arlington. He wanted to ask who they were, where they were taking him and why. But he couldn't find the courage to face what inner terror told him the answer might be and he kept silent.

In the intense summer heat everything seemed dead. They crossed a stagnant creek on a bridge of old rail ties, splintered and grey from sun and rain. Chalky dust rose in a white cloud behind them. This morning he had risen, showered, breakfasted and had driven across the Potomac into the capital, to the monolith that housed the Department of State. It seemed a lifetime ago.

He worked for the INR, the State Department's Intelligence Research Bureau where he headed a relatively important department. At nine-thirty, a senior executive, looking suspiciously uneasy, had appeared in his office door to summon him upstairs and he'd had an instant stab of premonitory fear. As they silently walked to the elevators, he tried to think of some place along the line where he might have slipped up.

There were a number of people present at his interrogation, mostly top-level men and one he later decided was from the FBI's counter-intelligence unit. It was immediately clear there was no point in his professing innocence. They had him cold. There was only one thing to do. Co-operate.

They seemed appreciative. Coffee was brought in, cigarettes were lit and there was his unexpected overwhelming relief at getting it all off his chest as step-by-step he painstakingly reconstructed every move he had made from the very first day he'd been approached; every phone call; the night-time meetings in the dark anonymity of Rock Creek Park; the cash money paid in advance, and precisely to the last detail, what information he'd sold. He'd withheld only his employer's identity. He did not know it and never had.

'Was he American?'

'Yes.'

'What part?'

'North-east, I should think.'

'Well educated?'

'Yes.'

In the end, and to his surprise, they had sent him home. But they cautioned he would be under strict surveillance, and would be formally arrested within an hour or so. He would face further intensive questioning, but would have the right to a lawyer and, since he was an alien, the right to contact his embassy. Because of his co-operation, he might get off with nothing worse than deportation.

He had felt a surge of loyalty to them, a bond. They'd been extraordinarily decent. But Americans were like that. After all, this wasn't Iran or Paraguay or Chile where interrogation success was usually guaranteed by electric shock or rape or high-pressure water hoses or blow torches, or fingernail extractors or vices designed to slowly crush your testicles. True, here they did train some foreign police in interrogation methods, and had developed certain new techniques using electronics and sound, that was well-known. But apparently it stopped there. Even Amnesty International had not documented torture in the United States.

The narrow dirt road burst abruptly on to an abandoned, summer-parched pasture. Soon they came upon some barns and an old farmhouse, which sat back from a driveway under some stately elms.

As they helped him from his car, he suddenly realized

with a new dread that this place fitted rumours he had heard for years, and which he had always dismissed as nonsense. Some, they said, believed capable of resisting normal interrogatory methods, occasionally and discreetly disappeared to a farm way off in the country. Not officially, of course. Such a place was disowned by officialdom. But the very nature of clandestine authority, as with police power, unfortunately bred men, regardless of country, who felt liberty had to be defended at any cost, and officialdom silently allowed them to exist because they were an indispensable convenience.

He felt rapid and painful blows against his ribs. It was his own heart. It had to be just rumour. In every organization there were always people who whispered and made things up.

They went up worn steps and into an old-fashioned kitchen. There was a man at a table, writing on a note-pad. He was about forty, tall and muscularly thin, and had an air of authority. His facial skin, some of which seemed to have been badly burned, was stretched tight over his cheek-bones. His very short, curly hair was so blond it was nearly white, and he had pale almost albino eyes. He was impeccably manicured and tailored, and had hung the jacket of his business suit neatly over the back of his chair. His voice was slightly nasal, and had the hint of a south-west accent. 'Sit down, won't you?' He accepted a folder from one of the young men from the car, glanced at it and said, 'Ask the doctor to step in, please.'

The prisoner felt a chair move behind his legs, the guiding pressure of a hand. He sat heavily, and heard his own voice, very far away, asking what the doctor was for.

A casual answer. 'Just a routine check-up. We may want to keep you a while.'

His own voice again. 'Please. Why am I here? They said I could have a lawyer. They were going to inform my embassy.' There was no reply. He went on. 'I answered everything this morning. Everything.'

The man at the table studied him fixedly, pale eyes unblinking. He said suddenly, 'Did your anonymous "employer" ever ask you to supply him any information about Dallas?'

'Dallas?'

'The Dallas Research Foundation. Dallas or BAC?'

He tried to think. Dallas Research had recently been formed by certain American oil interests with the ostensible purpose of advising on joint American-European Common Market action against the encroaching energy crisis. Beyond that, he knew nothing about it. BAC meant the Bipartite Advisory Commission on International Affairs, a group of concerned and distinguished public figures who acted as an independent think-tank. He felt bewildered. He knew nothing about BAC either.

He could hardly find his voice. 'Neither one. I'm sorry.' He stared helplessly, gripped even harder by an increasing and nameless terror.

His interrogator looked down at the folder. 'All right,' he said. 'We can discuss them later. Let's go on to France.'

He felt a certain relief. He was on familiar ground again. Virtually all the information he'd turned over to his employer had to do with how much the Americans knew of French military and diplomatic secrets.

'Let's go back to 1962,' his interrogator continued blandly. 'The plot by certain French generals to assassinate Charles de Gaulle when he granted Algeria her independence. De Gaulle always suspected American involvement. Do you know what I am talking about?'

'I know about the plot. Of course.' He'd begun to feel confused again. This was a whole new tack.

'In fact,' his interrogator said, 'he became obsessed with the idea, didn't he?' It was a statement rather than a question. 'So obsessed he ordered his Intelligence to infiltrate ours. We don't mind, really. Everybody does it, especially to their friends. We have people in France, Britain, Germany.' A thin smile. 'Tell me about the French infiltration of our Intelligence.'

Again he found he couldn't speak. Had they confused him with some French agent?

The pale eyes never left his face. 'There were only a handful, as you know, and mostly lower level.' A shrug. 'Technicians. Except for one. One burrowed in with far greater success than all the others put together. Apparently first into the State Department. We understand he worked his way up quite high, that perhaps he had even transferred to another more sensitive agency, perhaps even to the National Security Council.' The thin smile again. 'Tell me about de Gaulle's mole. You know all about him, don't you?'

It was another statement of fact. He shook his head dumbly. He had no answer.

A knock, the doctor came in, a woman. She was young, attractive. Her brown hair was brushed back and tied with a small velvet bow at her neck. She wore a light denim skirt and had slender, nyloned legs. She brought in with her a delicate air of perfume, and her stethoscope seemed out of place against the soft-swelling femininity of her blouse. She smiled and said 'Hello', and put down her medical bag and took out a blood-pressure apparatus. Someone helped him remove his coat and shirt. The doctor glanced into his face and frowned, and then carefully studied each of his pupils with her flashlight. She wrapped the blood-pressure tourniquet around his arm and pumped it up and listened to his heartbeat.

'When was your last medical? Did you by any chance have a cardiogram?' Her voice was matter-of-fact and pleasant. She looked at him reassuringly, eyes warm.

Presently she said to the interrogator, 'He's going to need a tranquillizer.' She finished with his blood-pressure and heart and rummaged in her medical bag for a hypodermic. She smiled. 'Just Valium.' There was a needle prick. She made some quick notations in the folder. He felt very faint.

One day at the office someone had shown a photograph he claimed proved the rumour. It was supposed to have been taken a month after the nuclear-power accident in California and the subsequent Washington sit-in with all its arrests. It was underexposed and crudely developed but you could make out stained tile walls lit by an unshaded bulb. A carcass was hung from an overhead rail by flesh hooks pushed through the tough gristle of the ears, and although

11

there were no longer any breasts or genitals and the skin had been flayed away apparently with searing heat, so that it hung down everywhere in tattered strips, you could still recognize it as human. And female. But, of course, the picture could have been taken anywhere. Others like it, documenting foreign police horrors, passed through the office quite often.

It took an immense effort to speak. 'I told them everything this morning. I know nothing about French infiltration.'

Nobody answered. The doctor packed up her medical bag.

'You've got to believe me. I didn't hide anything.' He was crying. Actually crying like a child. He couldn't stop.

'Would you mind standing, please.' A firm hand helped him to his feet. He was asked to strip. He looked at the young doctor for help. She smiled sympathetically and then left the room and he realized dully that they probably wanted to search him. Prisoners sometimes tried to destroy themselves. They had to guard against that. But he wanted her back. Somehow she was safety.

'Your shoes, please.'

He kicked them off. Only his underpants remained. The frail fabric suddenly seemed ultimately protective.

'And your pants, please.'

He fumbled. They dropped with a hush to the linoleum floor.

'Now spread your legs, please. That's right. And bend forward slightly, and hold your buttocks apart.'

Yes, it was an anal probe. Embarrassing and uncomfortable. And they would find nothing.

He obeyed. The interrogator nodded faintly to one of the young men, who went behind him.

And just then he knew instinctively it wasn't to be a probe at all. But it was too late to stop it.

The unexpected sound of a body in sudden exertion. A lightning scrape against the inside of one thigh and the shoe slammed into his softly pendulous testicles.

His scream became everything. Even before the pain

roared in a wrenching tunnel up through his body and straight to his mind. It had the sharp substance of a knife and was dark and deafening and went on and on and on, twisting and cutting, until finally it receded slowly, and he was lying on the floor, curled up, his mouth opening and shutting against its soiled surface, his face and chest wet from his own puke, and his screams died to a whimper. Hands pulled him to his feet and propelled him into the blinding heat of the yard and towards a small stone building near the barns. His legs wouldn't work, his feet dragged. The doctor reappeared buttoning on a white smock. She studied him briefly and professionally.

She shook her head. 'I think you're wasting your time. He isn't going to talk.'

'They all do.'

She smiled. 'Oh, I'm not saying he won't *want* to. I didn't mean that. I meant I really don't think he has anything more to say.' She lifted his chin from his chest with two slender fingers, grimacing slightly at his vomit, searching his eyes. 'Can you remember anything you didn't tell them?' She was gentle, caring. 'Try.'

Words formed in his mind, an answer, but wouldn't reach his mouth. She shrugged at the others. 'I'll be along shortly, then. Not more than a minute or so the first time. I'm not certain of his heart.'

She went back to the house.

Incoherent sounds finally tumbled out. His mouth babbled. Hands dragged him forward again. When they shoved him into the damp coolness of the stone house he felt a hot flood sheet his legs. Somebody cursed. His bowels had voided.

They turned on a light. He saw the stained tiles and the overhead rail with its hanging flesh hooks and tried to breathe so that he could scream at the injustice. He hadn't lied. He'd told them everything. He had nothing more to reveal. Nothing at all.

Washington–Oxford, Maryland

Chapter One

It was mid-August and Washington suffered an unrelenting heat-wave. For days there had not been even a thunderstorm to clear the muggy, suffocating air. Only early in the morning was there any respite. Then, the sleeping city cooled briefly and was bearable for an hour or two before it heated up again.

Aaron Zeismann awoke at seven in the small duplex he and his wife owned on a quiet back street of Georgetown. Their basic home was in the country at Oxford across the Chesapeake Bay but it was too long a daily commute, and since Juliet worked too they usually both stayed in town during the middle of the week.

He felt the momentary freshness of the early morning on his naked skin and sat up. Beside him, Juliet slept face upward, her slender, long-limbed body still sprawled against the heat of the night, her deep, full breasts sagging impersonally, her rich, straight, dark hair partially fanned over the pillow and partially over the gentle set of her almost perfect features.

Outside, a tree rustled in the last vestiges of the light breeze which had risen at dawn. Down the block, someone started up a car and there were footsteps on the sidewalk. A new day had begun.

Aaron rose quietly and went downstairs. He collected drink glasses from the night before from the living-room and took them to the kitchen. Crossing the front hall, he caught sight of himself in the mirror over the sideboard. He was always surprised at seeing himself. In his inner mind he felt himself fair and rather powerfully tall, some vague memory of his long-dead Air Force stepfather, when in fact he was only of medium height, hardly an inch taller than Juliet, and lean and Semitic and dark-skinned. And his hair, hardly blond, was like his mother's; a thick, unruly, black

17

mane low on his forehead above deep-set eyes. A faint, jagged scar ran across his left cheek and into a nose which had been broken several times. There was another, smaller scar where glass had once nicked the outside corner of his right eye, making it at times appear to be sightless. None of it went with his voice which was cultivated and confident, nor with his smile which was gentle and often touched with a kind of sadness. He was thirty-four, six years older than Juliet. They had been married eight years and were childless, largely due to his own insistence. There would be time for children later.

In the kitchen he put on the kettle and had just made coffee when Juliet appeared, still half-drugged from sleep and smiling shyly because they had made love during the night and now it was morning and suddenly she felt as defenceless in her daylight nakedness as he himself did on seeing her.

She put her arms around him to be kissed, and when he smelled the sleepiness of her face and neck and felt her warm skin and the softness of her breasts against his chest, he awoke sexually and in spite of himself.

She laughed and touched him affectionately with slender, cool fingers. 'You're incorrigible,' she said. 'And I love it.' And then more seriously, 'And I love you, too. Do you understand me? I love you.'

She studied his face and read his eyes. It was the truth. She loved him almost unreasonably and always had. She loved him even though she had never quite been able to touch a vulnerability she was sure lay deep and lonely beneath an exterior often coldly remote and difficult to live with. And she loved his body and his scarred Semitic face which always made her think of a fighter who had stayed in the game a year too long.

She kissed him again, quickly and hard and pulled away. 'We'll be late for work and we have a long day. And a dinner tonight, remember? Is Senator Strachey still coming?'

'He hasn't called to say he's changed his mind. Did Helen?'

'No. So they are.'

18

Juliet took her coffee, and they went back upstairs. They showered together, and he shaved while she dressed and went downstairs to call Esther about the vegetables she should prepare that afternoon. Esther was their nearest neighbour at Oxford, a black farm-woman who lived down the road and whose husband raised tobacco. She helped Juliet with freezing garden produce in the autumn and if they were having important people for dinner as they were tonight. She also looked after Robert Quincy when they were in town. Robert was the young Irish setter Aaron had given Juliet a year ago for her birthday, and Esther had persuaded them she didn't mind looking after the dog for three days every mid-week. It was far better, she said, than taking the poor animal into the steaming heat of Washington.

When Aaron came back downstairs, Juliet was off the telephone and had made more coffee and set out toast. At eight they picked up their briefcases, and Juliet pulled a comb through her hair a last time. She wore it shoulder length as a straight, dark frame to her face.

'Aaron, can you get away about three?'

'Sure.'

'There are things I'll need to buy in town.'

They went out and he mortice-locked the front door for the week-end. 'You haven't told anyone Strachey's coming?'

'No. You said not to.'

'Okay.'

'Although you still haven't said why.' She smiled but there was a faint resentment in her tone.

Aaron didn't answer.

'You're a bastard,' she complained. 'It has to do with Dallas, doesn't it? Richard Ender doesn't like Strachey.'

'If you insist.'

'No. But he doesn't. Well, you can tell Richard Ender your wife doesn't like *him*!'

'All right. I'm not particularly in love with him myself.'

'And I don't like Dallas, either.' Juliet was suddenly vaguely petulant.

Aaron again didn't answer. They came down the white limestone steps of the old house's front stoop and headed for their car, parked a block away.

Richard Ender was Aaron's boss. When the current administration had taken over two years ago, he had been appointed first assistant to the White House Chief-of-Staff, a position which had made him an important member of the Oval Room's new inner circle. Nine months ago, with the unofficial blessing of the President himself, he had quietly resigned to set up the Dallas Research Foundation. With little prior knowledge of Europe, Ender soon found he needed help. Aaron, in charge of French economic and political evaluation for the National Security Council and an expert on the Common Market, was recommended by none other than the NSC chief himself, the President's all-powerful National Security Adviser. Offered a fifty per cent increase in salary, Aaron did not refuse and in the last few months, since Dallas also had offices in Paris, had spent a great deal of time in France.

'I wish to God you'd stayed where you were,' Juliet said.

'Dallas isn't going to last forever,' said Aaron. 'We'll light up the world and I'll come back to the NSC and steal the old man's job from him, and the Zeismanns will live happily ever after.'

It was meant to bring a smile back to her face and it did, but only partially. Besides being away so much, Aaron nowadays often seemed totally distracted and Juliet could not get through to him. On Monday, and quite unexpectedly, she had flared up. They had been driving to Oxford, and she had suddenly burst out, 'I don't like your goddamned France.'

He had been surprised by her vehemence.

'Oh?'

'And I don't like you when you go there. That's some other life you have. It has nothing to do with us. And you become some other person.'

'Hey, calm down.'

He'd reached out to touch her. She pulled away and was

silent, ashamed. It was totally unlike her, she simply wasn't that sort of woman. But when they came over the South Capitol Street bridge, she had lost control again.

'You can't spend all your free time over there alone.'

'Where? Who?' He'd lost track. 'What are you talking about?'

'Fucking France!' Savagely biting off each word, deliberately using bad language, which again wasn't like her, to let him know she was serious, and hating herself for what she was doing but unable to stop.

He'd said, wary now, 'What are you getting at, Juliet?'

'You have evenings and weekends. Days on end. You've been in France for months this year.'

His smile had slowly vanished. 'What the hell are you trying to do, build a case for my having a girl friend?'

'Well, don't you?'

'No. I don't.'

'A man as virile as you? You mean you actually save it all for the little American wife back home?'

'Shut up.'

'Telling me to shut up is hardly an answer is it?' She'd cried and then said, 'I hate my goddamned job, too. I'm going to quit, and come with you next time you go.'

Of course she wouldn't. It was simply to get in the last word and he knew it. When he dropped her off at the Smithsonian where she worked, she'd apologized, leaving them both awkward and vaguely uneasy.

Bloody Dallas Research, Aaron had thought. What would her reaction be if she knew the real reason for it? What would she think of the torments of sleepless nights and perpetual fear that had been his lot for the last nine months? And what would she say if she knew that since yesterday he had been under surveillance again? The man parked in the new blue Chevy, a few trees down from the front door of their Georgetown duplex, had been there since yesterday evening. And their phone was again tapped.

A blonde little girl was out on the sidewalk playing hopscotch. She stopped to let them walk by.

'My turn,' Juliet cried spontaneously. She leapt nimbly

from square to square and back. 'Beat that,' she challenged Aaron.

He did. 'Hold this,' he said to the child. He handed her his briefcase. He made it to 'in' and back without putting a foot wrong and triumphantly stuck his tongue out at Juliet.

They reached their car, laughing, and drove away, and even the presence of the Chevy behind them didn't upset him the way it had. Instead of fear and unease he suddenly felt a bright, hard anger. He wanted to stop and reverse full speed into whoever it was. Perhaps at some later date he damn well would.

Outside the Smithsonian, Juliet stretched across the seat and turned his face to hers and pressed her mouth against his. It was the sort of kiss a woman gave a man only when she wanted him to make love to her.

'That's not playing fair,' he said.

She laughed. 'Did you ever know a woman who did?'

She got out of the car and he watched her long legs swing across the pavement, and then the huge glass doors of the Smithsonian opened to swallow her behind them.

Aaron headed for the Watergate offices of the Dallas Research Foundation and the Chevy followed discreetly behind.

Chapter Two

The same day, British Airways Concorde, Flight BA 579, landed at Washington's Dulles International Airport at 12:05 Eastern Daylight time. The plane had left London's Heathrow Airport at 13:00 London time, three hours and thirty minutes earlier. The temperature was ninety-three degrees Fahrenheit, with humidity at ninety per cent, air-pollution level at one hundred and nineteen, visibility a hazy four miles, and the wind south-west at only two miles per hour.

The British passport of one of the passengers said his name was Anthony Williams, and that he lived at 14 Thurgood Crescent, London SW7. His age was given as sixty-two, his profession was reported as computer engineer, and his next of kin was listed as a sister, one Miss Margaret Williams living near Coventry.

In physical appearance he was of medium height, tending to overweight, and his business suit, typically middle-class academia in style, was almost permanently rumpled. Above bland, green eyes which seemed to miss nothing, and whose brows were perpetually arched in vague surprise, wispy, grey hair gave him a benign and clerical look. The permanently stained index and third fingers of his right hand testified that he had once been a chain smoker. As did a battered old silver cigarette-case. But the case now seemed to contain nothing more harmful than a plentiful supply of life-savers which he sucked on with near compulsion as a customs officer rifled his luggage, one valise and a substantial but rather shabby briefcase. On the plane the air hostess had placed his accent as Midlands, and, sizing him up through the protective blue screen of her mascaraed lashes, she had also dismissed him as probably either asexual or queer.

Customs formalities completed, he entered a cab and gave the driver the name of a downtown hotel. His valise went in the cab's boot, but he kept his briefcase on the seat next to him. In it were colour slides and a mass of printed material pertaining to the use of computers as applied to medical pathology, both in diagnosis and data management. There was also a schedule for workshops to be held in medical schools in Washington, New York and Boston, and several introductory letters from the President of the Royal College of Surgeons.

When the cab was well free of the airport and on the way to Washington, he glanced once more at the headlines of the *Washington Post* he had brought off the plane. They were filled with the usual horror Americans as well as others had nearly but not quite learned to live with. The world as man had so long known it was unravelling. Fear, and a sort of anarchistic chaos, stalked everywhere and everyone.

He put the paper down and stared at the green blur of trees that was the passing roadside. On the editorial page he had read a sober warning by one of America's more responsible Elder Statesmen of journalism.

'In the emergencies we live with,' the old man had written, 'there are some who prefer not to wait for legitimate legislative wheels to turn in their favour. In the guise of patriotic expediency, how easy not to consult people, either their cumbersome congress or their fallible executive, but to present them at some later date with subversive illegality made palatable by public-relations sugar paid for from their own taxes. In such a way the Nazis took power in Germany.'

He wondered if the old man had any idea how close he had come to the truth, that the American giant, still suffering the traumas of divisive war and unprecedented political scandal, should be already spawning an equal if not greater monstrosity.

Perhaps, though, it were better he had not. Recently, one George Whitney Babcock, a British subject, had unwittingly, while selling some minor State Department secrets, come only within shouting distance of it. He had been interrogated, then had disappeared. Few suspected what had actually happened to him, that at a remote farm in West Virginia he had suffered an obscene and senseless death, undeserved by a non-professional who only needed money to sustain a Washington lifestyle beyond his means.

In spite of the intense heat, the passenger from BA Flight 579 shivered. He was on the ground now, in their country, totally exposed as Babcock had been, and protected ultimately by no one except himself. He forced his mind off it, and leaned back and closed his eyes and dwelt on the business he'd come for.

Before he knew it he was at the hotel. He checked in, and was shown to a high room with a splendid view of the whole Mall from the Capitol to the Lincoln Memorial and even beyond to the wide Potomac, moving sluggishly past the white flanks of the Kennedy Center. Washington, he'd always thought, was paradoxically the most European of cities, the Potomac one of the most American of rivers.

He washed his hands, enjoying the coolness of the room's vital air conditioning. And suddenly the telephone rang. The caller said they were delighted he had arrived safely and to come around as soon as it suited him. Awful weather. Unbearably hot. They'd have some iced tea ready. It was the headquarters of the American Society of Pathologists.

He hung up. Parts of the sky had darkened perceptibly. Perhaps there'd be a thunderstorm. He tucked his walnut-handled umbrella under his arm, and with a firm grip on his briefcase went downstairs again.

Out on the street, a well-shaded thermometer said the temperature had risen four more degrees to ninety-seven. He eased into the back seat of a waiting taxi, and gave the address of the Society. It was suffocating. He began to roll down a window, the driver complained; outside air would spoil the air conditioning. He obediently rolled the window back up. Beneath his jacket, his drip-dry shirt was already soaked.

As they came down K Street, he spotted a public telephone booth. He ordered the driver to stop. When the cab had disappeared into traffic, his slightly surprised eyes confronted the avenue. It was habit. He was certain he had not been followed. They had become such technocrats, the Americans, and so dependent on electronics, that they had nearly lost the simple art of keeping an eye on someone.

The door of the booth closed. He selected a number from memory, put in a dime, inwardly grumbling at the minute size of American money. He dialled. The phone rang four times. A switchboard voice answered, professionally crisp.

'Good afternoon, French Embassy.' And when he did not immediately speak, '*Allô . . . l'Ambassade Française!*'

He had covered the mouthpiece with a Kleenex, then his handkerchief, protection against a possible voice print. Like everyone else these days, the French Embassy taped all phone calls. He spoke slowly and in appallingly accented French.

'*L'Attaché des Affaires Culturelles, s'il vous plaît.*'

In a moment he was connected to a secretary. He asked again for the Attaché. The response came in perfect English.

'I'm afraid he hasn't returned from lunch yet, sir. May I help you?'

He felt a certain satisfaction. He'd timed it well. He really didn't want to speak to the Attaché at all. He had nothing to say to him. He said, still in his insistently awful French, 'Will you please tell him Mr Williams called?'

'Williams?'

'Anthony Williams. From London.' He spelled both names.

'Was there a telephone number, Mr Williams?'

'He'll know where to reach me.'

'Very well, sir. I'll see he receives the message as soon as he comes in. Thank you.'

He came out drenched from the steaming booth. The message he'd left would make sense to only one person, the man who would phone the Attaché that afternoon from some other public phone having received a non-committal postcard addressed to a box-number in Washington's Central Post Office and signed with a pseudonym. The man would ask if a Mr Anthony Williams had checked in. Although neither the French Ambassador nor the First Secretary could any longer be considered reliable, the Attaché still was, and would say 'yes' and the caller would thus verify a prearranged rendezvous.

He hailed another taxi and once more gave the address of the Society of Pathologists.

The driver was listening to Cincinnati playing Boston. No one was at bat at the moment so there was time for him to note that his passenger was English, kept lifesavers in a cigarette-case, and was more the type to ask to be taken to the National Geographic Society than to where he'd find 'go-go' action.

He was right in every observation but the first. If he had been among certain people high in governmental circles in Paris, he would have known his passenger was in fact not English at all but profoundly French and that his real name was not Anthony Williams but Paul Henri Bejerec, a Breton by birth. Bejerec was indeed going to visit the American Society of Pathologists. Just as he was later going to conduct a series of workshops for he was indeed an expert on the use of computers in medical pathology.

But there was a little more to it. Computers were just an engrossing sideline and the workshops only part of a complex cover for his real work. That work was covert intelligence and espionage. Paul Henri Bejerec was director of the North Atlantic Treaty Section of the SDECE, the Service de Documentation Extérieure et de Contre Espionage, the French Central Intelligence organization, and this visit to the United States had been unexpectedly precipitated by the recent 'terminal interrogation' in West Virginia of George Babcock, a relatively innocent incompetent who had been deliberately employed by one of his own agents as a decoy.

Chapter Three

At eleven the following morning, Aaron was playing tennis at the Congressional Club with Richard Ender. They played every Friday; Ender insisted on it. They left the office the moment they had answered their mail and squared away a day's work for their secretaries.

Ender was tall, athletic, his hair beginning to grey at thirty-eight but his boyish face still unlined. He wore heavy horn-rims when reading, and besides tennis indulged in *avant-garde* films, backgammon and downhill skiing with his three children.

He and Aaron were good and played hard. The first to win two sets bought drinks, and usually Aaron paid. It was worth it. Beating Ender, he'd found, helped keep him from becoming over-authoritative and demanding.

By eleven-thirty, however, Aaron had lost the first set four–six and the score was five–all in the second. He'd let the blue Chevy get under his skin. It was waiting for him in the club parking lot.

He tore sweat from his forehead with his wristband and readied himself for Ender's serve. The heat was unbearable.

'Forty–thirty,' Ender said. His white tennis shorts and shirt were drenched and sweat rivuleted his tanned legs above his high tennis socks. He bounced a ball to gain concentration. It made a small yellow blur, up and down, up and down.

Something about it reminded Aaron of another game, one he and Ender had played on a far more exclusive court. It was the summer before. He had not yet joined Dallas Research, and had been asked by the National Security Adviser, still his boss, to meet Ender and the President at Camp David. When their appointment was postponed until lunch, Ender had suggested tennis.

Only twenty-four hours before, Aaron had been briefed

by the Adviser for the first time on the real reason for the Dallas Research Foundation and on an unprecedented, top-secret recommendation made to the White House by BAC, the prestigious Bipartite Advisory Commission.

He had always thought himself a hardened cynic. Certainly he had tacitly accepted that the 'Bipartite' in BAC was hollow public relations. BAC's board was composed of men from major chemicals, heavy industry, banks and oil and by no one else. Just the same, he was unprepared for what he learned. Energy and runaway inflation were inseparable and unless the President could get both under control, BAC said, he would almost certainly lose the next election when they would be major issues. BAC, whose vital interests lay entirely with his winning, suggested that the only possible solution lay in an immediate double-edged, covert action sponsored by the White House, but in private hands. Its aim would be, first, to gain control of as many European oil reserves as possible and second, to use this control to force European co-operation in markedly reducing exports to the US while accepting massive increased US imports into Europe. The resulting vast new market-place would stimulate an anti-inflationary rise in American productivity with the American public enjoying simultaneous relief from crippling oil shortages.

BAC had also recommended they first make a test case of one nation and France had been decided on since in many ways France, even more than West Germany, was the kingpin of European economy. If all went well, Britain, Germany and Italy would follow suit. And then Japan. In whatever economic chaos was sure to ensue, BAC judged that the US would come out on top and thus the operation would be worth the risk.

'But French oil is almost entirely nationalized,' Aaron had protested.

The Adviser had smiled. 'Yes, but nationalization, as you know, is often only as good as the government in power. Our friends in the present French government guarantee us at least a fifth of their reserves. With energy as scarce as it's fast becoming, a twenty per cent slice of it is enough to control any French government of the future.' He raised a hand at the protest written on Aaron's face and smiled again. 'Before one points the finger of treason, Aaron, look at it from their point of view. Euro-Communism is a serious threat. In the event of a Communist election victory in France where would France be if we didn't have real leverage over her economy? Out of NATO and into the Warsaw Pact, surely. That's what they're imagining over there. So you see?' He put a hand on Aaron's shoulder and added matter-of-factly, 'The actual procedure will be up to the Dallas Research Foundation, to Ender and you. Money is no object. Our source is unlimited. The operation will be code-named Tricolor.'

Nothing was mentioned about subverting the powers of Congress, nor about betraying a major ally, bound to the United States by tradition as well as treaty. That had all been somehow justified. Democracy could be sold out in an emergency in order to save it. Aaron thought, it's not the sort of thing we hand out to the Third World, but it isn't the Third World, it's France, and the French people, who were surely one of the greatest people ever, would know nothing until it was too late. Like everyone else these days, they were being sold south by a government which in the name of expediency did whatever it pleased in secret and behind closed doors, and to hell with those who elected it. He felt a sudden surge of fury and angry loyalty to the French. And at the same time, dull helplessness.

Lunch was low-key, the President affable, conversation general. Neither Dallas nor BAC were discussed. Aaron knew he was there only to be impressed by the silent participation of the President himself. Uppermost in his own mind was the appalling realization that his transfer to Dallas was simply taken as fact. What their contingency arrangements for him were if he'd said 'no' were unthinkable. They had disclosed something to him far more than just 'top secret'.

After lunch, when the President had gone to phone his wife back in Washington, the Adviser had taken Aaron on a brief stroll across the shaded lawns, and he'd said suddenly,

'Aaron, there is only one thing for me to add. Should anything ever surface, this country cannot afford to see its executive involved. Do we understand each other?'

'Yes, sir.'

There had been a sudden flurry at Aspen Lodge as the President came out with an entourage of Secret Service men.

The Adviser had thrust out his hand. 'Good luck, Aaron. We'll welcome you back at National Security when this is over. And my regards to Juliet. Wonderful girl.'

Five minutes later the presidential helicopter was on its way north to Gettysburg where the President was to make a commemorative speech.

The past rolled forward to the present and the soft Catoctin Hills beyond Camp David gave way to the distant Washington Monument, barely visible through a haze of summer pollution.

Aaron heard Ender say, 'Whenever you're ready.' Impatiently.

The service was his. He put his whole being into it. Ender could only half come up from his crouch, the ball was too fast for his reflex.

'Beautiful, Aaron.' Awed.

'Fifteen–love,' Aaron muttered. He picked up two balls. He felt a fierce anger. You're dead, Ender, he thought. You've had it.

But suddenly he remembered he mustn't beat Ender. Not today. Today he needed him happy and riding on the crest. Because of the Chevy in the parking lot, he was going to wreck Ender's afternoon and probably his weekend, too. It wasn't good politics to put him down first. He cursed inwardly. Goddamn Ender, goddamn all of it. The United States of goddamned America and France and the goddamned heat and tennis, too.

Ten minutes later, when they walked off the court, the only satisfaction to Aaron in losing was that Ender was unaware he'd been handed it gratis.

They showered and settled as usual in the club's quiet bar and ordered drinks. Aaron listened patiently to Ender's triumph, feeding it. He wanted him just right.

Ender ordered another round. 'Are we lunching?'

Aaron begged off, explaining that he had to leave Washington early. He was relieved when Ender didn't ask him who his dinner guests would be, but realized Ender's mind was already on his own afternoon and evening. Ender was no longer close to his wife. She'd become too militantly activist. It was not the moment for divorce, however, so Ender kept up pretences and along with them a downtown studio-apartment where he could meet whatever current eligible he'd impressed among Washington's veritable army of bright young collegiate women.

Aaron knew it was now or never to destroy it for him. 'At the risk of turning the day sour,' he said carefully, 'there's something I am forced to bring up.'

Ender concentrated. 'What's that?'

'I'm afraid it's Larsen again,' Aaron said. He told Ender about the blue Chevrolet and waited. Ender's face slowly assumed the crucified expression he increasingly wore these days. Much had happened since the Camp David meeting. The delicate, covert task of transferring ownership of certain French oil reserves into American hands was well on its way. But there was trouble, too. The major oil interests financing Tricolor had taken advantage of the Adviser's and the President's discreet withdrawal to force their man on Dallas Research as 'consultant'. He was the new Ambassador to France, Ryan 'Banjo' Collins, and he had emerged as a real executive-suite threat to Richard Ender. Among other things, he had forced on Dallas, as so-called Director of Security, the veteran, FBI, counter-espionage specialist, Arnheimer Larsen, a man suggested as responsible for the rumoured murder of the State Department's wayward George Babcock.

Ender had finally found his voice. 'You're kidding me.' He sounded in acute pain.

'I'm afraid not.'

'Collins gave me his word it would stop,' Ender protested. He drained his drink bleakly. 'Is there any chance, Aaron, it's somebody else? And not Larsen?'

Aaron gave him no quarter. 'Whom do you suggest? The

Washington Police with some old parking tickets?' He put his own drink down hard. 'I'm sorry, Richard. I can't live or work this way. And I'm not having Juliet subjected to it, either. I mean it. He's going to have to try out his half-baked paranoia about French spies on someone else.'

He waited. Briefly, he felt sorry for Ender. It was too late in the game to fire Larsen. He'd left it too long and Collins had become too powerful. So, like it or not, he would have to cancel his date and spend the afternoon on the phone to Collins in Paris. Wearily but angrily, he would again risk loss of prestige by defending his right-hand man, his brilliant record, his many total security clearances by the FBI and other agencies. 'If being born abroad makes him a spy,' he would shout, 'you can lock up a lot of people in Washington, including one former Secretary of State. Then he would attack Larsen, reminding Collins of Larsen's ugly past in Vietnam and Uruguay, and his work training secret police for the Shah of Iran.

It would get him nowhere. Collins would first agree and laugh at the 'de Gaulle mole' legend: no one could seriously believe the French had successfully infiltrated American intelligence. Then he would probably quote his favourite historic figure, Cardinal Richelieu; trust no man for more than thirty days, he would say, and advise Ender that what they were doing warranted continued surveillance of *all* personnel, themselves included. The history of covert activity was littered with unthinkable defections.

If Ender had any fight left when he finally put down the receiver, he'd remember that the call would be on record. If anything ever did go wrong, he would be personally liable for refusing to take what Collins could justifiably claim were routine security precautions. His chagrin would be bitter. For the sake of politics, however, Collins would order Larsen to lay off for a week and in ten days' time, Aaron knew, he would be back in Paris where he stood an even chance of being able to handle Larsen himself and where if anything went wrong he could blame it on the French.

Ender suddenly squared his shoulders. 'You are right, of

course, Aaron, and I'm very sorry about it. I'll see to it immediately.'

'Thank you,' Aaron said. He put as much sincerity as he could into his smile. 'You needed this like a hole in the head, Richard.'

Ender managed a smile back. 'It's not your fault, is it?'

'Hardly. But I still feel badly about it.'

Ender ordered another round of drinks. It was bad, Aaron thought. More and more, Ender would be victim to a lurking suspicion: 'What other reason for Larsen's persistence except that he's right?' He would push it away but it would stay just the same. Evil was like that. Larsen's face rose briefly before his eyes, a dream figure of unspeakable horror, relentlessly pursuing.

They left half an hour later. Walking to their cars, Aaron couldn't resist pointing out the blue Chevy.

'That guy there,' he said.

As he drove away, he looked back. Ender was still staring at the Chevy, his expression one of disbelief and outrage, both at once.

Join the fraternity, Aaron thought.

Chapter Four

Out on Maryland's eastern shore, Esther Harris straightened slowly from weeding rows of carrots in the vegetable garden next to her farmhouse. She was a big, heavy, middle-aged woman and weeding was sweatwork for her. One time the children had done it but now they were all teenagers and racketing around some place, disdaining such misery as keeping the family food supply going.

Robert Quincy was missing again. Today he had already twice trotted back to the Zeismanns' house down by the estuary, once before lunch and once afterwards, and twice she had to go and fetch him back. He'd been after a rabbit and hadn't wanted to come, so the second time she'd taken his chain collar and leash and put them on and used the occasion to make him 'heel' the way Juliet always did. Back in her garden she had slipped the leash over a tomato stake so that she wouldn't have to watch him for a while. Now the stake was on the ground.

'Robert?'

The only answering sound was her husband's distant tractor out on their broad tobacco-fields.

Esther shaded her glistening, ebony brow with one dark-skinned hand. Her eyes swept the front yard, blistering in the heat, and she called again.

'Robert Quincy?'

She whistled.

'Drat the dog.' But she loved him almost as much as Juliet did and she laughed. After all, he was just a yearling, like one of her own children, really. Into everything, but nothing for more than a very short time.

She sighed, and wiped her hands on her skirt, and left the garden for the dusty dirt road which went by her house.

It was only a few hundred yards. Once past the biggest of

her husband's fields Esther could see first the red-brick chimney between the crowns of the acacias and sycamores that separated the two properties, then the white clapboarding and faded blue shutters of the old colonial house itself and the small adjacent barn which served as a garage and guest quarters.

She reached the brick walk which led between high rows of sweet-smelling box to the front door.

'Robert? Robert Quincy? You come right here.'

There was no sound. Only a dead stillness that struck Esther as out of place. Not a bird spoke, not a squirrel rustled.

She went up the walk and out on to the lawn.

'Robert?'

She whistled and called. The lawn was silent. She went down to the dock and pebbled beach. Fifty yards from the shore, out on the mirrored surface of the estuary, Aaron Zeismann's sleek, six-metre racing sloop seemed out of place in its total lack of motion, its mooring-line slack, its white hull's reflection unbroken by even the slightest ripple. Not a breath of air stirred.

Esther called again and then gave up and came back. Half way across the lawn she suddenly thought, maybe he'd got in the barn somehow. There were swallows up in the rafters, and although they had already nested and gone, sometimes Robert Quincy would sit by the hour looking up at where the nests were tantalizingly out of reach.

She entered the barn by the side door nearest the house and stopped dead. The main doors were partially open on to the road. That wasn't right. They had been closed earlier.

'Robert?'

The light pouring through the doors made the rest of the barn's beamy interior contrastingly gloomy and hard to see. Esther felt a vague, uneasy fear prickle up the back of her neck.

'Robert Quincy?'

Silence.

And then she saw him.

36

His dark-red body, stretched out lean and long by its own weight, hung suspended by its chain collar and leash from an overhead beam where someone had hooked the leash's loop handle over the shaft of a heavy bolt.

A scream rushed up Esther's throat to burst out in hoarse words. 'Oh, my God!'

She ran and pushed the barn doors wide open, and the hot August light poured in all the way, turned the red fur to flame. She reached out to touch the body and couldn't bring herself to. The tongue protruded almost black from the slack lips, which grimaced away to reveal the long rows of sharp white teeth. The brown eyes rolled grotesquely to one side and bulged vacantly. There was a pool of faeces and urine below the feet, and flies came to it the moment it was struck by the hot light from outside. Half an hour ago she'd playfully tossed a clod of earth to keep him quiet, and laughed when he'd chewed at it.

Who had done this? And when? Had she heard the motor of a car a little while back? Where were they now?

She went out. The road bent sharply for Oxford two miles away. There was no car in sight. Or were they still here somewhere? She could hear her own heart pounding, and almost couldn't move for the sudden terror that gripped her. She forced her feet towards her own house, walking more and more quickly, finally running, looking back repeatedly over her shoulder. Her husband would have to come and take the dog down. It couldn't be left there for Juliet to find when she came home this afternoon. And she was giving a party tonight. For important people. Aaron would know what to do. The police would have to come.

In the coolness of her own kitchen, Esther Harris found Aaron's office number and dialled it, and when the operator answered she asked for him desperately.

'Justa tell him it's his neighbour Esther Harris and I don't care what he's doing, I have to speak to him right away.'

And she waited. Who would want to do such a thing to the Zeismanns? And why? What could either of them have possibly ever done to make someone hate them like this?

And if they started with a defenceless dog like Robert Quincy, where in the name of God would it end, in what evil and darkness?

When Aaron came on the phone, Esther finally felt her first rush of tears. She could hardly speak.

Chapter Five

Paul Henri Bejerec had the taxi drop him off on Capitol Hill at a random 19th Street number. As was his habit, he waited until it disappeared, then with practised eye studied the quiet residential street. It was peacefully village-like, its thick, arboured trees a dark, cooling shade over its cracked sidewalks. At the corner two young wives, the backs and underarms of their summer frocks dark with perspiration, were talking over shopping trolleys. Nearby, another, older woman, still in her dressing-gown, watered thirsty window-boxes and talked in cultured tones to her husband who weeded the flagstone walk to their front door.

There was nobody else.

Bejerec tucked a book under his arm and headed slowly in the direction of the Library of Congress Annexe a few blocks away, a vast, neo-classic, six-storey monstrosity of cluttered offices encircling a massive centre core of reading-rooms and stacks.

Once inside, he took an elevator to the fifth floor. There, relieved by the carefully modulated air-conditioning, he made his way down a vaulted marble hall to the high-ceilinged Science Reading room, where scores of readers, heads aglow from green-shaded brass reading-lamps, bent silently to the printed word at long, highly-polished oak tables.

He crossed the room, and at the other side casually exited into a long corridor flanked by busy clerical rooms governing the functionary work involved in the library's foreign collections. At the end of the corridor he glanced behind him for the first time. It was empty. He turned down a narrow fire stair, and at the half-landing pulled open a heavy steel door clearly marked 'Restricted Area'. It thudded shut behind him, and he found himself in a vast and faintly-lit place whose endless close-spaced bookshelves were crammed, floor to low ceiling, with books. It was one of the main stacks.

Bejerec carefully counted his way ten rows along a tight, shoulder-wide aisle and waited in the tomb-like silence and gloom, inhaling the unique musty smell little-used books give off. It was so quiet he could hear his own wrist watch tick and the beat of his own heart which seemed inordinately loud. It was two o'clock. He was dead on time.

Presently there was the muffled sound of a door opening and shutting, and a whispered scuffing of moccasins that grew increasingly audible until a young black woman appeared. Her hair was close-cropped on a finely aristocratic head; her hands were slender and her young body slim in tight jeans and a white shirt. But her dark eyes were impenetrable, and she didn't smile. People who are blackmailed seldom do and she was an illegal immigrant from French-speaking Martinique in the Caribbean. The man she had come to meet had that over her and it guaranteed her silence which was all-important.

To identify himself he held out his book, a copy of Camus's *The Plague*. He had borrowed it the last time he had visited Washington. 'Would you be so kind,' he said, 'as to see that this is returned?'

She took the book, glanced at it, and looked back at him, satisfied. Then she turned, still without another word, and led him a different way out of the stacks. They went up another flight of stairs and down a different corridor. When they reached a door marked 'Modern French' she knocked and held it open for him. He entered a small, cluttered place whose ceiling sloped to low windows with a steep view down on to a tree-lined street below. A desk was piled with untidy manuscripts, and the pallid walls were hung with tattered posters of the French countryside.

Aaron Zeismann, jacket off, rose from a leather couch, smiling. The secretary quietly closed the door and they were alone.

Chapter Six

'*Alors!*'

'*Comment vas-tu, chef?*'

'*Pas mal. Malgré le temps qu'il fait.* How was tennis?'

'I didn't say I played?'

'But you did. Friday mornings you play Ender. Always. Did you beat him?'

'You'll never convince him of it.' Aaron perched on the edge of the desk.

Bejerec laughed and said, 'I don't trust Richard Ender. He is always capable of doing what is least expected of him. Out of vanity. He has a terrible ego.' Then he said, 'While you were deceiving him, I paid a call on your wife.' He ignored Aaron's surprise. 'She has grown into a very gracious and lovely woman, my boy. Very. I regret I could not introduce myself properly.'

'Where was this?' demanded Aaron. He was at once on guard. The only interest Bejerec had ever shown in Juliet was when it was decided that he needed an Establishment wife. That was eleven years ago while he was taking his Master's at Harvard. Bejerec had pointed her out to him and said, 'That one.' She was not really grown up yet. She was a Junior at Middlebury College in Vermont, the youngest daughter of a renowned Federal judge, and she was coltishly shy and still unsure of being a woman and filled with all the cheerful naivety of American youth. It had taken longer to persuade her family than her. It was hard for sixth-generation *Mayflower* descendants to accept a self-made Jewish orphan from California and UCLA.

'I went to the Smithsonian,' Bejerec explained, 'and cunningly asked to see their non-exhibited collection of early American cooking ware. *Et voilà! La belle Juliet* appeared like magic, looking very business-like, and I could finally see why you are such a popular couple in Washington. Tell me frankly,' he held up a thumb and forefinger, 'have you never fallen even that much in love with her?'

Aaron avoided the question. He knew if he asked Bejerec why he had gone to see Juliet that Bejerec would not tell him. There was anger in the way he hooked a straight-backed chair and straddled it. 'Look,' he said, 'you didn't come all the way over here to talk about my wife. Not with the risk involved, and when I'm due back in France in ten days anyway.'

Bejerec, chastened, said, 'No, I didn't.'

'Presumably it has to do with George Babcock?'

'Yes,' Bejerec admitted. 'Partly.'

Aaron stirred. He didn't want to think about Babcock. A week after the man had disappeared, he had received an anonymous envelope. It contained detailed photographs: Babcock before, during, after. Nothing else. Larsen terror-tactics. He had fed the pictures into his office shredder and that night had got drunk.

And now, thirty minutes ago, just as he was leaving the office, Esther's call about Robert Quincy. He still felt numb with the shock of it. And heartsick for Juliet. She mustn't know. Not tonight. He and Esther had agreed to tell her tomorrow that Robert Quincy had been run over. Esther's husband was burying the dog in the rose-bed by the barn.

He looked down through a window. The street below was empty. Half Washington had already left the city for any country greenery and cool they could find. Ordinary people leading sane and ordinary lives.

Some time ago he and Bejerec had discussed eliminating Larsen. And had decided against it. There was the very great risk that Larsen had taken pre-emptive precautions against such a possibility, that he would leave behind false witnesses or some fabricated but unchallengeable evidence. People accorded a voice from beyond the grave a credence they didn't allow the living. It wasn't worth the risk.

'What is there to say?' he asked Bejerec. 'It didn't work. Larsen probably saw the poor devil as a decoy right from the beginning.' He added bitterly, 'So much for that clever idea.'

42

'You mustn't blame yourself,' Bejerec said. 'The idea was good.'

Aaron shrugged and then told him about the blue Chevy and about Robert Quincy.

Bejerec's eyes, usually so bland, showed a profound unease. 'He is mad, this man,' he finally said. 'Diseased. But he is also something else. Something more dangerous than that. He is obsessed. Without a shred of evidence, with no cause at all, he has smelled you and, like a dog himself, he will hunt you to the very end. He will subject you again and again to every sort of horror, like Babcock and this poor Quincy, hoping some day you will crack and make a mistake. I don't like it, Aaron Zeismann, I don't like it at all.'

He took out his old silver cigarette-case and offered a lifesaver. Then, suddenly and without ceremony, he said, 'Now I am going to tell you why I really came over.' He waited for Aaron's full attention. He continued. 'I want to call the whole thing off. It's finished, Charles de Gaulle's legendary "mole". De Gaulle is long dead, to hell with him. I want you to quit.'

It caught Aaron by surprise. He found himself concentrating on a poster of a French barge canal thumbtacked to the wall near the door. Heavy-uddered cattle grazed a soft pasture beneath tall Lombardy poplars lining the canal's bank and reflecting their pale, jagged-green images on the dark stillness of the water. France was his youth and that was a lifetime ago.

Bejerec said, 'I know, I know. Just when your being here has finally paid off beyond your wildest dreams. Twenty years of time and money.' He smiled. 'And sleepless nights. What has it all been for, the superb job you have done? But we must face the facts, Aaron, the truth. And the truth is we have failed. From the first day we have been helpless to stop them. From the very first day it was already too late to open our mouths without exposing ourselves and having our mouths shut forever at what benefit to anyone. As far as I am concerned, what we laughingly call a government in France these days wants to be America's fifty-first state. And those who should care, like the Socialists, don't any

43

more because they have decided their future lies in Swiss bank-accounts. So be it.'

Briefly Aaron thought, Christ, they've bought him off, too, Bejerec. Then he rejected the thought. It was impossible. Bejerec was only profoundly disillusioned. Everything he'd lived his entire life for was blowing up in his face. He said abruptly, 'And where do you suggest I go?'

'Go?'

'When I quit.'

'But you go no place,' Bejerec protested. 'You stay right here, Washington, Oxford. That's the beauty of it. You keep right on at Dallas until it's all over. Then you go back to the National Security Council. Can you think of a better protection than honest innocence? If you have severed all connection with me, American counter-intelligence, Larsen and anyone else are stymied, aren't they?' The bland green eyes showed rare laughter.

Aaron stared. A year ago he would have jumped at the chance Bejerec offered. Two weeks ago, he could still have availed himself of it. Today it was no longer possible. In desperation following Babcock, he had thought of a last-resort step. He had acted on it without consulting Bejerec, hoping not to reveal what it was until he had some positive results. Now clearly he would have to.

He said to Bejerec, 'I'm afraid it's too late.'

Bejerec was taken aback. 'Oh? What's happened?'

'Julian Strachey,' said Aaron simply.

'Senator Strachey?'

'Yes.'

'Ah. His father was the Mine Workers' president, am I right? He joined pickets outside a striking coal-mine in Ohio and company police shot him.'

'That's right,' answered Aaron.

'What about him, then?' demanded Bejerec. His tone betrayed alarm.

'Up to now,' Aaron explained, 'we've been thinking only in terms of French government intervention. I tried to create alternatives. Strachey wants his party's presidential nomination next year. Badly. But he's not doing well in the primaries. People are starting to say he's just living off his father's name. He needs something. Now. Something big. It suddenly occurred to me we had it.'

He knew Bejerec would quickly understand what it was. Revelation of Tricolor to Strachey, if an ordinary senator, could be a dangerous dead end. But Strachey wasn't ordinary. He was chairman of a powerful Senate sub-committee investigating abuses in international banking, and, since his father's death, on a dedicated crusade against 'big business'. Bejerec knew that, and he also knew that largely due to Banjo Collins's influence a key role in Tricolor's intricate financing and merger politics was now being secretly played by the International Investment and Credit Corporation, a commercial-banking megalith headquartered in Brussels but indirectly owned by five American banks, all of which had major US oil companies as clients.

'Strachey hates the IIC,' Aaron added. 'From way back. Hand him proof they're involved in something like this, and he'd be all over them. Something would be bound to come out.'

'Of course,' murmured Bejerec. 'I'd never thought of it.' And then he was silent.

Aaron waited. He thought, I've pulled the mat from under him and his pride has to be hurt. But it can't be helped.

Bejerec finally said, 'Of course, knowing you, you have already seen Strachey. How much did you tell him?'

'Enough,' Aaron replied, 'to make him want more. He's coming to dinner tonight.'

Bejerec's eyebrows arched. 'Presumably he knows you only as Dallas Research, formerly of the National Security Council.'

'Of course. Juliet went to school with his wife's younger sister. We bump into each other around Washington. He likes sailing, too.'

Bejerec thoughtfully opened his old silver cigarette-case once more, and discovered with regret he had run out of life-savers. When he spoke again, it was a little sadly. 'Yes, you are right. It could be very awkward if you came out now. It is interesting that you thought of this man. Even revealing. It suggests a sort of non-professional personal desperation. Or should I say, involvement?'

Aaron smiled and Bejerec went on, 'You've changed, you know. You are not the same person I picked up on the docks at Le Havre all those years ago. In those days you didn't care about anything except getting your own back. Now you do. That's because you are no longer pretending to be an American. You *are* an American. I have seen it coming for a long while now.'

'That was the idea, wasn't it?' asked Aaron.

'Yes. That was the idea.'

'You figured me out with one of your computers,' said Aaron. 'And my future. You only made one mistake. Computers can accurately predict everything except men. Men are unpredictable.'

Bejerec agreed. 'And you, for example, unpredictably find yourself defending from itself any country you set out to spy on.' He laughed. 'It's true. And perhaps you are right. In a way the murderer stands to lose even more than his victim. Much more of this sort of thing, and your new country will soon no longer be the precious democracy of its founding fathers. It will be Hitler's Germany.' He sobered. 'All right, Aaron Zeismann, I am suitably impressed. I am even glad of it. You were never really French anyway. But I have a request.'

'Try me,' Aaron answered.

'French Intelligence will back you all the way but if your Senator does not work out,' said Bejerec, '*then* you quit.'

Aaron saw in Bejerec's eyes an instant's unguarded expression he'd never seen before. For an instant the other's feelings stood completely revealed.

The memory of Le Havre came back then, strong and visual as it often did: the cold, blustery docks, snow dusted white on the silent, waiting ships; the scruffy little *brasserie* jammed with sailors and longshoremen; the two *flics* coming in to pick him up, and bringing him into Bejerec's presence for the first time. He saw, as though only minutes ago, the glaring detectives' room of the dockside, the police sub-station; the naked walls, the file cases, the barren desk. And the icy stranger who unexpectedly spoke in cultured English and who had seen something in him that he could mould and use.

'Your stepfather was an American? You were raised on an American air-base?'

'Why ask me? You know already, don't you?' Defiant.

'I understand you speak English fluently. Or should I say, American?'

A shrug.

'And I understand you are a chameleon. One day you are a worker; the next, a stupid tourist or a student from Paris. That's how you con information.'

Another shrug.

More questions. Before he explained who he was and what he wanted, Bejerec had forced him to answer one after another. Then he'd said, 'I'll give you precisely one minute to make up your mind. You can go on leading your dubious existence as an informer for whoever pays the most. Or you can decide you want something better. But I warn you, we are a tight family and once you join us, if you change your mind, that's too damned bad.'

And now Aaron finally realized why Bejerec so badly wanted him to love Juliet, and why he had gone to see her, and why he wanted him to quit.

The bland green eyes were cold no longer. In them was warmth and undisguised anxiety. Men who are truly heads of families ferociously protect their own. The thought was overwhelming and explained everything.

He remembered Bejerec's lonely personal life and felt a deep gratitude, and with it a strength of emotion he'd never experienced before. He got control of himself.

'It's a deal,' he said.

Chapter Seven

The elderly Admiral had roving hands. He sniffed and stirred the simmering *Pocheuse Bourgignonne* whose recipe Aaron had found in a country restaurant in France. One arm encircled Juliet's slender waist far too freely, and she thanked heaven she'd found mosquitoes an excuse to throw on a light cardigan. This time of year they came in swarms down the estuary to the Chesapeake, and some always managed to evade the anti-mosquito lights and candles out on the lawn. Aaron had teased her about looking beautiful for Senator Strachey whose reputation as a womanizer was legend. To tease him back, but really with Aaron himself in mind, she had worn a dress whose deep-plunging front was far more in keeping with a fast Georgetown cocktail party than a quiet candle-lit dinner in the country where the guests were older people. She felt completely naked. But where she had foreseen trouble with Strachey, it came unexpectedly from the old Admiral who was a friend and neighbour.

'Behave yourself,' she laughed. She gently steered him away from the stove and to the big butcher's block which served as a centre island in the beamy, sagging old kitchen. 'Here,' she said. She presented him with a tray of *hors-d'oeuvres* and went to open the terrace door. 'And don't eat them all on the way. I'm coming immediately.' Charmed, he went out, unoffended by Esther's deep laugh.

Looking after him, Juliet could see Aaron down by the dock with Senator Strachey and his wife and the new couple the Admiral had brought to be introduced. They came from Chicago, and had just bought a summer place not far off. The woman was middle-aged but clearly quite taken by Aaron. She stood closely attentive as he pointed out the quaint little four-car ferry churning through the fading light and across the estuary to Bellevue and St Michael's.

'She likes him,' said Esther. 'That red one with the shawl.'

'So do I,' replied Juliet.

'I reckon,' declared Esther. She went back to the stove. 'And I reckon with that pair of lace hankies you got flying up top tonight, you'll be the one to get him.'

Juliet went to get out a second ice-bucket. 'You can count on that,' she said and Esther's laugh rose again.

'Will there be enough for the Senator's bodyguards?' Juliet suddenly remembered the two Secret Servicemen, patiently sitting it out in their car parked in the driveway. Strachey had automatically been assigned protection when he entered the primary race, and he got rid of them whenever he could.

'Don't worry,' cried Esther. 'I'll get 'em in here and fill 'em up. One way or the other.'

When Juliet had gone, her smile faded. She found it hard to keep up a pretence. Aaron had said not to call the police, Juliet would be certain to find out through them how Robert Quincy had really died. So Esther had gone out to her husband in the fields, and he'd driven her back to the barn on the tractor, and had taken down the limp red body. She'd cried, and he had too, his tears mingling with his sweat as he dug deep down into the rose-bed to make a last resting place for the dog, and then had filled and smoothed so as to leave no trace for Juliet to see when she came home.

When Juliet had asked where Robert Quincy was, they'd told her he was tied up at their house, and Aaron had said that was best; Robert wouldn't be all over the guests during the dinner the way dogs his age usually were. They could pick him up in the morning. Juliet had accepted it without question.

Esther sighed, dreading the moment when the truth would finally surface, and then she went to stir the soup once more and to baste the roast, glad at least for Juliet's reprieve from sorrow, even if momentary.

Outside, Juliet crossed the lawn, breathing in the sweet smell of new-cut grass. Helen Strachey and the new woman had come back up from the water. They sat on the wicker garden furniture placed around the base of a big elm. The men were still at the dock, discussing Aaron's graceful six-metre sloop. The estuary, turned soft pink now by the setting sun, cast its colour across the lawn to the house.

'What a heavenly place, Juliet,' Helen Strachey said. She was a stockily short, quiet woman, totally involved with her large stable of hunters and apparently quite removed from her husband's controversial life, his amatory adventures included.

'Thank you. President Monroe spent a whole six months here once.' Juliet's eyes swept the faded white clapboarding of the house, the sagging green shutters, the slightly aslant, worn brick chimney. It was indeed perfect, she thought. She put the ice-bucket on the wrought-iron table by the *hors-d'oeuvres* and sat down, throwing her long, dark hair back from her shoulders.

'I understand your husband once worked for the National Security Council,' the new woman said. 'What exactly did he do?' Her glance flicked Juliet's full, half-exposed bosom before she retreated behind her drink.

She was pretty once, Juliet thought, but she uses too much make-up. She deliberately did not pull her cardigan closed, she wasn't going to give her that victory. She said, 'He specialized in French economics and politics. Now he's with the Dallas Research Foundation. They're involved in the European energy treaty.'

'Oh, yes, of course. I've read about it.'

'Julian says he was the best man the NSC had,' Helen Strachey declared. 'Absolutely brilliant.'

'You must be very proud of him,' the Chicago woman murmured. And then she asked the question Juliet always hated. 'You do have children, don't you?'

You know damn well I don't, Juliet thought. Just look around you. She smiled disarmingly. 'I'm afraid not.'

'Some day, of course.'

'I hope so.'

'Such a perfect place for them,' the other persisted.

Juliet's hackles rose. What was it, she wondered, that made people so insistent that you reproduce? Was it so unusual not to litter like hamsters the moment you married? Aaron was right; she'd fought him at first because she'd desperately wanted his child, but eventually she'd had to agree. She was young still and engrossed in her work at the Smithsonian and in him. They had the sort of total independence you could not have if you had children. There was time yet before giving it up.

She turned to her guest with a guileless expression, and said what Aaron had often told her to say because it embarrassed people and shut them up immediately. 'Aaron is a Jew, you see,' she explained. 'And I am not. We wanted to make certain our two worlds would mate permanently before we did.'

Helen Strachey said, 'Maybe Julian and I should have looked at politics and horses the same way.' She had four children in their teens.

Juliet joined her laughter and then changed the subject. 'Tell me about your new house,' she urged the Chicago woman. 'However did you find Oxford? Chicago is *so* far away.'

Presently, the men came back, talking boats and racing. Aaron poured drinks and Strachey suddenly noticed Juliet and coolly began to make polite advances.

It's compulsive, she thought. She politely rejected him, paid court to Helen, made amends for putting down the new woman, and plunged into being a good hostess and enjoying herself.

She twice caught Aaron eyeing her dress, and because he did, the whole summer evening suddenly became enchanted and fun.

Chapter Eight

For Aaron the evening was difficult. He was tense with anxiety over Julian Strachey's presence and everything it meant, and what had happened to Robert Quincy didn't help. Nor the fact that in a week's time Larsen would surely be back at it, even though Ender had called to say his talk with Collins had been successful.

Some time during dinner he found himself thinking of Bejerec. He had given him a ticket to a concert at the Kennedy Center and Bejerec would be sitting alone, listening to the symphony's first movement. It seemed sad and futile to Aaron that he could not do the one thing he knew would bring Bejerec real pleasure; he could not invite him to his home and say to Juliet, this man is not Anthony Williams as you thought when you met him, but Paul Henri Bejerec, a very old friend and in a way my only family.

He looked down the table at his wife. The old Admiral was telling a sea story to a rapt audience and she was whispering an aside to Esther, serving, her hair its usual dark frame around her classic American face with its wide-spaced eyes and firm jaw and even teeth. When she saw his glance, she smiled at him through the soft aureole of the dinner-table candles. They were alone for a brief but intimate moment and, without warning, his memory reached back to their wedding night, to Juliet's happy laughter, to her eager girl's body and to the love she so trustingly had given. For a short while that love had almost prevailed over his unexpected guilt at the lie he and Bejerec had coldly entangled her in.

He smiled back. Bejerec was right. She had grown up and was lovely. Her dress, in the nicest way, was undeniably provocative. He knew she had really worn it for him, and he wanted to reach down the table and tell her that even if their marriage was a lie there were moments when he did care.

Then he remembered Bejerec had offered him the chance to change his life and perhaps to let himself fall in love with her before he lost what she felt for him, and the present came rushing back.

While the others had coffee and Juliet organized bridge, he and Strachey excused themselves. Strachey had a word with his two bodyguards who were out in the kitchen with Esther, and told them where he'd be. Then they walked down to the dock.

They untied the dinghy and rowed out to the six-metre. The moon had not yet risen. It was very hot and very still. The estuary was enveloped in a velvet darkness which felt like a tangible wall around them and was relieved only by faint starlight which barely framed the jagged-black silhouette of high trees lining the opposite shore.

They boarded and sat in the cockpit, Strachey sprawled aft at the tiller and Aaron, when he'd made fast the dinghy, at the halyard cleats. Strachey lit a cigarette and his lighter's flame picked out the bold, linear features of his face and his unruly shock of prematurely-grey hair. He had a very strong resemblance to his dead father. He laughed.

'Are we bugged?'

'I shouldn't think so,' answered Aaron. He'd thought about it. A micro-wave listening device somewhere near by, perhaps in a boat. If there was one, he'd be in dead trouble but it wouldn't reveal his double status and jeopardize Bejerec. It was worth the chance.

He put a kapok cushion behind his head and leaned back and thought, this is what all the undercover years have been about. It didn't seem real.

When he'd met Strachey two weeks ago in the Library Annexe, he had only roughly sketched out the role the International Investment and Credit bank was playing in the Tricolor strategy. Now he explained the mechanics. 'As you know,' he said, 'France's oil reserves and oil refining are basically in the hands of two nationalized companies. Over the years and with a semi-official, hands-off policy by the government, both companies have become so big and diversified as to be virtually autonomous. Provided Paris decides to look the other way, they can pretty much do what they want.'

'Including, I take it, divest themselves of reserves,' remarked Strachey.

'Yes,' Aaron replied. 'If they don't go overboard. In the case of the reserves we're after, the divestment will take the form of a long-term, renewable lease of the reserves to a third company.'

'Who's that?' Strachey asked. 'Certainly not IIC or Dallas. That would be a dead give-away.'

'No,' agreed Aaron. 'The actual lessee will be a French outfit called COPIC, Compagnie Occidentale des Pétroles Industrielles et Chimiques. They're mostly in refining and petro-chemicals.'

'And IIC is buying them up?' ventured Strachey.

'One of IIC's anonymous, Swiss holding-companies is,' answered Aaron. 'They'll own a controlling block of voting stock in COPIC in about a month's time.' He shifted his weight and the boat stirred slightly, water gently lapping its hull.

'Jesus,' muttered Strachey angrily. 'Houston owns IIC, IIC indirectly through Switzerland owns COPIC, COPIC as good as owns the reserves. *Ipso facto*, Houston runs the show. I see now why Ender has that bastard Collins on his neck. What about the French oil-company boards? Surely some director will object.'

'We don't expect any to,' Aaron said. 'The lease will be billed as a necessary political manoeuvre to meet African and Gulf of Persia demands to participate in French refining. To make that sound real, we're putting some of their people on the COPIC board.'

'How is COPIC paying for the lease?' Strachey asked.

'Cash,' Aaron said. 'The French were willing for it all to be credit and book-keeping, but Houston didn't trust that. They wanted leverage that was real. So a loan to COPIC is being arranged by the French Treasury through one of the Bank of France's credit agencies. The agency, of course, will actually get the finance from IIC.'

'That means a lot of laundering,' Strachey said.

'It does,' Aaron agreed. 'It starts right back in Houston with the US oil companies.'

'Why didn't they just use Eurodollars?' Strachey protested. 'God knows IIC must have enough of them.'

'Because these days,' Aaron explained, 'so many Eurodollars disappearing off the international exchanges might cause embarrassing questions.'

Strachey seemed surprised. 'How much is it, for God's sake?'

'I don't know exactly,' answered Aaron. 'I'm not really on that end of things. But to date I'm told they've moved well over a billion.'

Aaron could feel Strachey's shock through the darkness. There was a moment's total silence. Women's laughter drifted across the lawn and fell muted on the water. Strachey emitted a long, low whistle. 'I can't believe it,' he said. 'Are you certain there is no way of stopping this through the French Government?'

'I'm afraid not.' Aaron listed the key government figures either co-operating or bought off or coerced. 'It doesn't take many, you know, and Dallas has spent money that makes the Boeing and Lockheed pay-offs ridiculous. Dallas has anyone who could seriously block them. And they have the right man in the opposition. The French Left will *not* win the next national election.'

'Nothing illegal,' Strachey said. 'Just a good old-fashioned, hands-off, free-market, banking deal.' There was hatred in his voice, and Aaron remembered that when the senior Strachey was murdered, a New York banker had publicly regretted that the assassin hadn't finished off the son at the same time, later saying the media had misquoted him.

Strachey flipped his cigarette. A red ball arced the darkness and disappeared abruptly in a hiss of estuary water. 'What son of a bitch is the actual financial brain behind all this? Richard Ender isn't up to it. Nor Banjo Collins. Some genius at IIC?'

Aaron said, 'As a matter of fact, no. He works for Dallas. Ender dug him up. Henry Jedder.'

'Jedder?'

'He was brought in by the Swiss to clean up the off-shore trust scandals years ago, all that Bob Vesco mess.'

'Oh, Christ yes, the merger genius. Huge, sloppy man. He wrote that book on Panama as a corporate tax shelter.'

Aaron said, 'That's him. When Vesco fled to Costa Rica, he moved to Paris. His wife, Rosemary, is big in the jet set.'

'I guess Ender got the right man all right.' Strachey's lighter flared again as he lit another cigarette. 'Is there any CIA presence in all this?' he asked.

'No,' replied Aaron. He allowed himself another wry laugh. 'It's a little unfair, but the feeling is these days that they aren't to be trusted.'

'They asked for it,' Strachey said. 'Which brings me to witnesses. There's always the chance you, by yourself, would be passed off as a sorehead simply because you worked for the government. That's what finally happened to most of the CIA whistle-blowers. No matter how important you were at the NSC. And especially since what you have to say is so awful everyone is going to want desperately not to believe it.'

'I understand that,' Aaron said.

'We can't take the chance of your being ineffective,' Strachey continued. 'It might blow the whole investigation. We need someone else. There's clearly no one in Washington and there's nobody at Dallas Research, so IIC would be your best bet. It should be an American and someone with so much authority that his defection might cause panic and get others to follow. When that happens it always works fine for us. The more witnesses, the more each tries to out-talk the others. Can you find me someone like that?'

'I'm going to try,' said Aaron. He thought of Bejerec and the deal they'd made, and for the first time there was light at the end of the tunnel. He'd done the right thing.

'We also need all the documentation possible,' said Strachey. 'Get me witnesses and get me documentation, Aaron, and I'll blow the bastards sky high. And don't worry for anyone's safety. Nobody touches my witnesses. Not even the President. They get protection and they get immunity.'

A voice suddenly hailed, coming out of the dark like a fist.

'Yo!'

It was the old Admiral.

'The ladies grow restless,' he shouted.

'Coming,' Strachey called back. Aaron felt his hand on his arm. 'Aaron, this is bloody dangerous, what you're doing. Be careful. I'll be in London next month if you need me. For a week at least.'

Aaron remembered there was an economic summit, scheduled by the finance ministers of NATO. The President of the United States planned a stop-off speech on his way back from visiting the Mid-East. In a bi-partisan gesture he'd asked Strachey to join him there, and Strachey unquestionably saw a chance to make political hay of it. It was comforting to think Strachey would be close.

He hauled at the dinghy painter, it was warm and wet to his touch, and phosphoros glowed where it emerged from the water. 'That could make things easier,' he said.

The dinghy bumped alongside. They got in and started back. Aaron sat in the after-thwart and sculled. He felt exhausted. He hadn't realized how much he'd pinned his hopes on Strachey or how much tension he'd built up waiting to see him. The short dinghy paddle felt like lead.

Then suddenly the darkness burst into white light. Himself and Strachey pale and unreal, the shore, the dock, the long hull of the six-metre, alien paper cut-outs.

A low inarticulate moan, an animal sound. Strachey sprawled heavily down across the centre thwart. Dark water foamed pale. The dinghy rolled violently and nearly capsized. Aaron braced and steadied it.

Strachey's two Secret Service bodyguards were running across the lawn towards the dock, one tugging at something in the waistband of his trousers.

And simultaneously with the instant heart-stopping conviction of another Strachey assassination, Aaron realized what had happened. The Admiral had found the switch to the dock's floodlight. He shouted to the old man and loudly enough for the racing bodyguards to hear. 'Thank you, sir, but I think we're better off without the light, if you don't mind.'

'Wilco.' The Admiral's silhouetted arm reached for the switch.

Everything went black. Twice as black as before. Except for the dark purple pin-wheels in Aaron's eyes where the dock light had been. He levered the paddle and the dinghy moved again.

Strachey slowly sat up. 'Sorry,' he said. 'I just reacted.' It was barely a whisper.

'You did the right thing,' said Aaron. For a split second, just before Strachey dived on to the seat, he'd seen the blind expression of terror. They did that to him, he thought, when they killed his father. And in his own country. He'll carry it with him for his whole life.

They reached the dock and the old Admiral lent a hand heaving the dinghy out of the water. The Secret Servicemen materialized, worried at their over-reaction. Strachey told them he'd be a while yet. He and Aaron and the old Admiral walked back across the lawn to the house and the bridge game that awaited them.

Chapter Nine

Remembering Margita Majerová happened quite unexpectedly. Aaron was at the bedroom window, staring at the dark shadow of the rose-bed by the barn where Robert Quincy now lay. Suddenly she was there with him, boyishly slim, her short hair a fawn-coloured tousle and her fine-boned, Slavic face filled with gay laughter.

He wasn't prepared for it and it jarred him badly. He and Juliet had said goodnight to their guests. They watched the red tail-lights of the departing cars disappear into the darkness of the country road beyond the driveway and Juliet had put an arm around his waist and they'd walked back to the front door between the high rows of box, her long legs matching his stride, not talking, just smelling the box and listening to the night.

Esther had returned to her own home hours ago, the kitchen didn't look as though there had ever been a dinner party. They'd made drinks, and begun chatting about Strachey and his wife and the Chicago couple. Getting out ice they met at the refrigerator; Juliet came to him and Aaron felt her body tremble and knew she wanted him badly.

They had gone upstairs, slowly, step by step.

'What did you talk to Strachey about?'

'He wants to buy you. Or the boat. He couldn't make up his mind.'

'You know something? I believe you.' And laughter.

Juliet had gone to the bathroom to shower and brush her teeth. It was the splash and hiss of water that must have triggered the memory. Suddenly he wasn't in Oxford with her but in Paris with Margita, a different suite of rooms that were high-ceilinged and Edwardian French. The image was vivid, Margita and himself in the deep iron-legged bath tub with the ornate Victorian faucets, and still half asleep from the long night. Margita's face and body and her caress, and

59

their rush back to the brass bedstead to make love once more with the eager blindness of first infatuation. And later, the autumn streets, the brown and yellow chestnut leaves falling in the sidewalks, the bookstalls warm in the morning sun, Paris to be shared, and sidewalk coffee on the Boulevard St Michel and watching the milling students from the Sorbonne.

Juliet came from the bathroom then, and Margita vanished, and in her place there was Juliet's scrubbed-clean American look, her lips softly parted, her naked skin warm against his. 'Hey! Where are you?' Her eyes cared, her hands slowly moved down his back to pull him close. He kissed her, and stretched out on the bed. Juliet sat at her dressing-table by the window and began to brush her hair.

'What's wrong, Aaron?'

'Nothing.'

'You're a liar.'

'It's been a long day.' He forced a smile. Juliet's seated hips were wide and soft beneath the tall, straight column of her slender back with its crown of dark brushed hair that poured down it, and her shoulders slightly rounded forward by the weight of her breasts. Aaron thought, this is my wife. Regardless of the reason I married her, we share a life, a home, furniture, friends; we share early-morning jogging and tennis and sailing; we swim nude on lonely beaches and go on picnics; we share our bed and our bodies and music and food and her family, and sickness and bad temper and money worries. And she loves me.

He tried to concentrate on just that and on what Juliet was saying about the weekend. He didn't hear her. Margita Majerová came back, bringing with her a sadness and a hurt which were tangible. It was early morning in France. She would be sleeping still, perhaps with a lover. He could no longer clearly see her face, her eyes and mouth had become a blurred vagueness, her voice confused with Juliet's. All that really remained of her was the pain.

'I'm married, Margita.' They had sat at a crowded sidewalk cafe, Paris swirling around them.

The colour slowly ebbed from her features until she was chalk white.

'When?'

'Two years ago.'

'Why didn't you tell me?'

He had not been able to answer. When he'd first met her, she had only recently escaped from Czechoslovakia. She'd left everything behind, friends and a widowed father in Prague, and she'd lost the ability to cry. She hadn't spoken again until she had finished her wine. When she did, her voice sounded as though her soul had died, and her body suddenly looked as thin and vulnerable as a child's.

'What about us?'

'It has to stop.'

'Not just occasionally?' She made futile rings on the table-cloth with the bottom of her glass, one after another. She spoke nearly in a whisper, 'When you come to Paris. I only need that, Aaron. Just occasionally to know you want me. That's all I need. Just to know it isn't finished forever between us.' It was begging. She'd humbled herself completely. 'I promise that's all.'

How did you tell someone you loved and loved desperately that your love could destroy her? You couldn't explain that if Bejerec discovered her, he would unquestionably protect his American investment by sending her back to Prague with a request to the Czech police to keep her there.

Not meeting her eyes meant she wasn't to hope.

She had finally accepted it. She'd been too proud to ask even Juliet's name. She had walked away down the Boulevard St Germain, hands in her pockets, her hair a splotch of colour against the grey of the day. She had turned a corner and disappeared.

For a long while he thought she might have killed herself. He had visions of her, sprawled and grotesque in death on the kitchen floor of her apartment, face swollen from gas. Or half out of bed, sleeping pills cascaded mutely over the sheets. Time had half-cured, until recently he had heard she was alive and still in Paris. Then the old pain had returned.

'Aaron?' Juliet turned from her mirror, her dark hair brushed and gleaming.

He said, 'Bring your drink over here. You can't make yourself any more beautiful.'

She shook her head. 'Turn out the light. Look.' She pointed. 'The moon.'

He obeyed. The room plunged into darkness except for the window which filled with an extraordinary golden light.

'Come and see the water,' she insisted.

He went to the window and knelt, his elbow on the sill. She was close. He put his other arm across her thighs and her leg was against his side. He looked out. The elm trees on the lawn were slender reeds, their high crowns sharp-etched by a corridor of gold that started at the water's edge and, broken only once by the black pencil shape of the moored sailing-boat, stretched out across the silent estuary to the enormous golden ball just separating from the trees of the opposite shore.

He tried to recapture their fleeting, intimate moment at the dinner-table. He turned his face into her lap, breathing in her warm, female musk. She stroked his head and he thought, this is what my life turned up. I must learn to be at peace with it. In a little while he took her to bed. He heard her cries of love, he felt the heat and strength of her body straining eagerly against his and afterwards accepted her grateful tenderness and caring.

She whispered, 'I don't think I could survive without you.'

'Of course you could.'

She raised herself on her elbow and switched on the bed-side light and sank close to him, one breast heavily soft against his shoulder, one long leg thrown casually across his, pelvis hard and warm against his thigh. She studied his face and then his body, brushing her fingers lightly down his side, as though wanting to be certain he was there. Presently, she turned the light off and pressed against him. He felt her shudder slightly; she was stifling tears.

'What's the matter, Juliet?'

'I'm frightened.'

'Why?'

'When you go away, there isn't ever any guarantee you'll come back to me, is there?'

'What are you talking about?'

'I don't know. The future's all a blank, Aaron. I can't see any more. I've felt that way for weeks. I'm frightened.'

He took her hand, feeling desperation in the tightness with which she held his.

When she finally slept, he sat up beside her and stared blindly out of the window into the luminous estuary night. Bejerec had said Larsen some day might drive him into making a mistake, and as each day passed the chances of his doing so multiplied. When would it happen? What would the mistake be? Bejerec had said he was an American now. Was he? All the way? And if not, what was he then? Life led you to certain unsigned roads. You chose one, heedless, and when you found out where it led, it was too late to re-decide. You had to walk it to the end, no matter what.

Juliet stirred in her sleep. Her head, damp with the heat, moved against his hip and her steady breathing resumed, childlike.

Memory flickered again, disjointed sections of old film. Then steadying, each scene clear. The bare, dockside police-office, the barren walls and sterile desk, the late-afternoon winter sun; Bejerec.

'Who will you be in your new life, my boy?' Cold and precise. 'Because we're going to give you a new life. We're going to give you new parents, a new nationality, a new childhood, a life nobody, I don't care who they are, not even God Himself, will ever be able to challenge. Do you understand me? Not even God!'

A folder pulled spontaneously and at random from the file case. 'Here you are. This will do for a start. Aaron Zeismann. Born at Voiron, Department of Isere, August 20th 1912. Thirty years for armed robbery and manslaughter. Died in prison hospital at Le Havre, September 8th, 1948. Knife wounds.' And then, 'Ha! No known relatives. Perfect. It's a file we can bury forever. Aaron Zeismann gets a second chance.' He laughed, and leaned across the desk, green eyes appraising, missing nothing.

'Tell me, my boy, my little informer, any objections to being a Jew?'

And less clear than that, from even further back, the cramped kitchen of the pre-fab at the American Air Force base near Dijon. The confused faces, the filtered voices. His stepfather shouting 'Arab whore!' His blue uniform covered with blood and the broken bottle in his hand glinting vengeance. His mother's screams as the glass ripped at her dark face and heavy boots cracked her ribs. The wild swing that caught the child, him, the salt taste of his own blood in his mouth and the red of his own blood in his eyes. The blast and cordite smell of the suicide automatic, the unreality of the exploded head. Neighbours and police, the white glare of the hospital emergency ward.

And in the grey dawn of a month later his mother gone, and her few, pitiful things with her, and the fifty francs she'd made from the two soldiers the night before left on the kitchen table for him.

Suddenly the moon had disappeared, the window framed a similar pale grey of first light. Years had fled. And hours. He lay down and buried his face in the refuge of hair around his wife's neck and rolled against her. She came awake and he thrust despairingly into her. She cried out, but in a moment responded, still half-asleep but yearning, and he found momentary safety.

But when it was over, there was again the long, echoing corridor of time now stretching back and back to the Algerian *bidonville*, the appalling Arab shacktown on the outskirts of Paris where the child had hidden from the police and the priests: gone to earth among his own kind, his mother's people.

Juliet whispered to him to stay, but his feeling of hopelessness turned too bitter. He eased away from her, his sweat and hers turning cold on his skin.

The last thing he thought of before he finally slept was the mocking irony of his Jewish name.

Paris–Lyon

Chapter Ten

At seven-thirty on a late September morning, Paris was well into a new day. The Métro disgorged its packed cargo at a score of stations with strong Gallic names such as Hôtel de Ville and Reuilly-Diderot. Commuters thronged platforms at the Gare de Lyon, St Lazare and other major stations. Near Orly airport, the wholesale food markets had been busy for several hours, and the length of garish Rue de Clichy cut-rate shops unshuttered, while along the Faubourg St Honoré uniformed porters unlocked the brass-handled doors and hosed down the sidewalks of more hallowed establishments.

In an eighteenth-century town-house in the residential district of Levallois-Perret, a big, coarse-haired and bearish figure shambled out of bed and unsteadily crossed an ornately-furnished bedroom. His head pounded and pierced and as further mute testimony to the previous evening, his T-shirt, all he wore, was liberally stained by wine and lipstick.

It was Henry Jedder. In the bathroom, he flung up the toilet seat and relieved himself, feeling worse every second. Where had he been? Elsie's? Had there been a girl? He could remember neither her name nor what she looked like. He flushed the toilet, braced himself on the alabaster basin and forced down a glass of Alka-Seltzer. Then, still half-naked, he lumbered barefoot out of his suite of rooms and down the marble stairs. The carpets were at the cleaners, the marble felt cold to his feet and eased some of the misery of his body. Nights were freshening and the house was chilly. He scuffed across the silent front hall with its fountain and mute, neo-classic statuary, pushed the heating thermostat up and went to the modern kitchen Rosemary had installed in one of several useless reception rooms. He had to make his coffee himself. The Portuguese couple were still with Rosemary at their summer villa at Portimao on the Algarve. The

French chauffeur–handyman had taken a September vacation instead of his usual August one. Their one child, Michèle, was back at college in Grenoble where she shared a scruffy student apartment with two militant girl friends. He was alone.

He put on the kettle and tried to pull his mind together. Yesterday slowly came back; oh God, yes; Achille Reymond who ran COPIC, aggressively suspicious, all his questions on the oil-lease finance nearly impossible to answer without blowing the whole deal, and this with IIC control of COPIC only a month away, when it wouldn't make any difference what Reymond thought or said because he'd be out. Jedder muttered a curse. Hadn't he promised Reymond he'd go down to Lyon again on Saturday? Yes. It was to have lunch with him and his wife and to try to stall off his coming up to Paris today and showing up again at the Bank of France with more embarrassing questions.

Suddenly, getting down instant coffee, Henry Jedder felt a wave of panic. The meeting this morning, when was it? He looked at the kitchen clock. Eight. Was it nine-thirty Collins was coming over from the Embassy? There'd be Collins, Ender and Zeismann and himself. No, it was at ten. He had time. Relieved, he thought, thank God for Zeismann. At least he spoke French and knew what the score was in Paris and didn't have his head jammed full of his own importance. Who the hell did Ender and Collins think they were half the time anyway? Cowboys, and Collins the son of a bitch who had insisted that IIC's imbecile accountant review the stock-cost analysis at COPIC. Belgian, the accountant? Yes, Belgian. Bloody little man. Couldn't keep his damn mouth shut. That's how Reymond got the idea the money for the lease was originally exported dollars and not francs as they wanted him to think.

He felt the presence of the girl before he saw her. She'd come in without a sound, nearly as naked as he and shivering. She was Asiatic, short and flat-bodied with straight, jet-black hair and rather prominent teeth, but pretty just the same. She had nothing on but white briefs, their near-transparency provocatively shadowed.

Last night rushed back. All of it.

'*Bonjour*,' she smiled brashly. 'May I have some, too?'

He gestured at the cups in the open cupboard.

'*Merci, alors*.' She stood on her toes to brush his cheek with her lips, and with one hand gave him a brief, teasing sexual caress.

He stepped back, repulsed. Night-time was one thing, day quite another. She laughed and arranged two cups. '*Merde!*' she exclaimed. 'It's cold in this fucking morgue of yours.'

He remembered the other girl, then, and picking them both up and bringing them home. He said dismissively, 'The cleaning lady comes in half an hour.' It was a lie; she didn't come until noon. 'I'm afraid I can't let her see you.'

The girl went out with the coffee, 'Don't worry, *Monsieur*,' she sarcastically exaggerated the word. 'We will not disgrace you.'

Then she was gone and he was alone with the resonant ticking of the kitchen clock.

He'd started drinking at Harry's Bar after the office. It was the uproar with Reymond. Zeismann who had been with him had said, 'Listen, you've had enough. Either come to dinner with me or go home. Tomorrow could be rough. Collins likes you about the way he likes me and he's just looking for somebody to bully.'

'Screw Collins. He's Houston's lackey. And goddamned Ender is soon going to be his. So screw him, too.'

'Just the same.'

'I've bought and sold assholes like Collins and Ender. Dozens of them.'

He'd gone on to Elsie's. At two in the morning you found half Paris there, jet-set strays, airline girls, models, débutantes in revolt. Skilfully, they hadn't asked him for money until he'd brought them home. By that time he hadn't cared that he'd been tricked by a couple of professionals, and he'd really made them work for it. They'd used Rosemary's room, and vaguely he remembered taking a perverse delight in thinking Rosemary's mirrors could somehow secretly record everything they'd seen, so that when Rosemary returned they would silently taunt her.

He unsteadily sipped his coffee. Had they done any damage? Little bitches. He'd have to see.

He went back upstairs through the empty, echoing house. He heard laughter and water splashing in Rosemary's mirrored and marble bathroom. He slipped past the door to her suite. There was time to look later.

He sat on the edge of his ornate bed. It was only eight-fifteen. He was feeling cold now. He hated his room. A Paris decorator had been responsible. He hated the heaviness of the Empire furniture, he hated the barren parquet floor with its oriental throw-rugs and the gilded bedside tables with their baroque lamps. It was a room where there was no place to hide. Above all, he hated the gallery of framed photographs Rosemary had hung near his desk: himself and Bob Vesco, himself and the Chicago political group, the various shots of himself with prominent French and Swiss bankers he'd advised and with President Pompidou, and then, more personally, with Rosemary and some friends on the Riviera. Every run-of-the mill corporate executive kept photos like that.

He went to the bathroom and turned on the shower. Ender had said, 'Henry, when things simmer down, you can have Reymond's job. That's a hundred and fifty thousand a year for a start.' He hadn't told Rosemary. Ender had urged secrecy until it happened. But he knew just what she would have said. Take it. She would not have seen where it could possibly be a trap, that once locked into a specific, corporate structure there was little time for playing for the successes that really mattered and set you apart. He heard her voice, 'Henry, I don't wish to be negative, but what about *us*? What about this place and Portugal, too? And all our friends?'

In the end he knew that what she would say made sense. The cold, dread, fear of total failure had prevailed, because even money finally ran out. He hadn't earned any, not big money, since Vesco. Being everybody's adviser made them rich, not himself, and the more he thought about COPIC, the more he thought perhaps it was not such a bad idea. It would give him a solid platform on which to build better things. There was the coal cartel, his chance of pulling it together was still good; there was the solid-state market in Russia, still wide open; there was the new tax-exempt scheme on Eurodollar re-sale, what a killing that could be. He'd find time for it all somehow.

If Reymond didn't wreck everything. Damn him, anyway. Someone would have to find some solution to his trouble-making. It really wasn't his responsibility, and he damn well wasn't going to let Collins or anyone else try to blame him for it.

When he came out of the shower he felt distinctly better. Last night had been fun and Paris in the morning was filled with men getting up and sending girls off. He dried and went back to the bedroom and the second girl was there, dressed only in an unbuttoned cardigan and rummaging in his ciga-rette-box. She was French, a tall, natural blonde and, except for flaccidly pendulous breasts which seemed alien to the rest of her, was very attractive in an athletic, outdoor way. But he felt instant anxiety. She was very young, more so than he remembered. Suppose someone should see her leav-ing. She said apologetically, 'Oh, hello, I've run out.'

He covered himself with his towel. He was surprised by her manners and her educated accent. She clearly came from a good family.

She lit a cigarette. 'Is that your wife?' She looked at a framed photo of Rosemary on his dressing-table. 'She's at-tractive.' She unselfconsciously straddled a stiff-backed chair. 'We put away all her perfume and everything and straightened up and stripped the bed. The sheets are on the hall chair. Don't worry, I'm used to doing my mother's room the same way.' She smiled and then said, 'Look, I'm sorry to ask, really, but I'm pretty broke.' She hesitated. 'Could you possibly spare a little something extra?'

His stomach tightened. She hadn't suggested blackmail, but she might as well have done. 'How much?'

She shrugged and began buttoning her cardigan. 'Any-thing you like.'

He went to the teakwood valet where he hung his clothes

and produced a five-hundred-franc bill from his wallet. She stared at it. 'You couldn't possibly make it another?' She smiled wistfully.

He gave her a second note.

'Thanks. You're very nice. I left my name and phone number on your note-pad. The best time to call me is before lunch. I work in the afternoons. Daddy got me a job at Orly.' She glanced at the door and lowered her voice. 'And listen, if you want someone different next time, I can arrange that easily. I only met her last night.'

Ten minutes later he watched them both leave by the garage which gave on to the cobbled mews beyond the back garden; two respectable-looking girls, the blonde in a smart skirt and with an expensive St Laurent shoulder-bag. Nobody could possibly think them anything other than friends of Michèle.

He dressed, buoyant with sudden optimism. Even if only half of what he planned came to fruition, his worries were over. As for Reymond, Dallas had successfully to date quieted far bigger people. He went down for another cup of coffee and then left by the front door. The tree-lined street was early-morning peaceful, there was an invigorating autumn nip in the air. The hired limousine was waiting for him at the kerb, the temporary chauffeur respectful. They pulled away on to Boulevard Victor Hugo and autumn leaves, fallen from chestnut trees, swirled in a small cloud behind them.

It had been autumn, too, when he and Rosemary had gone back to his home in upstate New York right after Vesco and the Swiss scandal. His mother had died. Following the funeral, they stayed for a week at his sister's house on a quiet, tree-lined street of the small town, and shared the same bed for the first time in ages. The local university had offered him an Economics professorship and he'd felt far from Europe and nostalgic for his and Rosemary's early-courtship. She hadn't responded. 'If you ever had actually wanted the academic life of a small provincial town, Henry, then surely that's what you would have done.' She'd been upset at his plans to write a book, and perhaps she'd been right. You might reap glory but never money from a product which sold, no matter how successfully, only to a narrow market of experts.

They slowed at a crowded crossing and his thoughts turned back to the present. In a way he would soon be virtually in charge of the destinies of all these ordinary people hurrying to their offices to do their very ordinary work, and that was no small thing. He thought again of the blonde girl. She was exciting and surely she must be older than she looked. After he saw Reymond on Saturday, he could perhaps stay the night in Lyon at the COPIC suite in the Hôtel Royal, and take a room down the hall for her and a friend. But somebody new, he thought. He hadn't liked the Asiatic at all. She didn't know her place.

Chapter Eleven

Some areas of Paris are seen by few tourists. In the distant 19th Arrondissement not far from the cattle yards and the city *abattoirs*, the sludge-grey waters of a barge canal end at a hub of ten streets, appropriately honouring the many Communist workers of the area with the name Place de Stalingrad.

There are several *brasseries* on the square and at eight-fifteen in the morning they were already empty. Some time ago their regular clientèle had had their coffee or cognac and had gone to work.

Outside one, the Brasserie du Cochon d'Or, a nondescript plumber, dressed in the faded blue trousers and jacket of the French worker, was bending over a pipe and a portable workbench. He and his apprentice had arrived only a few minutes earlier to dismount it from the back of a vintage Peugeot truck. A waiter, round-shouldered, thin, serving-towel hooked in his belt, slouched in the doorway and picked at his Fernandel teeth with a matchstick while he watched.

Inside, Aaron Zeismann also watched. He'd ordered an espresso coffee and sat with it at a table a few feet back from the window. He'd spotted the Peugeot twenty minutes earlier. It had followed him two mornings running and he'd stopped at the *brasserie* to flush it out. They moved pretty fast, he thought, truck parked, bench and a few tools out, a pretence of work. Their easy familiarity with their equipment told him they were Europeans.

He was due at Dallas for a ten o'clock meeting with Ender, Collins and Henry Jedder; Achille Reymond had become an unexpected, minor embarrassment and Jedder was upset about it. He was a *bona fide* genius, Jedder, in many ways, and few could have so meticulously advised on the whole Tricolor operation or so successfully doubled the anonymity of the Swiss pay-off accounts for those French who needed paying, with Bermuda, Panama and Curaçao registrations. But he was also a neurotic man with illusions that he was a *force majeure* in high finance and thus difficult. Collins hated him.

Aaron drained his coffee. Was there some subtle way he could exacerbate the situation? He'd been in Paris over three weeks and he still had no sign of a witness for Julian Strachey up at IIC in Brussels where he and Ender spent a considerable time. Soon, it might be too late. He needed to exploit any dissension, foster any discord wherever possible and hope something might come out of it.

He glanced at the plumbers and the Peugeot, and then at his watch. It was eight-thirty. He fished in his pocket for money, and his thoughts turned to Juliet. Yesterday he had telephoned her and she had been warm and loving, but something within him blocked up. It had been hard to identify with her news of herself, of her father's new honours she'd flown up to Yale last weekend to share, of Esther and gardening. The longer they talked, the more she had seemed a stranger, Oxford unexpectedly alien and his American life slipping slowly away from him. Today the call still nagged and troubled like a bad dream.

He stood up. He'd planned precisely what he was going to do and how to do it. It was dangerous, it was also vicious and it was fostered by necessity and by a cold rage he was beginning to feel which had nothing to do with the respectable, Washington executive. That was a different character. It had to do with the homeless child of an Arab whore, fighting for his existence in an Arab *bidonville* and with the police informer later on at Le Havre.

He needed respite for a day or so; he had to see Bejerec, and the two men outside weren't the same clowns Larsen had used back in Washington. They were good and were backed up by others like them, but this was the last sort of thing they or Arnheimer Larsen would ever expect.

He left two francs on the table for his coffee, went to a wall telephone, dropped in a *jeton* and tried to make himself relax. The phone rang for some time before it was answered.

The man on the other end had a husky Marseilles accent.

'*Je vous écoute.*'

'*C'est moi.* The Peugeot. Same story as yesterday.'

'*Putain!* Where are you now?'

'Place de Stalingrad.'

'De Stalingrad? What's out there? A Party meeting?'

Aaron smiled at the speaker's sarcasm. 'It's a good place. Not too many witnesses around and maybe *Sûreté* will blame it on the Reds.'

'You're crazy. Do you know that? *Fou!* You'd do better to let me arrange it.'

'Thanks, but I want their boss to know it's me. Listen, anything goes wrong ring this number three times, hang up, then twice. Tell whoever answers. And then forget it. *D'accord?*'

'*Oui, oui. Entendu, alors.*' Aaron gave him Bejerec's private number and hung up. The voice he had been talking to belonged to the owner of the Relais Maritime. It was a very *recherché* small hotel in the 11th Arrondissement not far from the Place de la Bastille, a wholly Parisian quarter. It was very French-old-fashioned, there were few hotels like it any more, and on the same narrow street were several small *bistros* sandwiched between bakeries and grocery shops which more than made up for its lack of a restaurant. Its clientele were for the most part French: intellectuals, theatre and film people, a scattering of provincial gentry, politicians of all parties and the occasional English or non-French European 'in the know'.

When Aaron had first come over a year ago, Ender had offered him a penthouse apartment in the fashionable 16th Arrondissement. He had refused it. 'If I'm going to keep an ear to the French,' he said, 'then I have to be where the viewpoint is not solely that of the prejudiced rich.' The real reason he stayed at the Relais, of course, was not that. The real reason was Louis Tattel, the man to whom he'd just spoken.

Tattel was a middle-aged, beefy paratroop veteran of the Algerian wars and a one-time secret operative who had

76

helped unearth the OAS plot to assassinate de Gaulle. In recognition of his loyalty, Charles de Gaulle himself had wiped clean certain running controversies the old para had with the law. Tattel had bought the little hotel and slipped from view, although he still had the best contacts in France for almost anything you wanted, from forged documents to illegal arms, and half the police inspectors in *Sûreté* in his pocket as well.

Aaron had met him soon after he'd gone to work for Bejerec and before Bejerec had sent him off to America. The SDECE had stationed a watch on outlawed OAS officers intent on slipping into France through the Pyrenees. When a shot from a colonel's revolver had shattered Tattel's shin-bone, Aaron, his own life in acute danger, had carried the wounded man twenty kilometres through a raging storm to a hospital. He had bound Louis Tattel to him for life and the hotelier was the only person besides Bejerec he had ever trusted.

At the Relais, Aaron had access to Tattel's private telephone. It was located in the small bedroom-office behind the Relais Maritime front desk that was Tattel's home, and, courtesy of a technician friend Tattel had under his thumb, was unlisted and unmarked at the central telephone exchange. More sophisticated bugging methods were made possible by a small intervention device Aaron had brought over from America, and which operated from within Louis Tattel's television set.

A few nights ago, Tattel and Aaron had talked about Larsen's newly re-established surveillance. Aaron wanted to make certain it was not someone Bejerec had surreptitiously set to keep an eye on him, which Bejerec would never admit to if asked. They were in the innkeeper's office, Aaron at a small round table that served for eating and for cards. Tattel, who had spotted the stake-out the moment it had begun, was sprawled on the Algerian rug which covered his sagging iron bed beneath a wall plastered with photographic mementoes of old comrades, and faded magazine pin-ups. It was an ambience far removed from the old-world charm of the lobby, and the countrified character of the guest lodgings upstairs. The only hint of all that was Tattel's immaculate concierge's uniform with its proud lapel-badges of crossed keys which hung from a hook behind the door.

'They're not French,' Tattel said. 'At least nobody from Paris. Guaranteed.' He accurately flipped the yellow butt of his *cigarette au balayeur* into a brass 105 Howitzer shell case. Then he rose to pour himself and Aaron another *eau-de-vie*.

'Are they Belgian?' asked Aaron.

A startled look came over the hotel-owner's heavy face. '*Tiens!* As a matter of fact ... Yes, I think Emile had that impression. Forgot all about it. I can ask him again.'

'Don't bother. It fits.'

Perhaps his rage had started then. The IIC in Brussels, French-speaking, Belgian private goons; only a Frenchman would know the difference in their accents. IIC had always offered Dallas any 'facilities' the bank possessed.

Thus this morning, when the Peugeot truck had once more filled a discreet area of his rear-view mirror, he'd let it hang on a few hundred yards back, then he turned north on to Boulevard Sebastopol, to lead it eventually to the relatively untrafficked outskirts of town.

He had parked his Citroen DS 21 a few yards from the Brasserie du Cochon d'Or. Once inside, coffee ordered, he watched calmly as the Peugeot pulled up to park just in front of him, and its two occupants got out to blatantly put on their pretence of work. They had fallen for the bait.

Now he came out of the *brasserie*. He paused by the idle waiter and studied them. To anyone but himself they would appear legitimate. But the work-bench was set up for immediate dismantling should he unexpectedly move on, and the pipe they cut wasn't going to be put anywhere except back in the Peugeot.

Without looking at the waiter he said four short words under his breath, '*Foûte-moi le camp.*'

It wasn't the words, their abrupt vulgarity. It was his tone, his lack of facial expression. The matchstick poised an inch from the corroded Fernandel teeth, the flat feet stiffened in their down-at-heel shoes. The watery eyes stared straight ahead. Rigidly. Then the waiter went back inside.

Aaron crossed the sidewalk. The hair on the back of his neck was electric. It had occurred to him that he might have double-guessed himself. If this was an elimination, they'd set it up well and the waist-banded .25 Louis Tattel had forced on him last night would do him little good.

But he made it to the Citroen. He got behind the wheel, started the motor, backed up ten feet, grateful there was nobody behind him, slid into first gear. He knew they were watching. The moment he pulled away they'd radio their back-up and somebody else, probably parked close to the square, would take over their job. He didn't plan for that someone else to have the time to do it.

He started to turn his wheels away from the kerb. Then abruptly he heaved the steering-wheel over and slammed his accelerator to the floor.

The DS 21 is powerful. In one second it leapt the kerb. There was no time for the plumbers to get out of the way.

He kept his foot down. There was a ghastly, abrasive sound, the car rolled up and over work-bench and men alike and crashed back on to the street beyond the Peugeot. It had one man by the leg and dropped him shrieking after ten yards; the other man, still back on the sidewalk, was a huddled, broken blue sack, tangled in the shattered work-bench.

In the middle of the Place de Stalingrad there appeared the white kepi and traffic baton, the familiar blue uniform of a Paris cop, passing by and rooted by what he'd seen. He came to life, his whistle rose to his lips.

Aaron gunned straight for him, horn blaring. In seconds someone would have his number. The *flic* tugged at his holstered .32, then jumped for his life. The revolver slithered along the cobbled pavement. Tyres and brakes screamed on outraged vehicles, cut off. The Citroen shot diagonally and at speed across the light stream of traffic. Three more seconds and it disappeared up a side avenue.

Next door to the Brasserie du Cochon d'Or, a startled woman clerk was the first to emerge from a bakery. She ran to the bundle of blue cloth on the sidewalk and bent down to help. Her eyes settled on what had been a face and she began a long, horrified and piercing scream.

Chapter Twelve

The offices of the Dallas Research Foundation were located all the way across Paris at 37 Avenue Kléber, a wide boulevard of expensive shops and offices. It was not far from the Arc de Triomphe, and a relatively short walk from the verdant lawns and woods of the Bois de Boulogne. The offices occupied one of several converted eighteenth-century townhouses encircling a small cobbled court reached from Kléber through a deep arcade.

Rush-hour traffic was ferociously heavy. It took Aaron nearly an hour to cross Paris. He came up the Champs-Elysées to join Kléber, and after a few hundred yards signalled to the cars behind him, slowed and turned right into the arcade. An elderly porter appeared through the rattling glass door of his office. He recognized Aaron and swung open tall iron gates. Aaron drove through into the courtyard itself.

He quickly spotted cars, parked according to licence numbers stencilled on the paving blocks. Ender was there, so was Jedder. The black English Rover in a visitor's slot just beyond the stone fountain was Collins's. To forcibly goad Ender with his position, Collins had turned the conference room at Dallas into a personal office which he insisted on using if there was a meeting requiring his presence. On those occasions, which were fortunately rare, he did not use an Embassy limousine.

Aaron parked his own car. He'd stopped on the way to inspect the damage. A smashed left front headlight, the grille crushed in, the bumper badly dented and scarred. He was lucky; he could have put the car out of action.

He asked the downstairs security guard if Larsen had come in yet.

'Yes, sir.' The guard pointed to a neatly precise signature in the log book. 'He came in ten minutes ago.'

He would have heard by now, Aaron realized, have heard and be silently raging behind his near-albino eyes, because there wasn't a damn thing he could do about it. He signed in himself and took the elevator upstairs, grateful to be in its confines alone.

The ground-through-third floor was devoted to Dallas's French cover, the *bona fide* economic research and evaluation organization providing both French and American governments with independent information for the future energy treaty.

Aaron got out at the fourth. A wide spiral stairwell looked dizzily down to the ground-floor hall. Around it were his office, Ender's, Jedder's and Collins's, their secretaries', and a communications room with a telex to the Washington office as well as two special direct-line telephones. He glanced at his watch. It was a quarter to ten; he had another fifteen minutes.

Jedder's door was closest to the elevator. It was open and Jedder was behind his desk, a bearish shape, back-lighted by a window which looked out across the courtyard. In sheer size he looked important, and this morning especially aggressive although, Aaron knew, he would have a hangover. Sometimes it was hard to reconcile the man who was the financier with the man who had a miserable marriage with a jet-set social power and an unfortunate predilection for drink and under-age bar-girls. If you were an Ambassador Collins and tried to apply middle-class Alabama standards, you could reach no reconciliation at all. Aaron put as much good cheer into his voice as possible. 'Do you want a revolver or will you settle for Alka-Seltzer?'

Jedder looked up slowly. He saw it was Aaron and managed a smile.

'You look as though you'd kept on going after I left,' explained Aaron. Jedder's suit habitually looked as though he'd slept in it, another thing Collins scorned him for.

'I should have taken your advice.'

'Nobody ever takes anybody's advice. I'll see you down in the hall in fifteen minutes.' Aaron went on to the next door and his own office.

He was struck immediately by the very irony of its normality. What was there, the well-furnished executive haven, seemed irreconcilable with the realities of the Place de Stalingrad forty-five minutes earlier. The big oak desk, the excellently framed prints which decorated the papered walls, the thick-pile carpeting; none of it went with murder.

On a side table a stack of European periodicals and French daily newspapers awaited his perusal. An expensive tuner and amplifier would put him in touch with any radio stations in Europe. A TV-set broadcast silent images, its sound turned off.

He closed the door behind him and went to his desk. His day's work had been carefully laid out by his secretary, his calendar opened so that he wouldn't miss the red-lined appointments. A flat blue file occupied the centre of his blotter. In it, sufficiently coded to avoid secretarial prying, was the sealed, weekly, three-page brief, 'eyes only', of Tricolor's up-to-the-minute position in France. It was his job to compile it. He'd done so on Friday evening. Nobody but the recipients of the only three copies, Collins, Ender and Jedder would understand its context. Once read, each copy was immediately fed to the small electric shredder with which each man's office was equipped, in Collins's case usually his shredder at the American Embassy after personal delivery by Ender or himself.

Next to the file, in a red folder, was a twenty-page draft, to be rewritten, an exclusive, quarterly progress memorandum slated for the National Security Adviser's and probably the President's eyes when Ender would make a fast trip to Washington in two weeks' time. This memorandum, elaborately coded, took the form of a report on the take-over of a French machine-tool company by a Dutch holding company, with suitably scaled-down financial figures.

There was a light knock on the door to the adjoining secretarial office, and Jacqueline came in. She was fair and slight, not especially pretty but with a wide sensuous mouth and steady eyes. She was married to an engineering student and helping to pay his way through graduate school. Although she was French she spoke English to Aaron, since in her eyes he must be American. It was an irony that hardly escaped him.

'Good morning. I thought I heard you come in.' She put coffee on his desk.

'*Bonjour* yourself, and thanks,' Aaron's eyes rested on her very pregnant abdomen. 'When do you produce that thing? At lunch?'

'I wish I were! Feel,' she ordered. She put his hand on her stomach. Something surprisingly close to the surface knocked hard at it.

'Ouch!' he said.

She laughed. 'Don't forget your meeting. You have five minutes.'

She went out, closing the door softly. Aaron liked her and for her sake was glad she was leaving soon, but lonely, too, because they worked well together and he'd miss her. In a way she represented all the really decent things he liked about France.

When he came through her office a few minutes later and left his coffee-cup on her desk, she smiled acknowledgment without looking up. She was hard at work, her typewriter flowing at high speed.

The door to Collins's conference-room-office was still open, and he could see Collins behind the huge desk he'd had moved in. Ender was there, too, on the couch, one leg on a cocktail table, the other slung across the couch's arm, jacket off and fingers laced behind his head. Ender always sprawled, no matter where he was. Near him, Jedder was just settling rather stiffly and formally into a straight chair, his manner more European than American. He looked slightly less ill.

A number of things had crystallized in Aaron's thinking. Unwittingly, an intractable French industrialist, head-quartered three hundred miles away in the industrial city of Lyon, had created in that room elements of potential discord which should not be too difficult to nurture.

Collins was trying to shoot down Ender and looking for any excuse to do it. Reymond and COPIC were Jedder's choice, and Jedder was Ender's. Any trouble with Reymond gave Collins a weapon. Knowing all this, Ender was on the defensive and edgy. Jedder himself was edgy, too, as well as directly worried by Reymond who wasn't a serious threat to Tricolor, *per se*, but who could certainly cause a lot of very uncomfortable moments if not now handled correctly and at once. And Jedder was fed up, too, with what he felt as incessant, insidious and deliberate erosion of his position and prestige.

Aaron cautioned himself to be careful and not overplay his hand, not to give Collins, gratis, anything specific to reinforce and lend credence to his already hostile opinion of him.

He crossed the carpeted threshold and closed the oak-panelled door behind him. It was soundproofed against curious ears and had the feel of closing the heavy door of a safe. It gave him an unexpected and odd feeling of isolation, and thus of vulnerability. For an instant he had an overwhelming desire to turn and run. Run and never stop. Run forever.

But run where?

He said an easy and friendly good morning to Collins and Ender and settled himself in a comfortable chair, took out his notebook and pencil and waited.

Chapter Thirteen

Ryan 'Banjo' Collins was an old law-firm colleague of the Speaker of the House. A self-made millionaire from Pickens County, Alabama, he had built his fortune as a Washington lobbyist, pitting southern and south-western money against entrenched, north-eastern finance capital. A number of years ago he had shed, courtesy of extensive public relations, a politically detrimental image as a one-time red-neck supporter of both the Ku-Klux-Klan and the American Conservative Party. With only his nickname to occasionally remind, he had begun adult life as a country-and-western music star, and without completely alienating his 'good-ole-boy' roots, had gone on to achieve the image of an esteemed Elder Statesman in the realm of American trade abroad. Eventually, campaign contributions to the tune of two-hundred-thousand dollars saw him rewarded with the office of Ambassador to France. Now in his unpublicized and unofficial side-capacity as 'co-chairman' of Dallas Research he was, in effect, still looking after his earlier clients, many of whom were heavy financial contributors to Tricolor.

He was a small, dry man a zealous Fundamentalist and a teetotaller. He had a narrow face, cold grey eyes behind tinted, rimless glasses and thinning iron-grey hair. In spite of a thick regional accent, he had a surprisingly soft voice and a southern courtesy, when it was to his benefit, that bordered on the unctuous.

He didn't bother to say good morning to Aaron. His feelings about Jews in general and Eastern-Establishment Jews in particular were well known.

Aaron sat at the opposite end of the couch from Ender and said to Ender in the guise of pre-meeting chat, 'I went sailing at Dinard on Saturday. The end-of-the-summer Anglo-French regatta.' Dinard was the North Brittany yachting stronghold of the French upper class, and his remark was, as he had meant it to be, a red cape to Collins. The Ambassador felt put down by the British and thus intensely disliked them, and had nothing but contempt for the French whom he considered decadent papists. Aaron knew he had refused a formal invitation to the regatta. 'Too bad you couldn't have made it, sir,' he went on. 'Would have done you good.'

Collins's eyes glittered. 'I'm afraid, Mr Zeismann, that this weekend my official position called me to duties slightly less pleasurable.' As usual, he very carefully pronounced Zeismann as though there were something unclean about it.

Aaron went on, deliberately blithesome and emphasizing the sarcasm. 'Guess who I saw. None other than the coalminer's prodigal son. He came across from Cowes.'

He had indeed seen Strachey who had arrived in London the previous week. In keeping with their Washington social acquaintance, he and Aaron had carefully kept conversation to casual chat about wives and sailing. Aaron thought Strachey had handled it well.

'Strachey?' Collins looked surprised. His telephone rang. He picked up the receiver. 'Yes?' His eyes flicked Aaron's way for a betraying second and Aaron guessed it was Larsen. If he were right, Collins wouldn't be able to say anything without admitting his own complicity in Larsen's renewed surveillance, something he couldn't do without in turn risking an open breach with Ender and forcing Ender finally to appeal to the Adviser. The Alabaman's hands were tied.

Ender leaned down the couch and said, *sotto voce*, 'Christ Almighty, Aaron, what the hell are you trying to do?' He was flushed and looked anxious.

Aaron shrugged apologetically. He'd angered Collins, seriously worried Ender. All in less than a minute. It was a damn good start, he thought.

Collins told his secretary, 'No more calls,' and put the receiver down. He said softly, 'Presumably, when the President asked Julian Strachey to go to London for him he knew what he was doing.' He turned abruptly to Jedder. 'Henry, what do you suggest we do with your little anti-American friend in Lyon?' He held up a blue briefing-file which, like Aaron's, had been centred on his desk blotter. Something in his manner suddenly told Aaron he didn't really care. Collins didn't consider Achille Reymond any real problem. He was going to amuse himself, however, by using Reymond to bait Jedder and then use Jedder's reaction to embarrass Ender.

Jedder rose to the bait. His answer was stiff. 'I take it you mean Achille Reymond.'

Collins laughed. 'You may have other French friends in Lyon suspicious of "Yankee imperialism", but I doubt if they concern us.'

It was pointedly rude. Jedder controlled himself. He said, coldly, 'The IIC accountant was the one who let the cat out of the bag. Not me.'

Collins jabbed at him again. 'That may be, Henry, that may be. But in the situation we are in we all must expect the cat, as you say, to be let out of the bag frequently in areas for which we are responsible. And each of us, according to the particular cat, must be just as responsible for putting it back in the particular bag from whence it came. Not some inferior. In Reymond's case, you originally recommended COPIC over many equally-commendable companies and you have known Reymond for a number of years. You can hardly say this is *my* cat.'

Jedder didn't answer. Ender saw his sullen anger and leapt in, conciliatory. 'I don't think it really makes any difference, Banjo. What *is* important is that Henry is the only one of us who is competent to rescue the situation.' He turned back to Jedder. 'Henry, suppose we could prove to Reymond's satisfaction that the dollars the accountant apparently revealed were French-owned. For example, they could be dollars owed to France by the US in some sort of a balance-of-payment deal. Or, say, return of overpayment on French debt-interest. We could tell Reymond the French Treasury found the COPIC oil-lease a convenient way of reabsorbing the money into the French economy. Something of that nature. You'd know better than we what he'd swallow.'

It was good, Aaron thought, probably even the solution. He could see, also, that Jedder's hurt pride was partially mollified. But Collins hadn't replied, which meant he had other ideas or wasn't sold. Aaron decided it was time to be destructive again. He said to Ender, 'It would have to be airtight, Richard. Achille Reymond's not stupid.'

Ender immediately looked exasperated. 'What do you suggest as an alternative?'

Aaron shrugged and deliberately asked what he suspected was in Collins's mind. 'What do you figure Achille Reymond's price is, Henry?'

Jedder was caught flat-footed. Buying Reymond simply had not occurred to him at all. And that in itself told Aaron a lot. It meant Reymond might well be someone you couldn't buy. There were still people like that. Not many, but they existed.

'His price?' Jedder demanded stupidly.

'You know him better than we do.'

'I think it would be pretty high,' Jedder replied finally. 'I couldn't say specifically. I'm not acquainted with his personal reference points.'

'His reference points?' Collins feigned surprise and his Alabama twang was particularly pronounced.

Jedder stiffened resentfully again. 'That's what I said.'

'Now, Henry, what does that mean? *Reference* points. Or is that some fancy French term a back-home boy like myself wouldn't have heard about?'

Jedder flushed. 'Some people put a higher value on money than others.'

Collins had leaned forward across his desk with a forced show of infinite patience. The Alabama twang now was deeply pained. 'Henry, with your permission, and pardon the old southern expression, even the most blackassed nigger in the cotton patch knows his price. Now just tell us, please, in plain, simple English, Henry, please, how much is this frog buddy of yours going to want?'

Jedder sat up very straight and quiet. He'd gone white. Aaron felt sorry for him but it was also the right moment to mix even more. 'Ambassador,' he said to Collins, 'maybe "how much" is something Henry ought to play by ear. There's always the possibility that Reymond might be the kind of guy nothing could buy.'

Collins lost his veneer. 'That's horse-shit, Zeismann,' he snapped, 'and you know it. The man who can't be bought doesn't exist.'

'Suit yourself,' Aaron said cheerfully. He laughed. A moment previously he'd seen Collins glance imperceptibly at his watch and knew the Ambassador was suddenly tired of the game and that it was time to help him out of it. 'You know, there's another way of looking at this,' he said. 'Suppose we stop trying to guess how much Reymond's silence is worth to *him*, and start figuring how much it's worth to *us*.'

As he'd expected, Collins rapidly gave way. He stared, obviously surprised. Then he asked, 'All right. How much do *you* think?' Aaron stalled a few seconds to make it seem as if he were seriously reflecting. He said, 'Five million.'

Ender exploded. 'Jesus, Aaron. Are you kidding?'

'Maybe six or seven,' Aaron said. 'To us.'

'You're out of your mind. Nobody's had that much yet.'

'We haven't had anybody yet,' Aaron shot back, 'whose refusal might force us to pay off a lot of other people. Who are you going to have to shut up if, for example, Reymond keeps coming up to Paris and asking questions?' He stood up. 'You asked me what I think. That's what I think. And that's what I'm here for. To assess the French. To tell you,' he grinned at Collins, 'what their reference points are.'

Collins's stare was icy. For a moment Aaron thought perhaps he'd gone too far. But Collins suddenly looked over at Jedder. 'Zeismann's right. Try three million, Henry. Wrap it up attractively so he can't really call it a pay-off. Stock bonuses, pension plans, you figure it. Five's your limit if he holds out. But I suggest you try Richard's idea first, making the dollars seem legitimate.' He swung back to Aaron. 'I was born poor and came up the hard way. Back in Pickens County we had to sweat same as the niggers to make a dollar. And I never saw giving away even one of them if I didn't have to.'

'Fair enough,' Aaron agreed. He turned to Jedder. 'Richard's plan will need documentation, won't it?'

'Yes,' Jedder said.

'What do you mean?' asked Ender.

'Something in writing,' Aaron explained. 'Am I right, Henry? Maybe an exchange of letters between the Bank of France and say the US Treasury. Proof Henry isn't making it all up. And secret in nature to explain why the lower officials Reymond asked questions of wouldn't know the full story. Any signatures must belong to somebody big. Otherwise, he won't believe it.'

'Like Roche-Corbon?'

'Since he's the Bank's president, he ought to do.' Aaron laughed. 'If you don't think that's the way, Henry, say so.' It was face-saving courtesy. Actually Jedder had little choice.

Jedder smiled wanly, shrugged. 'I'll take care of it.' He rose and started for the door.

It was all over, except that Collins, compulsively, couldn't resist a final sarcastic word. 'Will you now? Why, that's just plain decent of you, Henry. It leaves us all with no more worries at all.'

Jedder turned from the door and something happened to his heavy face. The elements of it seemed to contort individually. He became for an instant someone animal and nearly maddened. 'Go fuck yourself, Collins, you red-necked provincial hick. Who the hell do you think you're talking to? I have friends in this country. A lot of them. When this is all over, you'll never put a foot in France again. Accept that as a fact.'

Collins had won. He leaned back, triumphant, and smiled. 'Suit yourself, Henry. As a patriotic American I suspect I'll pass on being an expatriate like you and stay home in the good old USA, anyway. You see, as you said yourself, I'm just a provincial hick and by definition the sort of cornball who happens to believe simple, old-fashioned loyalty to the land of his birth is a virtue.'

Jedder walked out.

Ender said, coldly angry, 'That was hardly necessary,

Banjo.' He also had risen. 'He doesn't have to work for us, you know.'

Collins pretended innocent surprise again. 'Doesn't he? Well, maybe not. Maybe he can pay off a house mortgage that would bust Rockefeller with one of his pie-in-the-sky fast-buck promotional schemes. You reckon?' His smile disappeared and he leaned forward, his voice very soft. 'He also screws around with little girls, Richard. You know it, I know it. He had two in that fancy palace of his last night, one of them sixteen. Just. One was sixteen and the other was some sort of a hippie gook who shacks with a couple of drugged-out buck niggers in St Germain. We're talking about a key member of the Dallas Research team, Richard, a key member.' Then the smile returned. 'But that's all right. I suspect, 'cause of it, Mister Professor Henry Jedder will keep right on doing pretty much what we tell him to do.' He stuffed the blue weekly report into his briefcase and snapped it shut. Then he saw pure hatred on Ender's face and realized he'd gone far enough and was conciliatory. 'Shucks, Richard, no need for you and me to start rooster-flapping 'cause of a damn Yankee like Henry.' He laughed. 'When does he see Reymond?'

'He's going down this weekend,' Ender said.

'Any problem with the papers he'll need by then, I can give you Embassy help.'

Back in his own office, Aaron considered that Ender's chagrin had to be bitter. Collins was acting more and more like a boss and more and more getting away with it. From his own point of view, however, the meeting had been a resounding success. The favourite son of Pickens County had been so busy bullying he'd let himself be outsmarted, and Ender with him. Aaron had seen a crack in Tricolor's wall, and had used the enmity between the two men to drive in a wedge. Almost for the first time since he'd talked to Strachey, he'd been able to take real and positive action.

He told Jacqueline he was going out for coffee and, feeling exhilarated, went down the hall to the elevator. Jedder was back at his desk, staring blankly, his hands resting unnaturally each side of his blotter. He was still deeply upset. Aaron slipped by his door without being seen.

The elevator was occupied. He took the stairs. One flight down, he ran into Arnheimer Larsen, impeccably tailored as usual, coming out of his own office. Aaron stopped. 'Oh there you are. I was just on my way to see you.'

Larsen waited. Aaron went on, authoritatively: 'There was an incident this morning. I had to take some rather radical protective action. Not sure who they were. French probably. I don't think anyone got my licence number but in case they did, you may have to do a little fixing at the Palais de Justice. If you don't know anyone there, I can give you a couple of names. Place de Stalingrad, OK? Have a nice day.'

He smiled. Larsen stared back, unblinking. He continued down the stairs.

Chapter Fourteen

Bejerec grumbled. 'You should have left it to me,' he said. 'I have specialists for that sort of thing.'

Aaron explained once again. 'No, I'm the one who had to do it. If anyone else had and made a mess of it, Larsen would have known I wasn't alone. I would have proved his point for them.'

'*Quand même . . .*' were Bejerec's last words.

They had met at the zoo on the outskirts of Paris amidst the trees and green parks of the Bois de Vincennes. Bejerec often came there. He claimed the zoo had a certain mundane sanity which enabled him to maintain his perspective. He usually spent most of his time observing the baboons which occupied in their hundreds a huge outdoor rockpile, protected from the public and prevented from escape by a deep moat. There, several score of families had staked out individual territories from which they occasionally looked out to see across the moat that other and alien civilization which joked at and mimicked their mannerisms, ignorant the while of the mirror reflection they shared.

'Look at them,' Bejerec exclaimed now, delighted and waving one short hand. 'You, me, everyone!'

He was a different Bejerec to the one in Washington. He wore a neat, almost ministerial, pin-striped suit, a three-quarter-length worsted coat and a silk scarf, for it had turned grey and chilly and threatened cold autumn rain. He looked very French, the typically overweight, businessman bourgeois of the old school. Only the wispy hair and the life-savers emerging from the battered ever-present silver cigarette-case seemed familiar. And the pale-blue eyes which at that moment filled with rare expression.

'The human race,' he said. He produced a sandwich from his pocket and carefully removed the plastic wrapper.

Aaron glanced briefly at the baboons, then automatically

over his shoulder. It was only eleven o'clock and a weekday. In the few minutes he'd been there, the few visitors around them had not changed. There was the same mother with the same little boy, the same flirtatious pair of teenage Lycée girls, undoubtedly cutting classes, the same tired-looking man with his family, probably a night-worker or possibly unemployed. His aggressiveness at the Place de Stalingrad had unquestionably given him momentary respite, but he had nevertheless been very careful on the way to meet Bejerec. He'd left the Dallas office in the Citroen, dropped the car in a back alley near the Bastille, walked to the Gare de Lyon, boarded a train, slipped off it again on to an empty *quai* and then had taken to the *métro*.

'Very well,' Bejerec said. 'Outside of your little breakfast expedition into the macabre, where do we stand? The indiscreet accountant, as you predicted, has gone to ground. We tried Brussels. IIC reports a leave of absence which means nothing. Nobody answers the door-bell or the telephone at his home. His wife is with his parents in Bruges. They refuse to speak to anyone.' He shrugged. 'He could be hiding. Reasonably there is no need to eliminate someone who will probably never dare speak another word. But, on the other hand, Larsen and company are not known for their reasonableness.'

'It makes no difference,' said Aaron. 'He hasn't enough clout for Strachey. Even if he were American. Look, there's something far more important.' He described the meeting about Reymond.

Before he had finished, Bejerec had begun to smile. '*Tiens!*' exclaimed the SDECE chief, 'It is possible they've run into a patriot? I didn't think such a thing still existed.' Then his smile faded and he said, 'I think I know what you want of me. Counter documentation.'

'You're right.'

'Otherwise known, in the American language, I believe, as tossing a monkey wrench into the works.'

'Right again. When Jedder gets down with proof that the dollars were French and legal and Reymond already has proof from you that they aren't, something is bound to happen.'

95

Ignoring a sign which clearly ordered him not to, Bejerec flung a piece of his sandwich across the moat at a baboon. Several raced for it. A female, smaller by far than her competitors, won out by dint of the loudest shrieking.

'I will have some letters made up which will be irrefutable.'

'Who do you suggest should give them to him? I can't.'

'Anonymous.'

'Won't that make them questionable?'

'It depends on who you are, doesn't it? To some, anonymity means authenticity. To others it means smear. In this case it makes no difference. You don't need to prove Jedder wrong. Only raise doubts as to his credibility. Achille Reymond and Henry Jedder will do the rest. Jedder will have to resort to the pay-off alternative, or get in a panic and *feel* he has to. That will destroy his credibility even more because Reymond will be convinced, in view of the sum you jacked it up to, that something is very wrong. Something big, too. That was very clever of you, that insanely high figure. Where do you see it ending?'

'I don't know,' Aaron admitted. 'But if you throw a rock in a pond, the ripples eventually reach shore. I'm hoping for some sort of uproar at IIC. After all, they're about to own COPIC. That puts them in the picture, at least. And as Strachey said, I only have to panic one American up there and I'm in business. The rest will follow like sheep.'

'It would be suitably ironic,' said Bejerec, 'if the same sort of craven mentality that created Tricolor were the mentality that destroyed it. When does Jedder go down?'

'He has a lunch date with Reymond on Saturday.'

Bejerec was thoughtful. 'Three days. Pretty tight for a really good job on the paperwork but we'll manage somehow. Well done, Aaron Zeismann.'

He fell silent and flung another bit of sandwich; it landed short and in the moat. While others screamed frustration a big male came sedately to contemplate in silence, to scratch himself and to bow, fatalistically, to impossibility. Aaron waited patiently. Something seemed to weigh heavily on the Frenchman.

'You know,' Bejerec said suddenly. 'I have once again been asked for the de Gaulle mole.'

And there it was, Aaron thought. He hadn't expected it.

Another piece of sandwich sailed over the moat, this time cleared it. Several young males barked ferocious claim but the big male, still hovering, slipped it away from them without their noticing. Bejerec smiled.

'Your Minister?' Aaron asked.

'Of course.' Bejerec shrugged. 'I tell you simply, my boy, to illustrate that this business of Reymond has indeed upset them.'

Aaron tried to visualize the scene, the high-ceilinged, Quai D'Orsay office of the Minister of the Interior, the high French windows with their brocade drapes, the Louis XV desk and chairs, the polished parquet floors with the occasional very expensive oriental rug, the hovering male secretary, Bejerec expressionless while the Minister convinced himself that his own venality was actually patriotism. The personal plea, the silence, then the order, for after all it was not unheard of for an ally, *in extremis*, to ask you to remove your spy from their midst, and finally it was completely legitimate to expect obedience from a department head. The Minister, after all, was the civilian in charge of the SDECE.

A baboon chattered. Aaron heard Bejerec say, 'I, of course, denied your existence, which is not the point. The point is that they have again exposed their anxiety and thus their weakness. You must never lose sight of the fact that they are weak, no matter what. Weak, and thus just as vulnerable as we. You don't have the Larsens of the world around if you are really certain of yourself. And when you do have Larsen, you expose yourself, *de facto*, to even greater danger. It's paradoxical, isn't it, that men of great intelligence who are up to no good usually pick great idiots to do their dirty work for them? Witness Watergate, among others.'

Aaron pictured the confrontation. The Minister was comparatively young, he would have been beautifully tailored and groomed as only French officialdom can be. More important, he was a graduate of the exclusive and elitist ENA, the Ecole Nationale d'Administration, and from an important, aristocratic family as so many young men in French government were. He would at first have been well-mannered to Bejerec, and to a disarming degree. Next, he would have pretended indulgent irritation. Ultimately, in the face of intransigent silence, he would have been insufferably threatening and unpleasant. Nobody in the world could be as rude, as arrogant, as bullying as the French *aristos* when they dropped their drawing-room masks.

Bejerec, however, would not have budged. And he was a key man, not easy to replace. How did you get around him, then? If you were a Minister of the Interior, if you thought like a Collins or an Ender? What sort of money was a Bejerec worth?

Bejerec continued. 'I think we've been together long enough. And it's started to rain. Keep me up to date. Perhaps the Bois de Boulogne should be our next place. Yes, I think so. Night-time there is the safest.'

He tossed his sandwich paper into a trash basket and started away.

Aaron put an arresting hand on his arm.

'How much did he offer you?'

The pale blue eyes flicked him briefly, then rested for a last time on the baboons. 'Not enough,' Bejerec said. And smiled gently.

Chapter Fifteen

Aaron watched Bejerec until he was a small figure ambling around a bend in a path that led towards the giraffes, a mild, bareheaded, overweight and anonymous man to whom he had been tied for all the years of his adulthood by nothing stronger than the slenderest strand of mutual trust.

He left the park and hung around the entrance of the Vincennes Métro. He saw no sign of surveillance but he kept waiting until a vague and distant rumbling told him a train was coming. He tore down the stairs, threw a slug into the turnstile, and made it across the platform to the train just before its doors closed.

Nobody got on after him. He changed trains at the Place de la Nation and finally got off at Denfert Rochereau in the far fringes of the Left Bank and took a cab back to the Place d'Italie. From there, he walked to the alley where he'd parked his car. It had been a long trip but worth it because it laid to rest any worry that he might have been followed.

He turned into the alley, smiling faintly at the idle passing thought that if his car had been stolen, and if indeed someone had taken his licence number that morning, then its new owner might have to cope with police action beyond all imagination.

He stopped dead and the fantasy vanished. His car was parked where he had left it. But something else was also parked there. The unexpectedness of it nearly stopped his breath. It was the battered, vintage Peugeot they'd used at the Place de Stalingrad, its front bumper nestled up against the rear of his Citroen.

He tried to think quickly and clearly. If they were going to hit him, it was foolish to warn him first. The Peugeot had to be a scare, Larsen getting his revenge and adding up terror points at the same time. Almost simultaneously he thought, warning his victim was Larsen's way, the victim's surprise and fear the fun of it.

He had a choice. He could step back quickly and run. Or he could take his chance and walk into it. Something made him decide to take his chance, perhaps a sudden and overwhelming weariness with it all that produced an irrational bravado. He walked slowly towards his car, trying as he went to see over its roof and into the Peugeot's windscreen which was higher. He could see nothing. He kept going, his body completely alien to him, a frail shell belonging to someone else, and he inside it only because it was the sole refuge available.

The street remained empty, save for the owner of a shabby *droguerie* who was rearranging some of the wares he'd put out on the sidewalk.

He reached the car, still unable to see anyone in the Peugeot, and then, as if in a continuing nightmare and compelled finally to look horror right in the face, he found himself at the back of the Peugeot itself.

Time stood still. He yanked the doors open.

The truck was empty.

He drove out of the alley. Checking for surveillance seemed ridiculous. He cruised slowly and openly down the Boulevard de l'Hôpital until he saw a *bar-tabac* with an open kerb in front of it.

He pulled up and went in and ordered a double Scotch. Somehow, he thought, it would have been less frightening if in the back of the truck he'd come face to face with either of the two men he'd run over, even the one dead. Suddenly the whole morning caved in on him. He began to shake. Uncontrollably. He threw down the Scotch and ordered another.

He had a lunch date to discuss opinion polls. To hell with it. He'd had enough. Enough of Dallas Research and the United States and of France. Enough of Collins and Ender and Larsen and Reymond and Strachey. Enough, even, of Bejerec. He wanted to be alone with the deep inner self who wasn't even Aaron Zeismann. He didn't want to think any more. He wanted only to exist. An unthinking animal. He wanted to get drunk and go to bed with a woman. There was a wall pay-phone. He called the office and was put through to Jacqueline.

'Cancel my lunch. Any excuse will do, we're paying him. Cancel everything else, too.'

'Are you all right?'

'No. I ate something.'

'Is that what you want me to tell Mr Ender?'

'Tell him it was Dallas Research.'

She laughed.

He hung up. Let Ender figure out where he was spending his day. He had another drink and went back to his car again, and again didn't bother to look to see if he was watched. He drove towards the Bastille and Louis Tattel's hotel. There was the girl he'd turned down at Fontainebleau last week. She was tall and exquisite and had beautiful legs. She was chic and fun and laughed a lot. God, but how he needed to laugh. He had her office number. He knew she'd not only say yes, she'd also take the afternoon off. And she wasn't Juliet who made him feel guilty or the ghost of Margita who was still love's dull ache somewhere deep within his heart's darkness.

He parked the Citroen by the local butcher's and went into the hotel. He wanted to shower, to wash away the morning and have another drink before he spoke to anyone. He kept seeing the empty back of the Peugeot truck. That round to Larsen, he thought.

He went through the revolving doors into the slightly threadbare old lobby with its high-sculpted ceiling and Victorian front desk and creaking glass-sided elevator, whose shaft was a wire cage and whose door on the ground floor was emblazoned with a large brass cutout of an eighteenth-century Montgolfier balloon.

Louis Tattel himself was behind the desk at the antique plug-in switchboard, talking to an English guest and looking eminently respectable in his black uniform jacket, the golden crossed keys embroidered on the lapels.

'*Mais oui, Madame. Vous ne risquez rien.*' He rolled his eyes at Aaron to express his exasperation with his client.

Aaron went behind the desk to get his room key from the rack. It wasn't there. Tattel caught his eye, pointed upward towards his room, then, quickly covering the mouthpiece of the receiver, said, 'Your wife took it. Twenty minutes ago. At least she said she was your wife.' He winked. 'I let her up anyway.'

The telephone once again demanded his immediate attention: '*Mais non, Madame.* Paris, she is not *le Congo, alors.* We are not the *sauvages.*'

Aaron stood rooted dumbly. He ought to have expected it. Juliet had hinted it on the phone. She'd done it before when he'd gone for two weeks to Quebec, appraising de Gaulle's impact there. And she'd followed him another time to San Francisco.

He didn't bother with the ancient elevator. It took forever, if indeed it stopped at the right floor at all. He made the four flights two steps at a time, spiralling around and around the dusty open cage.

Damn fool. No telegram, no phone call, the sort of impulsive, idiotic, romantic thing Americans did. No hint, no warning. Just arrive.

His room was at the end of a sagging corridor. He raced along it and threw the door open.

She was standing by the window, looking down on to the street. She turned. He stopped dead on the threshold. The boyish, slender figure, the wide mouth and the steady grey eyes which took him in with direct unflinching appraisal.

The short tousled blonde hair.

'Hello, Aaron,' Margita said. She wore a faint smile and the delicate smell of her perfume had already reached him. Across the room and across the lonely years of time, also, that lay between them.

'I told the *concierge* I was your wife. I said I'd left my bags at the airport until I made sure I'd found the right place. I don't think he really believed me. How are you?'

Chapter Sixteen

The waiter brought fresh coffee and at the same time, as a discreet hint, the bill. The lunchtime diners who had packed the small Rive Gauche restaurant had long ago returned to offices or shops, taking with them the mantle of security their numbers had created. The owner, released from hosting his clients, had removed his jacket and was helping a waiter stack chairs, simultaneously arguing with the cook who sat near the kitchen door, enjoying an after-work smoke and a glass of wine.

'And how is your wife?' Margita asked.

Aaron gestured silently. He was more aware than ever of the gulf six years had created.

'Are you a father?' she asked.

'No.'

She smiled shyly, her chin resting on one hand while she made small circular indentations in the table-cloth with her coffee-spoon. She had seemed to hesitate before asking either question, almost driven to them by the long silences between them. She asked again, 'Is that because you don't want to be?'

'Something like that.' He looked up quickly and then down again. She, too, had averted her eyes.

He had almost immediately taken her to lunch to ease a panicked awkwardness at being alone with her. There had been a heavy weight in his chest. Her presence overwhelmed him. He had forgotten how very beautiful she was. And how magic her personality.

'I would not have come, Aaron,' she had explained, 'if Gisèle hadn't told me you asked about me and wanted to see me. You did ask her, didn't you?'

'Yes, I asked.' It was true. Gisèle was a Paris artist, the one who had first introduced him to Margita. A week ago in a moment of overwhelming loneliness and nostalgia he'd

103

called her studio. 'Aaron! I heard you were in town.' They hadn't spoken for several years. She'd laughed her deep, husky laugh and he'd imagined her dark, heavy-set beauty. She'd been in love with Margita herself. 'You should have got in touch long ago, darling, and come to Bordeaux,' she said. 'The water was beautiful this summer. Like soup.' She kept a love-nest hideaway near the west-coast city on the long flat Atlantic beach that stretched unbroken all the way south to Biarritz and Spain, two hundred miles away. He had spent many weekends there with Margita when they were first in love, swimming, talking, racing on the hard sand, naked and hand-in-hand, and at night lying in each other's arms, listening to the pound and ebb of the great rollers that walled up there after three thousand miles of ocean, all the way from America.

There was another long pause now between them. There were a hundred questions he wanted to ask Margita, but after what Gisèle had told him of her, he hadn't the courage. Besides, what right did he have to curiosity. Or to judge.

Suddenly, she seemed impatient, annoyed. Her passive expression changed. 'You've changed, Aaron,' she said. When he shrugged, she challenged, 'Do you think I have?'

He looked up, taking her in once more. He still wasn't sure. She was less girl now, more woman. Her clothes were very casual, very expensive. Her make-up was delicate. She seemed more sophisticated, more sure of herself. And yet she was still Margita.

He was evasive. 'I don't know,' he replied. 'Have you?'

Her smile was slightly mocking. 'That was a cautious answer. You never used to be cautious. Not at all. Or care about anyone. It used to be with people, simply "piff-paff".' She gestured a face slap. 'You didn't need anybody, you didn't want anybody. You never gave a goddamn.' She laughed. 'What happened? Too much America?'

'It's been six years,' he said. 'Maybe we both just have the air of survivors.'

She repeated the word and thought on it. Something in her saddened. She was silent, then her chin came up off her hand. Defiantly. 'Yes, we *survived* all right. Are you surprised I did? Oh, I did, don't worry. But you probably know, don't you? Gisèle would have made certain you did.'

Gisèle indeed had told him everything. She had never quite forgiven him for taking Margita away from her, even if her own affair with Margita had been for both only the briefest sort of feminine encounter. Her husky telephone voice had hardened mercilessly. 'You sent her to hell our Margita Majerová,' she'd said. 'And she needed love. Badly.'

Hardest to accept of all had been Guy Roche-Corbon of the Bank of France. It was too close to home and he had always profoundly disliked the banker. But it was not surprising and in a way natural that Margita would end up with someone like him. Gisèle was well born and travelled the world of the very rich who always clung together. Margita would have turned to her like a lost animal when he had destroyed what was between them and Gisèle would have steered her where it best suited her own interests.

He heard Gisèle again, coldly triumphant. 'She drinks too much vodka, she smokes too much and takes too many pills. But except for that she's very well. And why not? Roche-Corbon's immensely rich. She hasn't a worry in the world, she can most of the time come and go as she pleases. And he is powerful. She is still Czech, she's a foreigner here. If she ever has trouble with the police and they want to send her back, he can take care of that. Easily.'

Listening, he had seen in his mind the tall, haughty, grey-haired French aristocrat whose expression was always patronizing.

Margita broke in, 'She told you about Guy, I suppose.' There was bitterness in her voice now, 'The Baron Guy Jean-Philippe Valois de Roche-Corbon? He has a big house in Paris and a château on the Côte d'Or and two hundred million francs in Swiss banks.'

'I know all that.'

'And his wife is the Countess of Vezelay and a papal princess and they have two ugly daughters they can't find husbands for.'

Aaron said cruelly, 'And you have a penthouse apartment on the Ile St Louis.'

'Yes,' she said.

Gisèle had said, 'Of course, you don't have to worry that she seriously cares about him. Everyone knows he's virtually impotent. He keeps her simply because if he sees something very beautiful he must own it.'

'Let's drop it, Margita.'

'And bury it? Put it all nicely and conveniently out of the way?' Her eyes flashed. 'So there's nothing to worry about. All my revolting sins?'

His own anger surged. 'Goddamnit, I said I didn't care.'

She ignored him. She rushed into it. She looked down at the table-cloth and in low hurried words said, 'After you, I slept around all over Paris, didn't I? Did she tell you that, too, Gisèle?'

'Yes, she told me,' he answered dully.

'For a while I practically had a different lover every month.'

For the first time ever he saw tears in her eyes. He heard his own voice suddenly rise to a shout. 'So what! Am I supposed to feel guilty for it?'

'I don't know,' she cried. 'Yes, I do. Why the hell do you think I did it?'

'Other women have gone through break-ups without going overboard.'

'Other women! I am not other women. I am me. And more of them have than ever tell.'

They stared at each other across the table, hating. She brushed back her tears fiercely. Aaron finished his coffee. It was cold and flat. The owner came by. 'We are closing now, Monsieur.'

'Just going.' Aaron rose. Margita picked up her shoulder-bag and went out. He paid the bill and followed. She'd put on her trench-coat and was waiting by the door, staring at nothing. There was a cold drizzle and her hair was already dusted with it.

They started walking, not touching. Aaron said suddenly, 'What happened to Prague?'

'Prague?'

'You wanted to go back, maybe get involved with the counter-revolution.'

She looked blank. 'The revolution? Oh, yes.'

The rain fell more heavily. Suddenly, she stopped, hands thrust into her pockets, and looked up at him. She studied his face and then burst out, surprisingly heated. 'There's not much point in fighting them any more, is there? I mean it's hopeless. A whole new generation has grown up in the communist schools and they don't want to be "liberated". They *like* being goddamned communists. Listen, I actually know a young student who can easily get out to the West to marry a boy she's in love with. Any time she wants to. But she won't. Do you know why? Don't laugh. She feels obliged to pay back the state for her education first. The goddamned, communist state. Can you imagine? And she will never be able to save that much money. Not in her whole life. Or even borrow it.'

She shook her head and laughed. There was nothing in her of the woman who had defiantly dragged herself down into degradation. Aaron saw for the first time the Margita he had loved.

They came along the Seine embankment to Boulevard St Michel, passing the Ile St Louis on the way, its hoary sixteenth-century buildings rearing proudly out of the greybrown river like massed medieval knights in battered armour. Her apartment was there, he thought, somewhere among them, the place where she was the creature of Guy de Roche-Corbon. That was one Margita.

There was another, the girl of all those years ago who strode beside him now, and whose deep-grey eyes shone with the passion of her thoughts while a gust of bitterly cold wind whipped her tousled, damp hair around the chiselled, Slavic bones of her indescribably beautiful face. When he first met her, she had only recently escaped from Czechoslovakia and her French was bad, her English almost nonexistent.

'How did you get out, anyway?'

Laughter in answering, like a schoolgirl. A bubbling, broken description of a forged diplomatic visa and privileged rank in the Party. Of occupying Russian soldiers at the Austrian border and feigned disdain for snub-nosed machine-guns and the unwinking blood-red stars dominating military caps. And finally raw, stubborn Czech determination.

'I said, "Rawsian officer go and fock yourself. Here, diplomatic passport. Party orders. Can not you read and write in focking Moscow?" '

Now, at a bookstall at the foot of Boulevard St Michel, there was a swirl of university students, youthful and fresh as she had once been, and there was again laughter. She threw her hair away from her face and teased an elderly bookseller.

Nothing had changed.

The weight suddenly lifted from within Aaron. He seized her elbow and spun her around and wordlessly pulled her tight against him. He looked down into her face and saw her as she had always been and she was crying again, and then gently holding his head between her slender hands and touching her mouth to his.

He took her back to the Relais Maritime and to his room and there was no longer any time between the last day they had been together and now. But somewhere in the late evening when they'd been out to dinner and come back to once again envelop themselves each in the heartbeat of the other; somewhere there in the naked darkness of their ecstasy he remembered Larsen and then Bejerec and Juliet and why he was there at all. A cold spark of indecision flared briefly wtihin him. Then it blew out, to be forgotten in the night.

Chapter Seventeen

In the morning he said, 'I have to go to Brussels for lunch. I have conferences there this afternoon and probably tomorrow. My weekend is free, we could meet in Amsterdam.'

'Oh, yes please, Aaron. Couldn't I come with you now?'

Aaron inwardly cursed Ender. 'I'll be with my boss.'

'I can't imagine you having a boss.'

'Sometimes I can't either.' He knew Ender would want weekend company. He'd have to find some sort of an excuse to get rid of him. He decided on personal family business: a cousin of Juliet visiting London.

They made love and Louis Tattel himself brought up croissants and coffee.

He dropped her off at her Ile St Louis apartment. The building was very old, five stories, and it was leaned against by others, even older, on each side and had a sloping slate roof and a view of the buttressed *choeur* of Notre-Dame over the chestnut trees bordering the Quai Archevêché and across the narrow intervening waters which separated the St Louis from the Ile de la Cité.

He pretended light-heartedness. 'Not bad.'

She turned steady eyes on him. 'Aaron, I made all my confessions yesterday. You'll have to take me or leave me on that basis.' She looked up at the building. 'I live on the top floor. The one with the studio windows looking up the river at Notre-Dame.' She went on, voice tinged with an odd bitterness, 'It has old beams in the ceiling and wall-to-wall carpeting and a sunken bath. And a blue Maserati in the basement garage to go with it.'

There was nothing he could do but accept it. He drove away and in his rear-view mirror he saw her still standing on the sidewalk watching him go.

He picked up Ender at the office and made the shuttle

flight to Brussels at the Charles de Gaulle airport at Roissy, north-east of Paris. Two hours later they were in the giant tower that was the International Investment and Credit headquarters near the site of the old 1958 Belgian Exposition.

In spite of a balanced number of European executives, IIC was that peculiar sort of American world that a group of Americans abroad sometimes makes around it and which often ends up a self-conscious parody of the real thing. They were filled with condescending self-importance, pretending not to be a major economic power but, for all their self-effacement, making certain you knew it just the same. Aaron felt embarrassed for them.

On the agenda this week were discussions on the eventual slow transfer of IIC-trained personnel into COPIC, possible removal of COPIC headquarters from Lyon to Brussels and security; how to compartmentalize executives so that no one person knew everything, and how to avoid the sort of leak which had just caused the trouble with Achille Reymond.

The IIC president was a colourless little man who, like most major bankers, gave grudging lip-service to a social conscience he didn't possess. The world outside banking simply didn't exist. He was, Aaron knew, what Henry Jedder would like to be, but Jedder for all his ruthless dreams was far too human and thus too weak. The president, who owed much of his position to brilliant advice from Jedder, said during breakfast the following morning, 'If Henry doesn't pull Reymond into line this weekend, get rid of him.' Jedder's first failure as a man was not to be brutal enough to similarly dishonour a personal debt; his second was not to recognize that failing in himself.

It seemed a lifetime to Aaron before Ender grudgingly swallowed his weekend excuse and he was able to board an early afternoon plane for Amsterdam. The fact that Larsen must unquestionably know where he was going didn't disturb him. If forced to, he could always pass off his lie to Ender as normal male secrecy. Ender, given his own extra-marital record, would have to accept it.

He met Margita in the bar of the Hôtel Donen. It was a

110

three-sided, intimate room of old wood and Delft tiles and with a lead lattice-work of tiny window-panes which commanded the merger of two tree-lined canals bordered by old Dutch town houses. It was too early for cocktail hour and only a few tables were occupied.

'I thought you'd never come. I checked in this morning and slept for hours.'

Her fawn-coloured hair had been beautifully fresh-cut by the sort of expert only found in Paris. It seemed impossible that only six years ago she had been so homeless and alone and so belonging to nobody, and the six years fell away as if they had never been. Aaron felt powerless against her emotions.

'When I go back to the States, I want you to come with me.'

'To Washington?'

'Washington first, yes.'

He'd decided on the plane from Brussels. He'd get out. All the way. Make a complete break and a completely fresh new beginning. There'd be no trouble with Bejerec. Bejerec would let him go gladly and the de Gaulle mole would cease to be an albatross around his neck. He thought of Bejerec's advice. He'd need to stay with Dallas until he could justifiably admit defeat to Strachey. Then he would go back to the National Security Council, at least for a while. There'd be a divorce. Juliet already felt the inevitability of it: he had sensed that.

He heard Margita say, 'It would be hard to leave Paris.'

'That's only because you are used to it.' He covered her hand with his. 'It's not the only place in the world.'

'No, but any other place might seem second best.'

'San Francisco?'

'I've never been there.' She laced her fingers happily with his.

He told her about it. He described the hills and the wharves and the bay. And northward, the forests and green fields falling in sheer cliffs into the booming surface of the Pacific. 'Not right away, but in a couple of years' time.'

She laughed. 'But it's going to fall down any day now. All of it. All the experts say so.'

'We'd be among the lucky ones.'

'Yes?' She seemed to muse on it and then suddenly said, 'Aaron, what about Juliet?'

It shocked him. It was the first time he had ever heard her call Juliet by name. The outside world rushed in.

He was cautious. 'What about her?'

'You have lived with her for eight years now. There must be something between you. Does she love you?'

He shrugged and thought resentfully, you don't have to stay married to someone because she loves you, not if you don't love her. If you do, it's a one-way street and is no good for her either.

By way of answer he said, 'She wasn't a child when I married her.' It was craven and he knew it and that made things even worse. He tried to hold on to their earlier mood by calling over the waiter and ordering more drinks, but it didn't do any good. The mood began to slip elusively away.

'If you were not in love with me,' Margita insisted, 'would you leave her just the same?'

'Eventually.' It was another evasion, and her expression told him she'd seen both and the guilt in him, too. He wondered how many other couples had been through this and if any had ever found the right answers. It didn't seem fair. It had nothing to do with what he felt for her. Or what he wanted for them both.

He said resentfully, 'I don't understand, Margita. We were talking about your coming with me to America. Where you're concerned, Juliet has nothing to do with it.'

Margita was thoughtful. Finally she said, 'No, Aaron, you're wrong. *You* said I was going to America. I didn't say anything. And Juliet has everything to do with it.' Her deep-grey eyes met his. 'I'm sorry, Aaron, but please try to understand. I've become selfish, I couldn't live twice through what happened before. I've just buried all that. Can't you see I must be very certain before I risk it all again?'

A few moments back he'd felt rage at Roche-Corbon. Now it was the eight years he'd lived with Juliet, the whole wasted lie which had come home to roost. He surrendered grudgingly. 'What do you want me to do?' he asked.

'Talk to her,' Margita replied. 'Then come back to Paris and tell me it's over. Isn't that fair?'

He had no answer. It was fair.

After a while Margita said, 'What about this weekend?'

'What about it?'

'If you said you wanted to call it off, I'd understand.'

She sounded downcast.

'Don't be ridiculous.'

They were silent again, awkward with each other, Aaron angry at his own truculence. Outside, the lights along the canal came on. The bar began to fill up. Suddenly Margita enfolded both his hands in hers. 'Aaron, can we go up now? I want you to make love to me.'

Her expression was soft. She was the way she had always been. The bad moment was over, the outside world went away and everything was right again. The only thing that mattered was them. He and Margita.

On Saturday morning they sat in their huge hotel bed and hugged terrycloth *peignoirs* around them and ate caviar and drank champagne for breakfast. And talked about old times and told stories about Gisèle and her lovers and laughed like children.

In the afternoon they walked the canals and Amsterdam's old, winding streets and shared *crêpes* in a tiny restaurant and window-shopped antique stores. It rained again. Yellow leaves fell from trees along the canals and onto the grey water, drifting together in slowly turning sheets of colour.

Very early on Sunday, he was awakened from a deep sleep by the insistent ringing of the bedside telephone. He moved his body gently away from Margita and lifted the receiver. Habitual caution stopped him from immediately speaking. He tried to think of who would know he was there.

Louis Tattel's husky voice came over the line, querulously urgent.

'*Tu es là, alors? Réveilles-toi!*'

'*Qu'est-ce-qu'il y a, donc, bon Dieu.*'

Louis Tattel told him.

The early-morning first editions of the Paris newspapers carried the late-wire story of Achille Reymond's Saturday night suicide. The Lyon industrialist had jumped to his death at ten-thirty p.m. from the window of his seventeenth-storey office where he had gone, according to his wife, to dictabelt some important letters and to collect some papers he'd forgotten.

Even before he put the receiver back, every instinct told Aaron that Collins and Ender, probably thanks to Larsen, had made the human error Strachey had predicted and that he and Bejerec had finally been handed the break they had so long waited for. He knew, like it or not, that he had to act on it, and act immediately. It was more than duty or obligation to the past twenty years. If he did not follow through now, some day it might in some way come between him and Margita.

He woke her and ordered coffee and they took a shower. It was four-fifteen a.m. They caught the six o'clock plane to Paris. He put her in a cab at the airport and then, after the most elaborate precautions he'd ever taken to avoid professional surveillance, used a special police pass to avoid the queue for the seven-thirty air-bus to Lyon.

He boarded the plane as a baggage loader and was in Lyon by eight-thirty.

Chapter Eighteen

A man's life has to do with the existence of a unique universe of thought locked in relative safety within a body. People call it a soul and claim to know about it, but actually don't. They don't know where it begins or ends, or how it is separated from its body shell, or even if it is. Only two things are clear, the body makes certain demands on its locked-in thought, and thought makes equal demands in return. Existence requires both, and in the end, when the chain of life that makes it all run is broken, thought, for all its infinite abstract qualities, becomes suddenly finite and is extinguished, too. It goes out like a snuffed candle and with it the personality it has given to the body's individual warmth and animation. The whole becomes simply useless, rotting organic matter; unfeeling, unknowing, and sharing with all other corpses the total similarity of non-personality.

Achille Reymond, for all his lifetime dynamism, was no exception. The mutilated mess that had been the industrial captain and man was extended on the slightly corroded zinc top of a Lyon city morgue table. A twenty-litre pail hung at the foot of the table for *matière détachée*, pieces of body which, due to the manner of death, might have been separated from the whole. In Reymond's case that meant considerable visceral matter hopelessly snarled around the top of the parking-meter on which he'd landed. The meter had entered the body at its lower abdomen just above the pelvis and had protruded out between the shoulder-blades as the body cannoned on to the sidewalk. To facilitate things for themselves and leave further unpleasantness to others whose job that was, the police had simply cut the meter off with a hacksaw and sent it along to the morgue as though it had belonged to the body all its life. It had not yet been extracted from the remains.

The scene was bathed in the intensely blue-white glare of overhead strip lights common to morgues, and which always renders death even more sterile, if possible, than it already is.

Aaron reflected on the light and on Reymond, on what Reymond had once been and was not and on life and death. He paid scant attention to the clinical pathologist whose youth and modish moustache gave the lie to his occupation. He knew what the pathologist would be saying. No alcohol in the blood past an acceptable dinner glass or two of wine, no drugs; the widow had been spared the sight of what she had once tenderly held in her arms and whose once warmth she had perhaps eagerly admitted into the very privacy of her own body. A son had made the required identification and had subsequently needed some medical assistance. The police had come and fingerprinted and footprinted; tissue samples had been gathered and preserved for future laboratory analysis which would show the man to have been healthy at the moment of impact except for a massive surging of adrenalin throughout his vascular system; the remains would be picked up by a mortician in the course of the afternoon. It was all that predictable.

Lyon stands, a grizzled giant, proudly astride the confluence of the Saône and Rhône rivers. It is one of France's most modern industrial cities and, at the same time, one of its most ancient. Immediately upon landing at the municipal airport, Aaron had gone to police headquarters. He met with the *commissaire* assigned to Reymond's suicide and showed identification that said he held high-ranking *Soûs-Préfet* status and was responsible directly to the Minister of the Interior on matters of national security. It was one of several useful identifications Bejerec had provided him with.

He received required co-operation, nothing else. That meant telephone calls to the morgue to announce his impending visit, a request to have Reymond's secretary surrender her Sunday and come to Reymond's office to meet him, and the use of an official car with driver. Nothing more. Local police chiefs are not known to look favourably on the

116

interference of high-ranking colleagues from Paris.

After the morgue, he ordered the driver to take him to that world once ruled by the dead man, the Compagnie Occidentale des Pétroles Industrielles et Chimiques.

COPIC headquarters were in a suitably imposing high-rise building in the sprawling, modern business-complex which looked across the grey Rhône from its east bank towards the hoary stone walls and steep-pitched tiled roofs of the old town opposite.

The sidewalk had been thoroughly cleansed. Some city workmen were putting in a new parking-meter. Sunday strollers ambled the sidewalk under a warm autumn sun. The night was over. And with it the weighty rustling sound of a man falling.

The executive suites were on the seventeenth floor and had the ghostly quality common to empty offices. Reymond's secretary met him at the elevator which opened directly on to the plush modern reception room. She was slightly overweight, beginning to grey. Behind dark glasses and too much make-up, her face was haggard. She had obviously been crying.

'I don't understand, Monsieur. Your colleagues were here half the night. Many of us were called in from our homes to answer questions.'

Aaron said abruptly, 'I'd like to see Monsieur Reymond's office.'

Taken aback, she opened her mouth to protest, then thought better of it. 'Just as you wish,' she murmured.

They went down a hushed corridor to a spacious modern room. Reymond had been an excellent amateur photographer; there were big blow-ups of his work on the walls, mostly lyrical scenes of the French countryside. There was a draughtsman's drawing-board. He had often liked to work standing up, ignoring the broad executive desk, cantilevered airily over thick executive carpeting.

An informal photo of Madame Reymond dominated the desk. She was a modern-looking woman, a natural blonde. The picture had been taken at a swimming pool and gave her a good body for her age which Aaron guessed at slightly

117

over forty. She had scrawled firmly across it. *'Je t'aime, Yvonne.'*

There were four windows, the view across Lyon magnificent. He wondered which one had been used. He glanced down. The street looked sickeningly distant. He turned away. The secretary was rubbing her forearms nervously. 'Tell me,' he asked casually, 'how long did you work for Monsieur Reymond? Five years?'

'Ten.' She said it proudly.

'Ten,' he repeated. He knew exactly what he wanted to know. It was simply a question of fitting the phraseology to the particular person. He felt he'd sized her up enough by now.

'Did he hold very strong views on things?'

'I – I'm not certain I know what you mean.' It was guarded. She knew exactly what he meant.

'I think you do.'

She surrendered reluctantly. 'Well, yes. I suppose he did.'

'For example?'

'I beg your pardon?'

'An example, please. Something he believed in very strongly.'

'Well . . .'

He could see her struggle to find something non-controversial. There was a full brief on Reymond in his file at Dallas. The industrialist had been a positive, emphatic person and had often made enemies over what he believed in. Aaron was beginning to like him.

He realized he'd have to help. 'He was in the Resistance during the war,' he said. 'Was he still particularly patriotic?'

She looked relieved. 'Why, yes. Yes, of course.'

He smiled. 'He was a Gaullist, I take it.'

She bridled, forgetting herself. 'As far as I know, the Gaullists do not have an exclusive right to patriotism.'

'I asked about your boss, not yourself.'

She lowered her eyes. 'Yes, he was.'

'How did he feel about the Americans, then?'

'The Americans?'

Aaron waved a broad generality. 'Multinationals, the almighty dollar.'

'Monsieur Reymond,' she answered, cautious again, 'had difficulty sometimes keeping his sentiments about the Americans to himself. That is well known.'

'He didn't like them?'

She hesitated. Then she dropped all defence. She coloured. 'He loathed them.'

'Ah?'

'He used to say if the world didn't do something, they would devour us all.'

'I see,' said Aaron blandly. He smiled again. 'And Gaullist or not, you seem to have shared his feelings.' He ignored her chagrin and went on, 'I believe he was anxious about possible American interference here at COPIC. He went up to Paris to see people at the Bank of France. Did my colleagues ask you about that last night or this morning?'

He waited. She'd paled visibly; her hand touched her hair nervously. 'No, Monsieur.'

'But it's true.'

'I wouldn't know anything about it. I am just his secretary.'

'Did he discuss his anxiety with anyone in the firm?'

She thought, then said, truthfully, 'I don't think so.'

'He hired a private detective agency this week to look up an accountant who came down here with an American named Henry Jedder. Can you tell me about that?'

'No, Monsieur.'

'Of course, you can't. Once again, you were just his secretary and businessmen never tell their confidential secretaries anything.'

She reddened, said nothing. Aaron said, 'I presume you can answer this one, however.' He nodded at the desk photo. 'His wife?'

'Yes, sir.'

'They were close?'

'Monsieur Reymond was always deeply in love with her. From the first day they met. He never once looked at another woman.'

Clearly the Lyon police had hounded her to know if there'd been a mistress in the picture. Aaron said, 'How did you get along with her?'

'Me?'

'Yes.'

'Very well.' She coloured again, this time with a certain indignation. Someone had also obviously tried to indicate that the mistress might be she. 'She's a lovely person and I have great respect for her.'

Aaron said, 'Thank you very much. Perhaps you would show me back to the elevator.'

She looked surprised. She'd clearly been expecting more. They went down the corridor to reception and waited in uncomfortable silence for the elevator. When it came, he said good-bye and then, holding the door open, asked suddenly, 'Why do you think Monsieur Reymond did this?'

Her eyes filled with tears. 'I don't know. Monsieur Reymond was very overworked and overtired. He could not have been himself.'

The emotion was real but there was no ring of truth about the words. They poured out glibly, a well-rehearsed lie. He was pretty sure of what it was she was hiding. But he wouldn't ask her; it would take too long to get confirmation, if indeed he ever got it at all. He pushed the down button, the elevator doors closed.

On the street the workmen had finished putting in the parking-meter. One of them tried it out, and the meter devoured its first franc.

Aaron dismissed his official car and chauffeur and the moment both had disappeared around the corner turned back to the COPIC building and the yellow sign of an Avis International car-rental office located off the main lobby. He wanted no record of where he was going next.

Chapter Nineteen

It was to the Reymond home, an old converted granary and flour-mill twenty miles out of town.

In forty minutes Aaron reached the high, wrought-iron gates which barred its gravel driveway from the winding, country road he'd arrived by. The gates were locked, the house barely visible beyond a screening copse of trees. He was deciding what to do when a Volkswagen truck pulled up behind him. A grey-haired, heavily-set man in working clothes leaned out. '*Mais alors*! What do you want?' His tone was unpleasant.

Aaron showed his police identification. 'I take it you are the gardener.'

'Yes, sir.' The man got out of the truck and reluctantly unlocked the gates, 'I'm sorry, but we've had reporters around, you understand?'

Aaron drove through.

The mill was very old. Its stone walls were pitted with the weather of five hundred years and the pink tiles of its various roofs had turned white from the sun. Beyond it and the sleepy, adjacent millstream, lay the long, barn-like structure of the granary and then some smaller buildings, converted to stables. The carefully kept grounds were silent.

Aaron left his car near some obviously family vehicles and went to a massive front door whose wide oak planks were studded with the heads of hand-forged nails. He pressed a bell. Presently, footsteps echoed within and the door was partially opened by a stoutish, middle-aged maid, her eyes hostile and, like the secretary's, red from weeping.

He produced his identification again. '*Sûreté*, Paris. *Préfet de Police* Silva.'

'We had you people all night. Can't you leave us alone?'

'It's all right, Marie-Louise.'

A girl appeared. She was about seventeen and in a dressing-gown. Her exhausted face looked as though her soul had been destroyed. Aaron guessed it was Reymond's daughter.

'You are Mademoiselle Reymond?'

'Yes.'

A kind of cold fury rose in him. Yesterday, Reymond was the man she called Father and loved, a familiar person she expected to be around forever. Today he was only a troubled image that brought an unspeakable pain nothing could stop.

He said, 'I'm afraid I must ask to see your mother.'

'Now?'

'Yes. I am very sorry.'

She hesitated, but authority prevailed. She said wearily, 'Will you come in, please?'

He followed her down the vaulted hall and then through a large but comfortable country living-room out to an old flagstone terrace, scattered with fallen leaves and separated from the millstream by a low wall bordered with autumn flowers, Michaelmas daisies and chrysanthemums. Garden furniture was casually placed about a huge grist-stone which served as a table and there were worn stone benches.

'I'll tell Mother.'

'Thank you.'

The girl disappeared. Aaron waited with a sense of unreality. From behind the granary came the steady sound of a tennis-ball in play. It seemed out of place, but part of losing someone you loved, he thought, was to keep yourself going at all costs because the alternative was unthinkable. Presently the sound stopped. Then Yvonne Reymond came around the corner of the granary and crossed the millstream by a small foot-bridge. Her son, stocky and athletic like his father, remained on the other side, watching.

'Monsieur Silva?' She betrayed no emotion. Her eyes were direct and honest, her mouth firm. She was slightly heavier than in the photograph on her husband's desk, and blonder. Her tennis dress looked as though she had slept in it and sweat rivuletted her cleavage and soaked dark under her arms.

'It must seem brutal to disturb you,' Aaron said, 'When you have surely had your fill of the local police. I am sorry.'

She frowned. 'You have come from Paris?' He could see her mind trying to put it together. Paris didn't interfere unless something was very wrong.

'Yes. I am from the office of the Minister of the Interior.'

A sort of wariness came over her. He glanced pointedly at her son. 'I must be alone with you, Madame Reymond. There are things I have been asked to discuss that are for no one to hear except yourself.'

She looked momentarily taken back, then called to her son to return to the court. When he had obeyed, she sank into a garden chair and with a weak smile apologized for her tennis dress. 'Yesterday I rolled it up and put it in a laundry basket. I never thought I would be using it today. There are times when you have to find some way to keep going.' She seemed to forget him for an instant, then she came back. 'Very well, what is it?'

Aaron said, 'What I have to say to you may be upsetting. But I want first of all to put everything out on the table. I don't have time to fence around and I don't think you would want me to.'

She hesitated, then nodded faintly.

'The *Préfet* at Lyon,' he went on, 'has officially put your husband's death as suicide. Do you agree to that?'

Whatever she had expected, it wasn't this. She had been nervously smoothing her skirt. She became motionless. There was dead silence.

'You don't, do you?' Aaron urged gently.

'No,' she whispered.

'Neither do I. Do you know who killed him?'

'No. I don't.' Her hand went to her throat.

'But you have a vague idea of why he was killed?'

'Do I have to answer that?'

'No. Because I know what your answer would be. Presuming, of course, that your husband discussed his business with you. He did, didn't he? You were known to be very close.'

'Yes, he did.'

123

'Did the Lyon police ask any questions about COPIC?'

'No. None.'

'And you offered nothing?'

'I didn't see what good it would do. Except maybe to burden the children more than they already have been.'

'I take it,' pursued Aaron, 'that you reached a telephone agreement with your husband's secretary about this.'

She coloured perceptibly. 'Yes,' she said. 'I spoke to her. But not on the phone. She came out here the moment she heard.'

'Don't worry about it,' Aaron said. 'Nothing you say will leave here.'

She looked relieved.

'In effect,' he continued, 'you agreed, both of you, to keep quiet.'

'Yes.'

'To go along with the official suicide story. Your husband had been terribly overworked, temporarily not himself . . .'

'Yes.'

'You have been very wise,' Aaron said.

'Mr Silva,' she began. She was confused as to what he was aiming at.

He interrupted. 'Suppose I try briefly, Madame Reymond, to tell you what I know. Your husband became anxious ten days ago that something was very irregular on the financial end of COPIC's plan to lease and manage certain important state oil-reserves. He was given to understand there was possibly American money behind it. When he got no satisfactory answer from Henry Jedder, he became more suspicious and hired a private agency to try to find out. Am I right?'

She was startled. 'Yes.'

'The agency confirmed to him that a Belgian accountant who had first raised his suspicions actually worked for the American-controlled IIC bank in Brussels. Not for an independent firm. Almost simultaneously, he received anonymous documentation in the mail verifying his fears and indicating that IIC was actually involved in a masked take-over of COPIC. In his own participation, he felt he was treasonably helping to sell out French oil to an American cartel. When Henry Jedder came to lunch yesterday with contradictory "proof", he didn't believe a word Jedder said, and when Jedder finally offered him a lot of money to keep quiet, he lost his temper and threw Jedder out.'

He waited. Far off, a horse whinnied, and sounds drifted from the kitchen.

She said, almost in a monotone, 'Achille was terribly angry. He called your Minister of the Interior. The Minister and he were classmates at the Ecole Nationale d'Administration. But the Minister was away some place for the weekend.'

But they knew Reymond had tried, Aaron thought. That meant his phone was tapped. It was fortunate Madame Reymond and the secretary had talked personally.

Yvonne Reymond was saying, 'What hurt him most was Henry Jedder. Achille was always one of Henry's biggest supporters. He arranged a dozen deals for him. To find out Henry was simply using him . . .' She broke off helplessly, smoothing her skirt again.

'Why did your husband go into his office last night?' Aaron asked.

'He had some idea of dictating a memorandum,' she answered, 'while it was all still fresh. Everything Henry had said.'

'Or didn't say?'

She shrugged; she was suddenly close to tears. Aaron knew it would be difficult for her not to visualize her husband's last moments. The broad shoulders hunched over the dictaphone, the knock at the door, his surprised anxiety at the entry of three or four men completely unknown to him. And his shocked realization of what he was in for when he was seized and dragged to the window, his impotent shouts rendered ineffective by the building's sound-proofing.

Finally, there would have been the last unthinkable and incredulous moment of paralysed terror when the window was thrown open and he was propelled bodily out of it into the night void.

Were the same thoughts, Aaron wondered, now marching

through the heads of those ultimately responsible, the various members of the government and key men like Roche-Corbon? Some must already suspect, as he had immediately done, the ready convenience of Reymond's 'suicide'. In the protected atmospheres of executive offices, private drawing-rooms or the candle-lit wealth of Maxim's, they had sold out their country in something that seemed nothing more than diplomatic and monetary power shuffling. Not people. Nobody had told them about the criminal mentality that lurked behind the slick, institutional façade of a Dallas Research Foundation. Murder and bribery and blackmail and torture were something you read about as happening in far-off, backward nations where the press was controlled and couldn't shout the truth. Certainly not in polite, civilized places like London or Rome or New York or Paris.

But now they knew it did. And it would be too late to stop it. They had unleashed irrevocable terror amongst themselves.

Madame Reymond got through to him, echoing his thoughts. 'I understand. This is France.' Her voice broke. 'My husband was murdered to keep him quiet,' she said. 'Who did it? IIC?'

Aaron was careful. If he told her the full truth she would never believe him, and he needed to keep his credibility with her in order to ensure her vital silence. But he had to tell her something because silence on his part would be equally dangerous.

'Not exactly,' he said. 'There were elements within IIC seeking to use its financial power for political subversion. COPIC's lease of oil-reserves was some of what was involved. We are working closely now with Brussels to bring a stop to it. Your husband's death has crystallized many things for us. He rendered his country no small service.'

'Oh, my God!' She finally began to cry. 'Achille, Achille. Oh, my God, what were you mixed up in?'

Aaron could only try to lighten one small corner of her nightmare. 'I think you ought to know,' he said, 'that he was unconscious before the fall. He died at the desk.'

Her grief came out then, with all its agony and raging. When he decently could, Aaron took his leave. 'To discuss the matter with anyone,' he said, 'especially the local police, could seriously jeopardize your family.' She gave him her promise.

The last glimpse he had of her was as he left the terrace. She was still seated and staring into space, her shoulders hunched, her hands twisted in her lap. There would be no more brave attempt at tennis. Her whole being belonged now to the shattered, ugly remains of the man she had loved and whom, tomorrow, she would bury.

Aaron drove back to town, dropped off the Avis car and took a taxi to the airport. Halfway through his talk with Madame Reymond, he had realized he might well have the witness he'd so patiently searched for. He wanted to get to Henry Jedder as quickly as possible and before anyone else decided to.

Paris–Bordeaux–Montreuil

Chapter Twenty

Bejerec lived in Montmartre, not far from the Basilica of Sacré-Coeur which from its high vantage point looks out, a great, white guardian angel, over a sea of Parisian roof-tops ending indefinitely at a smoky horizon. His small apartment, furnished with a jumble of antiques and with a certain erotic taste in paintings, was above a local stationery shop which specialized in artists' materials, for Montmartre, once the home of famous painters, still swarmed with their imitators, selling profusely to tourists enchanted by quaint old-world streets, cobbled alleys and little tucked away shops. Bejerec protested frequently that he meant to move to a corner of Paris more realistically modern-France. But the threat was an empty one. About Montmartre there is still an air of seductive charm.

He had come home earlier than usual, abandoning his office at six o'clock. He was dining with old friends, a botanist and his wife. After dinner there would perhaps be some chess.

He wanted to think before he went out. At four, he had received a coded message from Aaron Zeismann requesting an urgent meeting that same evening. It was almost certainly because of Achille Reymond's 'suicide'. Dallas, probably Collins, had blundered badly in giving Larsen free rein. Such unspeakable brutality as throwing a man out of a seventeenth-storey window usually created a chain of panic that boomeranged.

How had Aaron taken advantage of it? He must have gone at once to Lyon. Whom would he have seen? Business associates, the police, probably the body. Perhaps even the widow? What he would have determined, of course, was whether the 'suicide' was directly linked to Jedder's Saturday meeting with Reymond and the false letters they had provided. If so, he would probably have tried to see Jedder himself and as soon as possible. The financier's peculiar genius was not the sort to cope with terror, and the man had recently reached a state of near nervous exhaustion. He might well be cowering some place convinced that he, too, would die because Ender and Collins would no longer trust him but couldn't fire him because of what he knew about Tricolor and Dallas.

Aaron would be after him for Strachey; indeed Henry Jedder would make the perfect witness. And he would want help in getting Jedder out of the country. That could be difficult. If Collins and Ender had any sense they also might well foresee Jedder as a panicked defector. Through the Ministry of the Interior they had the police in their pockets. All the principal exit doors of France would be firmly shut.

Bejerec went to his living-room drink cupboard, pushed aside some heavy texts on computers as applied to pathology and fixed himself a cocktail, a mild Martini-and-Rossi dark vermouth on the rocks with a double twist of lemon peel and the tiniest dash of bitters.

Jedder, he thought, was more than ever their last chance. In his interview with the Minister just before he met Aaron at the zoo, it had been made immediately clear that the head of the famous de Gaulle mole was finally and irrevocably on the block. The Minister had received his orders.

'Please try to understand, Bejerec. Your mole, any intelligence he might chance to gather, neither are worth the loss of more important information elsewhere.'

It had amused Bejerec to goad the man into an explanation. He pretended innocence. 'What information is that?' he'd asked.

The Minister's voice rose in exasperation. 'I'm speaking of the sort of massive, world-wide satellite and electronic intelligence which we cannot afford and which they provide us with. They don't have to, you know.'

'But, Monsieur,' he'd insisted, 'can the Americans *prove* we have infiltrated them?'

'They don't need proof!'

'Suspicion is enough?'

'Yes!' The Minister had shouted. To regain control of

himself he'd arranged things on his desk. Bejerec had waited.

Suddenly the Minister had looked up with a new sort of expression. 'I have been authorized,' he said carefully, 'to see that you receive a substantial end-of-the-year bonus if you change your mind.'

And there it was, the bribe. It had been very hard not to smile. 'How much, Monsieur?'

The sum must have nearly stuck in the man's throat. 'A million francs,' he said after a moment.

It was close to what he knew the Minister himself had received.

He had let the man have a moment of hope. Then he had said quietly, 'A most attractive offer, Monsieur. But as it is, I'm afraid it's impossible for me to accept. As I have always guaranteed, we have no one in American Intelligence and never have had. For me to invent someone to fire would be not only ridiculous but dishonest.'

It hadn't worked. The Minister had kept control of himself and his response was icy and dismissing. 'You need invent no one, Monsieur, and I want his name as well as verifiable confirmation he has been removed. This week. If not, I shall be obliged to find someone to take your place.'

And there it was. Twenty years of intricate tightrope-walking at an end. Unravelled by the treason and venality of a cabinet minister. It had finally come to a choice between himself and Aaron Zeismann. There was no question of the decision. Senator Strachey was a last chance, and there was also Aaron's personal future with Juliet. He could only call the Minister's bluff and hope for the best. They would have to decide which was more important: offering the Americans their sacrificial lamb, or continuing to count for much else-where on his own long and distinguished experience and intricate knowledge of espionage. They would not replace him easily.

He shrugged. 'I will tender my resignation immediately, Monsieur.'

Except for a few words of icy dismissal, his reply was greeted with silence and with a strange and vindictive smile he had not been able to fathom. It was worrying.

Bejerec's living-room window looked out over Paris. The city was dark velvet now with onrushing night and laced with canyons of light, the horizon a deep mauve. Down below, the bakery had shuttered its windows, the *droguerie*-owner was taking in his display wares, and a waiter at the local bistro was bringing in sidewalk tables. People were going home, scurrying shadows when they faded from the overhead glow of street lamps. In a thousand other French towns and on a thousand other streets they were doing the same.

He went to his record player to put on Pietro Mascagni's *Cavalleria Rusticana.* He'd attended a performance of it at La Scala last year when on vacation. With a certain nostalgia he remembered that time. He had toured all of northern Italy's most picturesque Shakespearean cities, and briefly had been able to forget the affairs of France.

He refreshed his drink. The haunting chorus of *Cavalleria Rusticana* echoed through his apartment. He took a bath and dressed slowly, humming with it, and thought of what he would do with his life if his bluff didn't succeed and they accepted his resignation. There was always computer pathology. How ironic if he ended up lecturing at some American University under the name of Anthony Williams, and perhaps even living there. How very ironic indeed. But then that's the way life was. It was a carousel; you could not get off whenever and wherever you wished. You were obliged to wait for the unknown place and time when it would stop of its own accord, listening all the while, as you went round and round, to its wheezing calliope endlessly repeating your own particular song of fate. You never knew and that, in a way, was what made it so exciting.

The telephone rang. He let it go. Four times. It stopped. He arranged his tie before an ornate Louis XV mirror. The phone rang again. This time there were six rings before it silenced. It was Aaron, and they were to meet at ten o'clock and, as prearranged, half way along the Route des Lacs in the Bois de Boulogne. In recent years the vast park had at night degenerated into an open meeting-ground for those who sought hedonistic pleasures of every conceivable variety, either for free or for money, and cars and people, milling its dark winding roadways, created a general confusion ideal for any clandestine meeting.

Bejerec slipped into his dinner-jacket. He glanced around his living-room, left on one light and a small television, whose sole purpose was to convince a burglar someone was there, and switched off *Cavalleria Rusticana*.

Then he opened the door.

Two men stood on the threshold, respectable in ordinary business suits. He had never seen them before. Because he hadn't and because he couldn't account for anyone there at that hour, he sensed immediate and serious danger. It flashed through his mind that he had once considered carrying a revolver.

A third man materialized in the hall behind them. In spite of the dim light, Bejerec at once recognized the long, pale features, the almost albino eyes, the close-cropped blond hair.

There was no time to think further.

He stepped backwards silently as they came in and, turning his body slightly away from their view, slipped a hand into his breast pocket. There was a cyanide capsule there, tucked away in his old cigarette-case amongst the life-savers. The case clicked open and the capsule rolled into his fingers.

The door closed behind the men. Bejerec faced them again and found himself filled with a certain overwhelming regret. How very close he and Aaron Zeismann had come to stopping it all. Now Aaron was on his own and he, Paul Henri Bejerec, would never know.

Chapter Twenty-one

Shortly before this, Aaron stood on the wide front steps of the town house that was the hollow monument to Henry Jedder's financial finagling and his wife's social ambitions. No sign of life came from within the darkened interior. He rang the bell once more, faintly hearing it echo in the hall behind the heavy door. He'd been there some time now and he tried not to think that since he'd spoken to Jedder on the telephone Jedder might have panicked and fled, or that Larsen might have already come and taken Jedder away. He'd spotted what had to be a stake-out just down the street, two men in a tarnished yellow Renault. Nobody up to any good ever parked a car like that in Jedder's sort of residential area.

He'd caught the first available plane back to Paris, a late-afternoon flight. He had begun telephoning Jedder while waiting for it. Two busy signals amidst a dozen 'no replies' told him Jedder was probably home but didn't want to talk to anyone. Finally, just when his frustration had become acute, Jedder had answered, nervously guarded. Aaron had kept the conversation as undramatic as possible so as not to alarm him. Besides that, he remembered the phone was tapped.

'I presume you've heard about Reymond. It's a shame. But not a disaster. It could even work to our benefit. I think we'd better talk about it.'

'I'm going out.'

'Henry, frankly, she'll keep an hour. Call her. Collins may be difficult about this. I'll come over and pick you up. We can find a quiet bar and figure out how to calm his fears. Then you can have a fun evening with no worry, okay? Maybe if she had a friend, I could join you.'

Jedder had surrendered, deciding, Aaron sensed, not to risk losing him as an ally until he saw a clear and safe way

136

out of possible terror. It would be typical of Jedder to try to have it both ways even in a crisis.

Arriving in Paris Aaron had set up his rendezvous with Bejerec and then had taken a moment to call Margita.

'How was Lyon?' She sounded worried.

'Lousy. Look, there are a couple of things I must do, I won't be free for a while.'

'I'll be here. And Aaron?'

'Yes.'

'I love you.'

He rang Jedder's bell again and then frustratedly banged the heavy brass door-knocker. He felt inexpressibly weary. All he wanted was Margita in his arms and sleep. Then, to his overwhelming relief, a vague sound from within suddenly materialized into footsteps which approached the door with the peculiar hollowness common to shut-up houses.

There was the rattle of a chain, the massive *poignard* handle swung down and the door partially opened. It was Jedder himself. 'I'll get my coat,' he said. 'The house is still shut up. Rosemary doesn't come back until next week. Where do you want to go?'

He looked ghastly. There was no question in Aaron's mind now that the financier was indeed terrified by what had happened. Success would depend on his being quickly and firmly decisive. He pushed in past Jedder and closed and locked the door behind him.

'I'd just as soon talk here,' he said. 'And keep an eye on the street while we do.' He pointed to the door of a front room. 'What's in there?'

'My wife's study,' said Jedder.

'It will do.' Before Jedder could protest, Aaron flung open the door. If they had somehow managed to bug the house, they probably would have skipped Rosemary's part. He entered. The rays of a street light, coming through the slanting shutter-slats of tall windows, picked out furniture, shapeless and ghostly under dust sheets.

He glanced out at the street. One of the men had left the Renault and was passing slowly by. Nothing else.

Jedder came to stand hesitant in the doorway. 'See here,'

he began. Aaron ignored him and pulled away a dust cloth from a hardbacked chair and sat down. 'Henry,' he said, 'you're in one hell of a mess. Let's start at the beginning. What happened with Reymond on Saturday?'

There was a moment's silence before Jedder replied. He was truculent. 'Reymond? Nothing. There were no further problems.'

'Did he go for the documents we provided or did you have to offer the bribe?'

'The documents were enough.'

Aaron allowed himself sarcasm. 'So then, just to prove it, he went to his office and jumped out of a seventeenth-storey window?'

Jedder's voice turned thick. 'Look, I'd really rather not talk about it.'

Aaron controlled an intense desire to laugh. 'Henry, this one isn't going to go away and I'm not Collins or Ender. You have to trust someone. You can't carry it alone. So let's get down to it.'

'I'm sorry,' insisted Jedder stiffly. He moved towards the hall, heavy and bearish. 'If you still would like to go out for a drink . . .'

Aaron knew the time had come to halt gestures. His interruption was cold. 'I've just come from meeting Yvonne Reymond. Your lunch was not a success; it was a disaster. He slung you out and now I'll tell you something else. Something you don't know, just suspect. After you left, he got on the telephone to the Minister of the Interior.' He waited. There was no way Jedder could know Reymond had failed to reach the Minister.

Jedder slowly came back all the way into the study.

Aaron said, mercilessly, 'Reymond didn't commit suicide and you know it. He was too damn angry to.'

There was a scraping sound as Jedder fumbled for a chair and sat down heavily. Aaron could see his eyes. In the shadow-slatted light filtering through the window shutters they were dilated and unreal.

He went on more gently. 'You didn't count on this sort of thing, Henry, did you? Open your mouth and you get thrown out of a seventeenth-storey window. People like Collins and Ender mixed up in something like that. But sooner or later there had to be someone who couldn't be bribed. Or black-mailed. And in the sort of game we're all playing, how else do you keep someone quiet?'

The other didn't move or make a sound. Aaron again peered through the shutters at the stake-out. 'You know about those two out there, don't you?' he asked. 'What time did they show up?'

Again, Jedder didn't answer. His breathing was heavy.

Aaron said, 'Listen to me carefully, Henry. Collins and Ender think you bungled Reymond, and now they've silenced him they're afraid you might panic and become as dangerous as he was. Unless you're a fool, you've been adding that one up all day. You'll have those goons out there as company until it's decided whether you're still worth keeping or not. And it will probably be "not" because they really don't need you any more. You've done all the setting up, haven't you? The hard part? The rest is pure mechanics some second stringer from IIC can handle.'

There was a sudden stifled sound. Jedder's bearish bulk hunched over, and his hands gripped the seat of the chair. A hoarse whisper burst from him. 'What the hell do you want? What are you here for?'

'I want to make a deal,' said Aaron. 'Collins and Ender are blowing it. Fast. Dallas and Tricolor are in dead trouble and I want to be on the right side when it all comes apart. My deal is I get you out of here with me, whole skin, and guarantee your permanent future welfare, physical and financial. In return you talk your head off.'

It took a moment for Jedder to understand. When he did, a harsh laugh burst from him. 'Talk to whom?' he cried. 'Nobody's talking in this country. We've seen to that, haven't we?'

'I didn't mean France, I meant Washington,' explained Aaron. 'Specifically I meant Julian Strachey.'

It caught Jedder completely by surprise. 'Strachey?'

'His committee on international banking,' Aaron explained. 'His political career needs something very badly.

139

He's been after the IIC for years, you know that, and one whisper of Tricolor and IIC in the same breath and my guess is he would hog headlines for six months. Just what a presidential aspirant needs. To say nothing of what it would do to the hopes of the present incumbent.'

It seemed forever before Jedder spoke. 'It needs more than a guess, Zeismann,' he whispered. 'It needs guarantees. What you're talking of doing. Ironclad guarantees.'

Aaron knew he'd finally reached the point of no return. It was now or never. He plunged in. 'I have them already,' he said. 'I saw Strachey in Washington.'

He waited, steadying himself. He was shaking inside. He'd burned his bridges. He'd gambled on another man's fear and exposed himself completely. He didn't want to think of what would happen if it didn't work. If Jedder wouldn't agree, it wouldn't just mean the end of his and Bejerec's last hope. It would also mean Jedder would be mortally dangerous. In self-protection and with all the deadly risk entailed he would have to lower himself to the level of Collins and Ender. Worse. To Larsen's level.

He heard Jedder speak, his tone incredulous. 'You talked to Strachey? My God. When?'

'Two months ago. Right after they eliminated someone else back home. Someone like Achille Reymond. I began to look for a way out right then.'

'I never thought of the Strachey Committee,' Jedder said. He seemed dazed. 'Of course.'

'He offered me senatorial immunity,' Aaron said. 'Complete protection for myself and any witness I produced for him. In your case, I'm certain he'd offer even more. Political influence behind your business, for example. Here or in the States. We talked about you. He was pretty keen.'

There was no need to say more. Jedder was not a fool. He could come to all the remaining conclusions by himself and Aaron guessed he would have already started to. He would have begun to make mental pictures of the witness table, himself the star witness, flanked by counsel; the raised, leather-backed chairs and the wide, semicircular mahogany desk of the Committee; the packed spectators in the high-ceilinged room; the bright television lights; the batteries of clicking still cameras. And the damning indictment coming from his own lips. Names named, a righteous finger pointed irrevocably at the massive conspiracy that had begun in the White House. Not just revenge for every humiliation suffered at the hands of Ryan 'Banjo' Collins, but far more. Henry Jedder, guardian angel and saviour of American legality and liberty.

Aaron looked pointedly a final time through the shutters. 'Make up your mind, Henry. Every second that goes by makes it doubly difficult to leave Paris, let alone France. Turn in Dallas and probably end up a national hero, or take your chances with Ender and Collins.'

The man in the Renault had joined the man under the street light. They lit cigarettes. Aaron guessed they knew they were being watched in return.

Jedder said, 'I hope to God you know what you're doing, Zeismann.' And rose from the refuge of his chair.

They left the study and the ghostly covered furniture. Aaron said, 'We're not coming back. Do you have any documentation?'

Jedder seemed startled. Documentation underlined the reality of what he was doing. Once produced, it would make his decision irrevocable.

Aaron didn't give him time to think of alternatives. He steered him firmly up the broad marble stairs. 'Anything,' he said. 'Letters, notes.' He wondered briefly if Jedder's marriage would weather Jedder's turning coat. He doubted it. Rosemary Jedder was unlikely to be foresighted enough to guess the eventual result. It wasn't important. Jedder, once over the shock of having no one to be bullied by, would be well rid of her.

As though reading his thoughts, Jedder suddenly stopped. 'I have to telephone Rosemary.'

'Forget it. Your phone is tapped.' Aaron said it with a certain savage enjoyment as though it proved everything he'd previously said. 'Collins ordered it up last week.'

'But I can't simply disappear,' Jedder protested.

'It won't be for more than a few days.'

141

They were on the second-floor landing with only a faint shaft of light coming from Jedder's bedroom above. The street was visible down through the arched transom window above the front door. Jedder looked down at it. 'What about them?' Aaron heard terror in his voice again.

'We're going to do what they think is normal for you to do,' he answered. 'What we talked about on the telephone. We're going to have a drink with some girls. If we do that, nobody's going to decide you're not coming back here. We'll move from that point.'

'But what about yours?'

'My what?' Aaron felt a surge of irritation. Time was too precious for inane questions.

'You're being followed, too. I spoke to Ender this afternoon. He knew you'd gone to Lyon.'

Something in Aaron froze. He cursed. He'd been double-guessed and like a rank amateur hadn't covered himself for it. Larsen had figured he'd hear about Reymond and might go to Lyon, and he'd had someone at the airport there just in case, waiting to pick him up. This time someone truly professional. He'd seen no one. Had they tracked him to Yvonne Reymond's too? The thought was sickening.

'Don't worry about my goons,' he said to Jedder. He forced a light laugh. 'They'll take a coffee break with yours.' And then pick me up again, he thought, and no matter what I do to shake them, maybe hang on. A man like Larsen didn't let go at this point. Not for anything.

In Jedder's room he asked brusquely, 'Where do you keep your papers?' He didn't want to give Jedder time to think. 'Your desk?'

Jedder nodded. He was breathing hard again and sweating. Aaron thought, it's finally hit him, what he's into. All the way. He's going to go to pieces right in front of me.'

'Sit down a moment, Henry.'

Instead Jedder bolted for the bathroom. Aaron heard him retch and there was the splash of vomit.

He searched the desk himself. It didn't take long. In a bottom drawer he found something beyond his wildest

142

hopes. In two files, held together with a wide rubber band, there were thirty-odd Tricolor weekly briefings and eight monthly full reports. All should have been destroyed by Jedder in his office shredder. Instead, he had brought them home. They were unimportant in themselves. He had regularly consigned to beneath the sand at the bottom of Tattel's 105 Howitzer-shell ashtray microphotographs of everything that had left his own desk. The mass of notes Jedder had scrawled all over them, however, explaining every coded word and action, was something else. So was the sheaf of attached letters and other memoranda between Jedder and the IIC president, partially or wholly substantiating everything the briefings and reports contained. What shadowy thoughts of double-dealing had motivated the man? It made no difference. They were damning, and they made up enough documentation to tear IIC to shreds. And Dallas with it.

Aaron closed the drawer. A thought, a vague hunch, suddenly nagged. Such complete indiscretion could mean more. He was right. In a pigeon-hole he was rewarded by finding a small, tucked-away notebook. He opened it and it took only a glance to understand that in its careful listings of Bermuda and Lichtenstein Trusts, dummy Panamanian and Dutch holding companies, and numbered Swiss accounts, it pointed a merciless finger at the treason of a dozen major French political figures.

He heard movements in the bathroom. He pocketed the notebook. Jedder appeared, wiping his face with a wet towel.

'Sorry.'

Aaron held up the files. 'We'll take these.' Without waiting for agreement, he thrust one at Jedder. The other he pushed into the waistband of his trousers, then buttoned his jacket over it.

Jedder hesitated. 'I have a briefcase.'

'Men going to bars to pick up girls usually don't take their briefcases,' Aaron said.

Jedder stared at the file an instant, then secured it inside his shirt.

They went back downstairs. Aaron turned on the hall

lights. 'Act completely natural. They're not going to do anything. Only report.'

They went outside. The two men were still there, still out of the Renault. They turned their backs. Aaron could feel Jedder's tension. It had physical force. He said casually, 'Walk or taxi?' It was loud enough to be heard across the street.

'Taxi,' Jedder's reply sounded normal.

They found one near Boulevard Victor Hugo.

'*Chez Elsie, alors.*'

'*Chez Elsie? Oui, Monsieur.*'

The Renault followed them.

Chapter Twenty-two

Elsie's disco was remote from the usual night-club areas of St Germain, the Champs-Elysées, Montmartre and Pigalle which are strictly for tourists. It was in the converted loft of a two-storey warehouse in a far corner of the 15th Arrondissement which borders the Seine north of the Eiffel Tower. The neighbourhood was run down: small factories and semi-slum residential with the usual scattering of broken-windowed garages, and the occasional unimportant public building. It was a *pot-pourri* of ugliness, French style.

Elsie herself, a one-time Dior mannequin now middle-aged, had predicated her establishment on successfully pairing 'in' Parisians according to their sex preferences. The décor was designed to help. A square bar filled one corner of a dark irregular-shaped room whose four walls were occupied by booths, across each of which curtains could be drawn for privacy. Stereo speakers roared from amidst flashing strobe-lights set in the low ceiling. Packed tables surrounded a small dance area. In the back there was an uncovered washroom with three open toilet-booths which served everyone regardless. The young long-haired waitresses who pushed their way through the jammed and sweating clientèle wore skirts slit to the hip and thin bra-less tank-tops. It was a world of its own.

The taxi dropped off Aaron and Henry Jedder. They went to the door and rang; an electronic voice asked who they were. Aaron gave their names. They were inspected through an optic peep-hole, then admitted. Before he went in Aaron glanced quickly over his shoulder. The Renault was pulled up at the end of the silent, empty street. It had not tried to park.

The door slammed behind him. A couple of bouncers grinned a good-evening and he and Jedder started up. Noise poured down the stairs from above like water. When they reached the cloakroom at the top, it would be deafening. He said quickly, 'Sit at the bar, Henry, and wait, talk to anyone you want, look natural. But for Christ's sake, lay off the booze, okay?'

Jedder nodded.

Aaron tapped the file at Jedder's waist. 'I'll take that.' When Jedder handed it over without complaint, he added it to the one already in his own waistband.

'I shouldn't be more than half an hour. You'll be on your own but you couldn't possibly be in a safer place.'

In the taxi Jedder had wanted to know where they would go after Elsie's.

Aaron hadn't dared admit he didn't yet know. Temporary refuge was something he was depending on Bejerec for. He'd told Jedder he was arranging it.

They reached the cloakroom and another smiling bouncer opened the disco door for them and they were engulfed in a hot roar of deafening sound and by packed, shouting, sweating people. Aaron pushed Jedder forward and saw him in jagged strobe-lit movements slowly elbow his way to the bar, and saw, also, a leggy overbusted blonde, surely still in her teens, suddenly spot Jedder and rise from a table to follow him.

For a moment he tried to adjust his Dallas image of Jedder to the present atmosphere. When a man reached the higher levels of the corporate ladder, you expected him to have shed his animal self of lesser days. But few ever did.

He began his own tortured path through the room, fighting against the tight contact of hard, sexual bodies pressing from all sides. He could not leave by the way he'd come in. He wanted the Renault to think he was still there.

Past the bar, there was a short dark corridor. In it was the door to the washroom and beyond that, two other doors. One he knew was Elsie's office, the second announced itself with a faintly glowing red sign as the fire exit. He tested it tentatively. It was jammed shut by weathering and lack of use. Suddenly, with a blast of light, the door to the office opened. He had just time to look casual when a woman came out, probably Elsie, he thought. She smiled and closed the door behind her and slipped by him in a waft of blonde-ness and heavy perfume, provocatively tight-jeaned.

Aaron looked in the washroom. There was a man in a booth and two girls were talking before the mirror. Beyond them, on the blank outside wall of the building, there was no window, only an air-vent.

He had no choice.

The corridor was empty; he took a chance that no one else was in the office, and opening the door stepped quickly inside. It was a small, feminine place with a delicate Louis XV desk and brocade curtains partially drawn over French windows leading to a roof terrace. He quickly unlocked them and stepped outside, closing them carefully again. The disco roar faded to a low and distant vibration.

The sudden relative silence was intense, the cool of the autumn evening stabbed like ice at rivulets of sweat which ran down his shirt into his trousers. The Paris sky glowed red. He made his way by its light across the terrace to where he could see past the bulk of the loft room he'd just left and over the roof of an adjacent one-storey garage down onto part of the street in front. There was no sign of the Renault. He'd guessed right when he'd told Jedder they'd probably take a break for coffee.

An iron stair led from the fire exit to an alleyway. He climbed over a small parapet, lowered himself to it and went down and conned the street again. There was still no sign of the Renault. Nor of anything else. If Larsen had a special tail on him, they'd made the same mistake the Renault had and decided he was at Elsie's for the evening. Ten minutes later, he was across the Seine and walking fast along the right embankment, now absolutely certain he was not being followed. He needed a car and there wasn't time to rent one. His watch said twelve minutes to ten. His rendezvous with Bejerec was at ten, and Bejerec would not wait for him longer than five minutes.

At five to ten, he found what he was looking for. Close to the Trocadero there was an unlocked BMW, its keys in the ignition. The number-plate was Swedish, the owner obviously unused to the ways of Paris where nobody makes that voluntary a gift to thieves of their automobile.

At ten sharp, he had entered the Bois de Boulogne by the Route des Lacs and had pulled over under a street light so that Bejerec would have no trouble in recognizing him.

He waited. A steady stream of slowly cruising cars came by, desperate people looking for their kind of solace. Headlights flashed, a middle-aged couple in a Mercédes convertible had decided on him. He ignored them and reviewed what he wanted from Bejerec. Immediately, he'd need a totally safe place out of Paris where he could keep Jedder for a couple of days and leave him from time to time without worry. He needed a private aircraft to transport them from France to England. They would have to have false identities because they didn't dare take the risk of travelling under their own. He needed money.

A Fiat coupé stopped close alongside, roof down. There were two women in the front seat, smartly sweatered and above average attractiveness.

'*Bonsoir?*'

More headlights flashed, a grey-haired man slowed and called out, his apartment wasn't far away.

Aaron kept on adding it all up. He needed a lot of money because disappearing with Jedder was going to blow his cover and he couldn't count on Senate protection all the way. Not with Larsen still in the picture. He was going to need private guards, to be selected and paid for by himself, and a secure place to hide until the Senate hearings were over and Dallas and Larsen were destroyed.

A single woman waved. When she drove on, disappointed, Aaron suddenly became aware of time and felt, simultaneously, a cold, sinking sensation. He glanced at his watch. It was twenty-two minutes past ten.

Where was Bejerec?

The cold sensation accelerated. In seconds it became an identifiable, premonitory fear which he tried vainly to suppress. It was the first time Bejerec had ever failed to appear at a rendezvous and precisely on time.

He started up the BMW and drove out of the Bois. He wanted a telephone. There are few public booths in Paris, but he remembered the Hôtel Concorde was only a few hundred yards away at Place Verdun, a huge, garish, modern cement and glass monolith which catered for American tourists.

He parked and in the lobby pushed two people out of the way to gain access to the only free booth. They started to protest, then saw his expression and decided better.

He called Bejerec's home first, letting the phone ring the required twice then dialling again, the signal that he had to talk. There was no answer. He tried it again just to make sure then took out his notebook and decoded one of several numbers Bejerec had given him.

A woman answered, her voice cultured. 'Hello?'

Aaron asked for Bejerec.

'I'm sorry but he is not here.' She sounded vaguely worried.

'He had an engagement to dine with you and your husband. Has he gone already?'

'He never showed up. We assumed something pressing occurred. May I ask who is calling?'

'There is no message. Thank you.'

'But, Monsieur . . .'

Aaron dropped the receiver and came out of the booth.

Some time between seven when he had contacted Bejerec and seven-thirty when Bejerec was due at dinner, something drastic had occurred. A heart attack? Bejerec was the right age and under constant strain. An accident? Instinct and fear told Aaron it was neither. He felt physically ill and was pouring sweat. And helpless. The two files tucked in his belt pushed ruthlessly against his stomach, and Jedder's notebook was a thick wad in his inner breast pocket. There was nothing he could do for Berejec and he still had Henry Jedder on his hands. He had to try to push Bejerec out of his mind and think clearly. He knew Bejerec would want him to put Jedder first, above all else.

The lobby clock said ten-forty. The financier had been at Elsie's for close on an hour. If he had not already panicked

149

and gone home, he would surely do so shortly. There was no way of phoning him. Aaron knew he would have to return to the disco, and if the Renault was back on post he'd also have to find some way to slip in unnoticed. He didn't dare risk entering the office from the outside and getting caught there. Not while he still had to get Jedder out of the place.

Finally, what to do with Jedder when he did get him out? He could not leave Paris until he knew what had happened to Bejerec, not because he could help Bejerec, but because any trouble Bejerec might be in could have a direct bearing on himself and his own choice of action.

A minute ticked by. Another. Hotel guests swirled through the lobby, coming in from dinner. Suddenly Aaron saw precisely what he had to do and saw it with dazzling clarity. Another phone booth became free. He went into it, closed the door behind him, inserted a coin and dialled Margita.

Chapter Twenty-three

She picked him up on the Left Bank *quai* of the Pont d'Iéna. He'd abandoned the BMW and taken a taxi to the foot of the Trocadéro's brilliantly-lit fountains which descend in sculpted terraces of rushing water from the Palais de Chaillot down to the Right Embankment. He had walked across the bridge, collar turned up against a sudden cold wind and flying spray.

She was driving her Maserati. It was dark blue and looked rich, and as she pulled up at the kerb he had time to think bitterly that one of the rewards for being a banker's mistress was that sort of car. And to remember she loved speed and drove like a man and well.

He got in, grateful for the warmth of the instrument-glowing interior. She leaned over to kiss him. She was in jeans and moccasins with an open wind-breaker over a soft cashmere sweater. She laughed and said, 'I was taking a bath. I just threw on what I was wearing all afternoon.'

'You're fine.' He hadn't told her anything. Only to meet him and urgently. And with a car, if possible.

'Where are we going?' She put the Maserati in gear and eased silently back into the street.

'Elsie's.'

'Elsie's?' Completely surprised, she slowed. 'Aaron, Elsie's has turned into a real whore joint.'

He ignored the protest. 'Do you know Henry Jedder?'

She frowned, trying to remember. 'The financier? I think I've met him. Doesn't he mix with a lot of people in the Government?'

'He's waiting for me in the bar,' Aaron replied. 'I can't go in. You can. I want you to pick him up for me.' He didn't give her the chance to object. He said, 'It's important. I wouldn't ask you otherwise. Then I want you to drive him to Bordeaux.'

She turned her head to look at him, now with real astonishment. 'Bordeaux?'

'Tonight,' he said. She was speechless. He explained. 'Without going into details I have to get him out of the country and to the States. Immediately. But I have to get him to Bordeaux first and something's gone wrong and I have to stay in Paris tonight. Maybe tomorrow. I can't do it myself.' He looked back. Except for a little 2CV which had passed them going the other way, the *quai* behind them was empty.

He heard her say, 'But Bordeaux is five-hundred kilometres. Can't he take a plane?'

'No.'

'But why not?'

He thought, there isn't time to explain. And besides it would be too much for her to understand. He would have to depend on her sympathy. She'd been through escape from Czechoslovakia, after all. That and her feelings for him. He said, 'The French don't want him to leave. They'll be watching the airports.'

He saw the fear creep into her eyes, then, and half-perception that she might be getting mixed up in serious trouble.

'And you?'

'The same goes for me.'

'May I ask what it's all about?'

'Not yet. Later.' When she was silent, he said, 'Is there any reason you can't?'

'I don't know.' She gestured nervously, stalling. 'Why Bordeaux? What happens there?'

'Gisèle's beach-house. Remember it? It will be shut up for the winter. I need some place to hide Jedder for a few days. Some place nobody will possibly think to look for him. For a lot of reasons, mostly because he's not dependable, I can't keep him in town.'

'Does Gisèle know?'

'Of course not.'

They were at the street leading to Elsie's and in a moment they pulled up opposite the door. The Renault was back

152

from coffee, the two men in it keeping warm. They wouldn't recognize the Maserati and wouldn't be able to spot him as long as he stayed in it.

Margita stared straight ahead, not looking at him. 'Aaron, if you're in trouble with the French too, does that mean if you get out of the country you won't be coming back?'

'Probably not.'

'What about us?'

He'd hoped she wouldn't ask, not yet. There hadn't been time enough to prepare her for his answer. He said, 'I want you to leave France with me.' He waited. Her eyes were very wide and she was very still. 'Can you?' he asked.

'Now?' she whispered. 'I don't know. Must it be now? This is awfully sudden.'

'It's not what I planned either,' he said evasively. He'd thought of Larsen, of possibly leaving her vulnerable when it became clear he'd defected. The thought was intolerable. But he couldn't tell her. The risk of panicking her was too great. Selfishly, he desperately needed her. He could still do it alone, yes, forget the security of knowing what had happened to Bejerec, but his chances of failure would multiply drastically.

He glanced back at the Renault. There wasn't time any more to talk. They had to keep going. 'If you look in your rear-view mirror,' he said, 'you'll see a yellow Renault with two men in it. They're waiting for Jedder to come out.'

She looked and turned wide eyes to him, as though up to now it had all been just talk but wasn't any longer.

'I want you to take Jedder out the back way,' he said. 'There's a door from Elsie's office to a terrace and a fire-stairs. Do you know Elsie?'

'Yes, but . . .'

'Will she help you?'

Margita shrugged. 'Aaron, who are they?'

He ignored the question. 'When you reach the side alley, walk to the other end. I'll meet you there.'

'But maybe he wouldn't come with me.'

'He'll come. Show him this.' He took a card from his

153

wallet. He held it close to the green glow of the car's clock and took out his pen and scrawled on the back of it.

She shoved the card in a pocket of her jeans and looked back at the Renault again. 'Jesus, Aaron . . .' He waited. She started to speak again, but changed her mind. Suddenly she flung her door open. 'I'll get Jedder for you.'

There was a kind of reluctant desperation in her voice. She crossed the sidewalk and rang the bell and in a moment was admitted. Aaron slid behind the Maserati's wheel and drove away. The Renault didn't move.

He drove around the block and parked in shadows near the other end of the alleyway and cut the lights and motor and waited. He knew he'd thrown her badly. She hadn't said yet that she'd go to Bordeaux. At the same time, she hadn't refused. He tried not to think of failure and he remembered he'd forgotten to warn her to turn off Elsie's office lights before they came out onto the terrace which was partially visible to the Renault. It was too late now.

The Maserati's clock said two minutes past eleven. Then, three minutes past. The minute lasted forever. So much for the grandiose scheme that was Tricolor, he thought. It ticked out its life in a dirty alleyway outside a Parisian discothèque. Then he thought of Bejerec and the terror Larsen had started last summer with Babcock at the farm in West Virginia. It didn't seem last summer, it seemed yesterday and Reymond's broken corpse but an hour ago. When would it end? He forced his mind off it. There was transport to arrange. Louis Tattel could help there. For anything else he'd be on his own until he got Jedder to Strachey.

Suddenly the clock said eleven-twenty. What the hell had gone wrong? But even as he began to imagine the worst, the crack of light from Elsie's office was extinguished. He strained his eyes against the darkness, trying to see if the terrace door opened, if there were figures on the roof. He saw nothing.

Instead, the first time he was aware of Jedder was when the financier appeared close by, shambling up the alley towards him. Margita was with him and he was clearly very drunk.

154

When they reached the Maserati she said quickly, 'I think he ought to be somewhere where he can sleep.'

'He can sleep on the way.' He took Jedder by the collar. 'Henry, listen to me. We have to talk.'

Jedder tried to focus and couldn't. He stumbled against the Maserati. Aaron knew it was no use trying to get through to him. He half dragged, half walked him around to the passenger side and opened the door and shoved him down into the bucket seat. Jedder groaned and his body slumped and he was still, his breathing heavy. Aaron went back to Margita.

'Elsie helped,' she said. 'I told her the Renault was someone his wife had following him. But there was a young girl feeding him drinks, and she was going to make a scene because if I took him away she'd lose five-hundred francs, she said. Maybe more. I had to pay her to shut her up. I took the money from his wallet.'

'How much is left?'

'A couple of thousand. And a cheque-book.'

'That's enough,' Aaron said. 'All right, what have you decided?'

She looked up at him and quickly away, her shoulders hunched. In the cold half-darkness she suddenly appeared childishly slender and vulnerable. It had begun to drizzle, and her hair reflected a cobweb light. Her voice was flat. 'You mean Bordeaux?'

'Bordeaux and the States, both.' She didn't answer. He said gently, 'What does he have on you, your banker? Step out of line and you don't get your immigration visa renewed? Is that it?' It was partly a shot in the dark, partly because long experience had given him a strong intuitive sense.

She looked up very sharply, to stare hard at him. Then she smiled wanly. '*Touché*,' she said. 'That was clever of you. Yes, something like that.'

It had run through his mind when they'd met in Amsterdam. At certain unguarded moments, she'd seemed nervous and for no reason. He'd thought then that she might be taking a terrible chance of being caught with him. Some

French had that much vindictiveness and her banker had that much power. If her visa wasn't renewed she'd be deported and where would she go? Back to Prague and dreary communism? After her life in Paris, it would kill her. And if not Czechoslovakia, where else? Anywhere and alone, she'd once again be a lost refugee.

He said to her, 'You're frightened that if I screw it up somehow, or you do, or,' he jerked a thumb at the dark mass in the car that was Henry Jedder and smiled, 'he does, then you've burned your bridges behind you.'

She didn't flinch. 'Yes,' she answered.

It was why, he realized, she had insisted that he clear himself with Juliet before she came with him. She had to be certain. He was amazed he hadn't seen it. He thought again of her staying behind and of Larsen. He couldn't force her. He could only bluff. And hope. She'd said she loved him. 'You have to make up your mind,' he said. 'Right now. We can't stay here any longer. Keep going the way you have been, or take a chance and run for it. Don't look for reassurances, I can't give you any. I can only say I'm sorry. I didn't plan it this way. And if you decide "yes", it has to be all the way. You're going to need your wits about you. I don't want you trying to think with a divided mind. Otherwise, it *will* get screwed up. And it will be *you* who does it.'

He waited, hearing the far-off sounds of Paris at night. The *métro* rumbled distantly. A car turned a corner down the street where an old woman scavenged in a refuse basket. He wondered when one of the men in the Renault would get tired of waiting and go inside Elsie's to reassure himself that he and Jedder were still there, and that they hadn't somehow missed them coming out.

Suddenly Margita changed. A smile flicked her mouth and her voice was strong. 'You don't sound very sure you can trust me with it.' She looked like she had last week by the bookstalls, the way she'd looked when he'd first known her.

He knew it was 'yes'.

'Why do you think I'm asking you to do it?'

'Because there's nobody else to ask.' She laughed. She

shook her head as though she had to be crazy, and then reached up to kiss him. 'Do you want me to telephone when I get there?'

'Yes.'

'Then I will. As soon as.'

He pulled her to him. 'Don't let him cash a cheque.'

'It would tell where we are?'

'It might.'

She felt rigidly slender, her whole body pressed hard against his and she trembled. He held her close a moment, then let her go and she got behind the wheel. Her lips formed a good-bye and she rolled up her window. The Maserati pulled quietly away. It was a quarter-to-twelve.

Aaron watched her disappear and then he walked a few blocks and found a taxi. It took him back to the Relais Maritime.

The lobby was deserted with only a night light at the desk and light coming through the door behind it which gave onto the cluttered little room which was Louis Tattel's private world. Tattel's radio was on, and he saw the old para asleep in a chair, a newspaper fallen from his hand.

He took down his key from the board. There was a message from Ender in his box and one from Juliet dated Saturday.

He took the creaking, open-caged elevator up to his floor. Before he reached it, exhaustion finally came over him with stifling force. He made it down the corridor to his door, opened it, fumbled for a light and with what took enormous, methodical effort locked the door behind him and wedged a straight-backed chair under the handle. He dropped his clothes leadenly across the foot of the bed and yanked down the bedspread and crawled between the old quilt and the blankets, the wool rough on his skin. It was Sunday night and Margita's perfume still clung faintly to the pillows. He had made love to her there on Wednesday. He had been to Amsterdam and to Lyon and looked at the broken body of a man who had dared to protest, and into the terrified heart of another who didn't want to end up the same way. And if he wasn't a wanted man already, if he made even one mistake, he would be one and running for his life.

He thought of Bejerec. His mind went once more back through time to the dockside police-station at Le Havre. A teenage Arab tough stared defiantly into Bejerec's bland green eyes which without expression studied the dossier spread before him.

'*Alors, jeune Arabe!* So what do you think with your dirty, surly face and living off whores and thieving in *bidonvilles*? Shall I leave you to forget your English and have your throat cut for whispering nasty half-truths to the police about your fellow workers? Or shall I play God and father and give you a life?'

He stirred and something felt alien in his hand. He realized he was still holding the message slip which said Juliet had called. It would be seven o'clock in the evening at St Michael's and if she was not having people in for dinner, she would be seated by an autumn fire with a sandwich and a glass of milk, watching television and trying not to think of her husband because thinking of him was painful to her, that's the way love was.

He kept seeing Juliet for a long time and what his life with her had been. Then he let the message drop to the floor and in seconds was asleep.

Chapter Twenty-four

The telephone began to ring. Persistently. It summoned him up out of a dark, confused tunnel, but he couldn't make his arm respond to his brain and reach for the receiver. He thought for a moment he was in Maryland. Why didn't Juliet answer? When he finally picked it up, he dropped it and had to retrieve it from the floor. 'Hello?'

'*Dis donc, alors! Réveilles-toi! Bon Dieu. Tu es mort, enfin?*'

Louis Tattel.

'I'm listening.' He focused on his watch. It was six forty-five.

'Somebody is on my phone. Your sweetheart, I think.'

'Get her number.'

'*Merde!*'

The rattle of the house phone. He waited, hearing Tattel, muffled as he talked to Margita. Grey daylight created a still-life of his room; the old, provincial, pine bureau with its porcelain knobs, the hand-woven throw-rug a dark blob on the darker hardwood floor, the gilt-framed mirror reflecting the open, chintz-curtained window through which came the distant occasional sounds of a city beginning to wake.

Tattel came back. 'She says you can't and hurry up.'

Aaron cursed and raced into his clothes.

Downstairs, the hotel owner was behind the desk in his vest, his concierge's jacket thrown over his shoulders, his braces hanging by his sides. He was checking out an early-morning departure, a couple going off to catch a train. Aaron skirted their baggage and went into Tattel's private back room. He shut the door firmly behind him and grabbed the telephone from the cluttered table.

'Where are you?'

'Vensac.' She sounded very far away.

159

He remembered it, a cross-road and a cluster of non-descript old houses thirty miles seaward amidst the vineyard between Bordeaux and the pine forests which bordered the Atlantic. It was France's biggest wine area. She must have driven very fast.

'Any trouble?'

'No.' She spoke in English. He wondered why and remembered the only phone was in the *bar-tabac*. It was so that she couldn't be understood.

'Gisèle doesn't have a phone, remember? She always uses her next-door neighbours'. They're shut up, too, so I took him out to the house and then came back.'

'You left him alone?'

'It's all right. He's sleeping. There's no way he can leave unless he wants to walk. It's quite a way.' She laughed. 'Or have you forgotten?'

It was a long time, but he hadn't. He saw the cottage, driftwood-grey from the sun, and the wide, hard beach between it and the thundering, grey Atlantic. It was the very last of a sparse line of summer houses on a sand-drifted, tar road which then ran on emptily south behind the dunes as far as the eye could see. The neighbours' place was two-hundred metres away. Gisèle liked privacy.

It was summer when he'd first gone there, a long, hot, July weekend. Gisèle had asked half-a-dozen people and he'd met Margita. There'd been a lot of chilled white wine, swimming and sunbathing. They'd gone one afternoon to Vensac to buy cigarettes, and when Margita had come out of the little *bar-tabac*, her hair and skin laced by salt, her slender body bronzed dark, his heart had suddenly raced and he'd pulled her close to him and searched her cool, open mouth with his and slipped his hand inside her unbuttoned shirt. They couldn't wait, they'd made their first love by the side of the road on the drive back. Then the Jeep had refused to restart and laughing, they had to walk it, seven kilometres, and had made love twice more on the way on the warm, sandy floor of the pine forest.

He heard Margita again.

'I need a pane of glass.'

160

'A what?'

'I had to break a window to get in.'

'How big?'

'Upstairs, over the door.'

'Okay.' He could buy an oversized piece and bring a glass-cutter and putty.

'And I need food.'

'Can't you buy some?'

'I don't dare shop here. I'd attract attention. When will you come?'

'Maybe tonight.'

'Please, Aaron, I'm no good at this alone.'

'As fast as I can.'

'I love you.'

She hung up, and he sat down on the rough-woven rug cover of Louis Tattel's creaking iron bed. Tattel came in and lit a *cigarette au balayeur*. Rancid blue smoke curled up. Over the years the upper walls had turned yellow with it. He said in a hard voice, 'That was a pretty expensive phone-call.' When Aaron looked up, he continued, 'The deal was you would give the number to no one. I'm going to have to change the number. That means a lot of bribes around the central exchange'.

'The number's safe,' Aaron said.

'It's safe, is it?' There was heavy sarcasm in Tattel's voice. 'Let me tell you something about safe.' He put two shot glasses on the table and with his teeth yanked the cork from a bottle of *eau-de-vie*. 'In Algeria, during the war, we had some Arabs in our company, the smart ones who wanted to stay French. There was this one, fat little bastard reading up on Napoleon every night, getting ready to be a proper Corsican. Can you imagine? Fucking Bonaparte? Except we found the little cocksucker was also selling us out to the other side. Like that, he figured no matter what happened he'd come out on top.'

Louis Tattel poured the two shot glasses full. He shoved one across to Aaron, drank the other in one swallow, refilled it and recorked the bottle. He laughed. 'He had a big club, that little Arab, down to here like a donkey. One of the

161

sergeants gave him what we used to call a Foreign Legion circumcision and tied it to his helmet. What a sight!'

Time stood still for Aaron. Tattel, the cluttered table with its checked cloth, the wall of old calendar pin-ups and the faded photos of paratroop buddies loaded with out-dated weaponry. He felt a dull pain start in his innards.

'What are you getting at?' he asked.

'I'm getting at the tail you think you've had on you for a week.' Tattel's look was curiously sly. He poured another shot. 'Real pros. You've never actually seen them but they even know you went to Lyon yesterday.' It was a statement, not a question.

Aaron said sharply, 'How the hell did you know?'

The old para ignored the question and lit another cigarette. 'Of course,' he said, 'did you ever think that the fact you never spotted them meant they were never there in the first place?'

A sort of wildness surged up in Aaron. He leapt up and slammed his palm on the table. 'Goddamnit, Louis, what do you want? I'll pay for the telephone!'

Tattel's eyes narrowed. He went right on. 'There are tails and there are informers. You made up a tail, up here,' he tapped his head, 'to avoid the truth. Well, face it now. You've been sold out and don't tell me "no" because I happen to know better. Who knew you went to Lyon? I did. Suppose I told Ender. Me. Ever think of that? Or suppose Reymond's widow did.'

The pain in Aaron had doubled. 'Reymond's widow never told anybody anything,' he said.

'Sure?'

Aaron's mind raced back. Her dignity and her rumpled tennis clothes, pathetic armour in her battle against grief. He heard again the whisper of the mill weir beyond the old flagstone terrace and the far-off sound of her son's tennis racquet. 'She thought I was from the police,' he said numbly.

'Ah! So that leaves who else?'

Louis Tattel waited. Aaron sat down again slowly, and now the pain was nearly unbearable. If he had been informed on there was only one other person. It was almost impossible to think of. When Tattel said her name for him, the old para's voice sounded a thousand miles away and his room was like a dim light far down a dark tunnel. Nothing was real.

'When you took up with her,' Tattel explained, 'I had some friends put a bug on her telephone. I don't know why. Maybe because I saw you'd stopped thinking. I don't know what the hell you're up to but even if it's nothing, not to think is dangerous. Especially around women.'

He poured another shot and Aaron drank it. Last night, and again this morning she'd said she loved him. After a moment he asked, 'Whom did she call?'

Tattel shrugged. 'Her banker.'

'And?'

'Just her banker. She made three or four calls. One was from here.' Louis Tattel recited her reports; where Aaron had taken her to lunch, where they were staying in Amsterdam, what plane he'd caught to Lyon. 'If she didn't call him, he was on the phone to her. "Where's Zeismann now, what's he doing, where is he going next? When?" '

Aaron hardly heard. He wasn't listening. He saw her face smiling at him, her face and her sunburned body, racing naked and arrow-slim into the boiling Atlantic surf. He thought of last night on the shadowed back street, holding her cold slenderness against him and trusting her to get Jedder to Bordeaux. He tried not to remember but he couldn't help it.

And then he saw Larsen, his pale albino eyes and hair, his manicured nails and perfect tailoring. Somewhere along the line Larsen had stumbled on to his past with Margita and had skilfully used Gisèle to set it up again, Gisèle perhaps a willing accomplice because of her old jealousy. It didn't make any difference. Margita was the beginning of a straight line which ran through Roche-Corbon and ended at Larsen and Collins, with enough proof that Aaron Zeismann was dangerous to warrant the risk of seizing a Frenchman of Bejerec's imporance and influence to try to get more. He saw Bejerec, ageing and far off, his normally guarded expression anxious. What had they done to him?

The old-fashioned Bavarian clock on Tattel's bureau struck seven. A little wooden peasant boy and girl came out, danced stiffly around and around, but never touching, then went back in again to await the next hour.

'What are you doing with her in Bordeaux?' asked Tattel.

It was the first time the hotel-owner had ever asked him anything, for he had lived a life where early on you learned not to want to know other people's business. Aaron figured he deserved an answer. He thought a moment and then told him why he'd sent Margita to Bordeaux with Jedder and why he thought she'd been informing on him. Not all, because knowing too much would be dangerous to Tattel, but enough. 'I didn't think as far as her informing,' he added. 'I only saw her trapped and hoping I'd be a way out.'

Tattel said, '*Pauvre putain*, just like my little Arab, all right. You have to feel sorry for her. My guess is you're safe with her for a few days anyway. She'll probably bet on you until she thinks it's not going to work. The moment that happens, watch out. She'll run squealing back to him and claim she saved it for them, whatever it is they're doing.'

He was right, Aaron thought, and he knew what he had to do. Go to Bordeaux and con her the way she'd conned him, give her what she wanted to keep her from panicking, and get himself and Jedder the hell out of the country just as he'd planned. And fast. What happened to her then didn't matter. She could talk to anyone she wanted. She could go to hell.

The pain suddenly disappeared from within him. Suddenly it was as though she had never been at all. What he'd felt for her belonged to somebody else, not him. Making love to her belonged to an Aaron Zeismann who no longer existed, to a man who had found it easier to remain infatuated with her memory than to overcome the guilt he felt about his wife. How long had he actually loved Juliet without realizing it? Bejerec had seen his love and he hadn't. It didn't make any difference, there was now and the future.

He told Louis Tattel what he wanted. He needed money

and a plane to get him to England. He told Tattel he'd be in Bordeaux by evening. Tattel sighed and said it was impossible but promised results in forty-eight hours.

'Who else was into her telephone?' Aaron asked.

'Nobody,' Tattel said. 'You're lucky. I think her banker put his foot down at being listened to. The same for a tail. They don't know she's gone.'

Suddenly, it was seven-thirty, the hotel was awakening, guests were ringing for coffee. Louis Tattel slipped on his concierge's jacket with its gold-embroidered crossed keys and went off. Aaron was alone.

He had another drink and went upstairs. He went into his room. Something on the floor by his bed caught his eye. He bent and picked up the message-slip which said Juliet had called.

He stood looking at it until it began to blur and he felt the hot sting of tears behind his eyes. He hadn't cried the night his stepfather had cut him up with a broken bottle and almost killed his mother. He'd been too frightened. But he had cried at the end of the long day which had begun at dawn and with the pathetic fifty francs his mother had left for him on the kitchen table, and when he'd outrun the military police and French social workers and the *gendarmes* and the priest, whatever their good intentions. He'd cried then in the leaky-roofed, freezing, *bidonville* hovel in the bed of the old Algerian woman who had taken pity on a child of her own kind and let him in beside her to keep warm.

He had not cried since.

He went into the bathroom so that he could be alone with his weakness and not be heard. The only thing that was important any longer was Juliet and himself, their home, each other, what they shared. Nothing else counted and he was going to save it if he could, no matter what the price to anybody else.

Chapter Twenty-five

At seven in the morning, when most Parisians were still asleep or just rising, the little *bar-tabac* in the village of Vensac was busy. It was the time of year when the miles of vineyards north and south of Bordeaux were being cleaned up after harvest. The pale gravelly soil between the long rows of grape-vines was being turned, weeded, fertilized, the vines themselves pruned back to short, ugly grey-brown stumps. In the autumn cold of the early morning, vineyard workers fortified themselves for their day's work with cognac and black coffee.

The only telephone was right by the cash-register. After Margita spoke to Aaron, she called a Czech friend whom she could trust, and all the time was acutely aware of the proprietor and his several customers. Bad enough that she was the smart Parisian the locals barely tolerated during the summer, but worse that the line wasn't any good. She had to nearly shout and she knew everyone was listening, especially since she'd spoken to Aaron in English and now was speaking Czech. She arranged for her friend to call Roche-Corbon to say she was in Cannes, far to the south-east on the Mediterranean. Another Czech friend had been badly hurt in a car accident. She would stay in Cannes a couple more days. When she finally finished speaking and put the receiver back, her hands were damp and perspiration stood out on her forehead.

She had decided it wouldn't be safe to stay away from the banker very long and had given herself, and Aaron, an arbitrary deadline. If they were trying to stop Jedder from leaving the country, it was only a matter of time before someone in *Sûreté* checked out all of his connections and Aaron's, too, and thought to look for them at the beach-house. Besides that, if Roche-Corbon were to become suspicious of her Cannes story, he would perhaps ask his friends in the police to check out her Maserati. She would have to put it away out of sight.

She paid for both calls. There was pointed, smirking silence among the men lining the bar. Going to the door she saw a rack with potato crisps and biscuits. All that was lacking was coffee. The proprietor grudgingly agreed to sell her some of his own and fumbled endlessly about for a jar to put it in. Eventually she was able to leave, clutching her purchases. On the way she dropped some. There were whistles and comments when she bent to pick them up. She was grateful when, finally outside, the door of the Maserati closed on her. If she'd tried to fix herself clearly in everyone's mind she could not have made a better job of it.

A chill wind swept the empty intersection that served as a village square. Margita sat behind the wheel a moment, taking stock, angry with herself, angry with the sleek, rich lines of her car which was so *recherché* in Paris and so out of key here. A faded French flag hung over the door of a narrow two-storey building sandwiched between others across the way. That was the local *gendarmerie*. How long would it be before her presence was methodically and officially noted in the neat log-book handwriting of the resident *gendarme*? Probably by nightfall, for that was when most of the village, including the *gendarme*, gathered again at the *bar-tabac* for end-of-the-day *pastisse*.

Then, most likely in a day or so, the *gendarme* would settle his red braided *kepi* on his balding head and ease his rumpled bulk behind the wheel of his tattered Citroen 2CV. He would make a tour down the dunes. Unless they were very careful, he would see Gisèle's house occupied and very likely would stop to verify whether it was Gisèle herself or somebody with her permission and later would ask Paris to call her for verification. These days of squatters you could never tell. And if he stopped there, he might also look in the garage and note down the licence-number of the Maserati. Either could be as disastrous as if he saw Jedder himself and an alert for him had already reached out to the provinces.

She started the car but didn't pull away. A gust of wind

stirred the bare branches of a nearby plane tree, fallen leaves scurried. She was thinking rubbish, she told herself; scaring herself like a little girl, creating nightmares where perhaps there weren't any. She put the Maserati in gear and drove away towards the coast, first slowly, but once out of sight of Vensac very fast. Almost immediately the vineyards gave way to flat pine forest and after a few kilometres, there was the occasional salt-marsh and finally the long, low line of dunes that was the barrier against the wind and water of the Atlantic.

She reached a T-junction and turned south. Slowly the road became lonelier and more sand-drifted, the summer cottages spaced farther and farther apart. After a mile and a half, there was only one left, Gisèle's. The garage was separate, fifty feet across an open parking-area. She put the Maserati away and shut the doors behind her. Then she took the coffee and potato crisps and biscuits up the short wooden walk to the house and the kitchen door. The broken window upstairs caught her eye, its missing pane a dark, betraying blob which could be seen at a distance. It was mute testimony that perhaps the house was occupied by someone who was not supposed to be there.

When they'd arrived at dawn, she still hadn't known how she would get in. Her passenger slept the sleep of the drunken as he had all the way, and was slouched grotesquely big and slovenly against the door as though dead, his mouth partly open, spittle dried at its lower corners.

She'd found the kitchen door solidly locked, the front door also, as were the sliding glass doors to the living-room which faced the sea and gave directly onto a wide sun-deck. The downstairs windows were boarded up. It seemed hopeless. Eventually, cold and desperate, she had walked to the neighbours' house, also empty, and found a ladder which she'd dragged back and used to reach the upstairs window. Gisèle always kept extra keys in a kitchen drawer, she'd remembered. They were still there.

Margita bit her lip and went on. There were some old packing-cases in the garage. If she could nail the window up with boards then the *gendarme*, if he did come past, might

168

think it had been temporarily repaired against the winter before the owner had left at summer's end.

She closed the kitchen door behind her, muffling the low moan of the wind and the vibrating rumble of surf. Earlier, the house had had the dead-cold feel of a place shut up. She'd lit the oven and turned on the electric heaters in the bedrooms. Now the kitchen was warm and the edge had come off the rest of the house.

She put water on to boil and went to look for Jedder. Most likely he had gone upstairs and found a bed. But the bedrooms were empty. She called out. There was no answer. It took a moment or two to realize that he wasn't in the house. She ran back downstairs. Aaron had told her not to let him out of her sight.

'Mr Jedder!'

Silence.

In the kitchen, she flung open the door and looked out at the parking-area between the house and the garage. The only tyre marks in the wind-blown sand were the ones she had made putting away the Maserati. If Jedder had left or been taken away, it had not been by car.

She rushed to the living-room and yanked at the sliding doors to the terrace. They were still locked. But he could have gone on to the beach through the kitchen. She unlocked the doors, slid one open and went on to the sun-deck. The wind tore at her. Steps, then a narrow boardwalk, led to the beach. Frantic now, she looked for footprints. But first the sand was too soft and dry for any and then high tide had obliterated others he might have left on the harder surface.

The beach was empty. Some gulls swept raggedly overhead, silent, heads bent down to look at her. Margita hesitantly went to the water. But the foam was smooth and flat and behind it nothing rolled in the curling breakers, no nightmarish dark object to realize her worst fears and stop her heart.

She spun around. Where in the name of God was he, then?

'Mr Jedder!' The wind made her cry an impotent whisper.

The house stood a silent, grey bulk against the equally grey sky. She called again and was convulsed by a nameless dread. At any moment the sea itself would reach out for her. She raced back up to the sun-deck and, sobbing, flung herself on the sliding doors and burst into the living-room.

And simultaneously heard her own scream, a wild siren, shrilling unchecked. Her hands clutched the sides of her head, trying to shut it out.

Henry Jedder stood mid-room, blinking, expressionless. His shirt was half-unbuttoned and out of his trousers which were unzipped, and his tie was askew. He had a bottle of Scotch in his hand.

Margita sank to the couch.

'I'm sorry,' she said. 'I couldn't find you.' She was trembling violently. She couldn't stop.

He didn't answer.

'If you go anywhere, you must let me know. Please.'

He kept staring and then said abruptly. 'I tried sleeping. The beds are all damp.' He frowned, swaying slightly. 'Haven't we met somewhere?'

'Last night,' she said. She thought, could he actually not remember? Perhaps not, he'd been very drunk.

'I mean before.'

'Probably. Some party or other.'

'What's your name?'

'Margita. Margita Majerová.'

'You're Czech?'

'Yes.'

'Refugee?'

She shrugged. 'I've been in Paris quite a while.'

'Do you work for Strachey?'

Strachey? Who was that? The name was familiar. Wasn't it someone in politics and famous? Aaron must be connected somehow, otherwise Jedder wouldn't have asked.

She stared. What should she answer? 'You might say so,' she said.

Jedder frowned again and grunted, 'Where's Zeismann?'

'He's coming tonight.' She made it sound positive. But was he?

Jedder held up the bottle. 'Found this in the cellar. Want some?'

'No thank you.'

She bowed her head, feeling the tears begin. Wasn't it perhaps a senator? Maybe some day the President? If so, then perhaps she was mixed up in something big indeed and perhaps now too far in to get out even if she tried. She didn't want Jedder to see her tears. She wanted to hide and sleep and not have anyone ever see her again.

She heard Jedder shamble into the kitchen and cupboard doors open and slam shut as he searched for a glass. Then there was silence and she felt a loneliness which was a physical pain.

She thought back to the first time she'd ever come here, a lifetime ago. She'd only escaped from Prague a few months before and on that weekend she'd met Aaron and had fallen desperately in love. Every day had been filled with laughter, she'd always been able to see the end to not belonging. Now she was back here again but in a nightmare.

When Roche-Corbon had told her Aaron had contacted Gisèle and ordered her to take up with him at once, she'd been terrified. It was bad enough to inform, but to inform on somebody you'd once loved to the point of suicide, that was as impossible as having to make love to them again. To her overwhelming relief she'd found time had finally intervened, she had felt nothing for Aaron any more. Her only concern was to stay in Paris. Even if Prague's nostalgic beauty often haunted her dreams and made her heart break, she couldn't face its soul-killing Stalinism. And where else could she go? Italy where the police demanded favours of refugee women? Scandinavia where she couldn't speak a word of their languages? England? She knew no one there. Informing on Aaron Zeismann had not been so difficult. Nor using him.

Now she wasn't sure. Something had happened last night. In the carnal frenzy of their love-making Aaron had been only another man. But last night in a shadowy, cold and

171

misty back street he'd unexpectedly become someone quite different. When would he come and make it all safe the way he had years ago? She so badly needed his strength.

Margita couldn't stop crying. She had never felt so defenceless. Nor so frightened.

Chapter Twenty-six

When Aaron reached number 37 Avenue Kléber, it was five-past-nine. He was, he knew, taking a terrible, if calculated, risk. If they had seized Bejerec as he suspected and Bejerec had talked, or even if he and Louis Tattel were wrong about Margita and she was still reporting to her banker so they knew Jedder was in Bordeaux, then he was finished. The old para had expressed complete incredulity. '*Putain!*' he'd cried. 'Only idiots take chances like this.'

It was a risk Aaron felt he had to take, however. His and Juliet's future required that he stay above ground if humanly possible until as Bejerec had advised he could retire safely first from Dallas then from the National Security Council and fade into the American scene as an ordinary white-collar suburbanite with a wife and children to support.

Louis Tattel had shaken his head and had reached for the *eau-de-vie* again.

Ignoring the outrage of rush-hour Parisians behind him as he slowed, Aaron braced himself and turned off Kléber and drove under the deep-shadowed arch of the building into the morning-grey of the inner court. He would soon know whether he was right. He nodded routinely to the uniformed porter who stood in his office doorway and it occurred to him that there was real irony in the terrible mistake he had made in trusting Margita. Twenty years ago he would never have so let his guard down, whatever his feelings. She'd been right when she'd said he'd changed. Perhaps indeed that's when she knew she could get away with deceiving him. If he had not become so American, he never would have behaved so naïvely. The 'mole' risked being destroyed by the very earth into which he had tunnelled simply because he had tunnelled so successfully.

He pulled into his allotted parking-space and checked the other cars around him. Ender was already there. And so was

Collins. The Ambassador's unofficial English Rover was parked at the very end of the courtyard, its chauffeur and two bodyguards waiting discreetly. Collins and Ender would be talking about Reymond, and probably about him, too. Jedder would be notably absent this morning, and fear that eliminating Reymond might have pushed Jedder into a rash step would make Collins especially susceptible to Larsen and to hindsight. His own going to Lyon without consulting anyone could easily have been made to appear highly suspect, as could his going to Amsterdam when he'd told Ender he'd be in England. In the 'good-ole-boy' network, Margita was the sort of infidelity you boasted about to your friends. Why cook up a lie to cover it, and Collins might well use both to embarrass Ender into final loss of power at Dallas. In the high stakes being played for, Dallas control would then pass out of the hands of the President, the Adviser and the banks and into the hands of the oil men.

Aaron locked his car. His only defence was coming here in the first place and then playing the total innocent. He looked up at the silent stone façade of the Dallas building. He wondered briefly what other dramas it had seen down through the years. It dated from before the French Revolution. Of the privileged men and women who once arrogantly strode the cobbles of this courtyard, to be helped by obsequious footmen into ornate carriages, how many had heard the rattling rush of the heavy guillotine just before it struck them into eternity?

Cold in the pit of Aaron's stomach became a tangible weight. Ender had been under pressure a long time and every man had his limit. The easy way out might suddenly seem the least risk in the long run, and the easy way out for Ender was to pre-empt Collins by stabbing his own right-hand man in the back. Practising caution where billions of dollars and the necks of your superiors were concerned would never be condemned for long and might well be worth temporary loss of face.

He went into the lobby to sign in with the guard at the desk. He was greeted without guile. If they'd taken any decision against him, they hadn't yet formalized it.

He was grateful to be alone in the confines of the elevator. At the fourth floor, when the doors opened on the hushed sanctuary of the executive offices, a brief mental image of Babcock last summer flicked the back of his mind. Babcock on his way to be confronted by his superiors. Had he also been planning to bluff his way out?

He went around the open spiral stair past Jedder's empty office and to his own. His day's work had been immaculately laid out on his desk by Jacqueline: the familiar flat blue file containing the weekly briefing dictated by phone to her on Friday from Amsterdam, and next to it in its red folder his still unfinished, quarterly report.

He called her on his intercom. Her voice came back, boxed electronically by the machine but fresh and cordial.

'*Bonjour, chef.*'

'Good morning. Would you rouse Mr Jedder for me?'

'Hold on a second,' she answered. 'I have your coffee.'

The machine clicked and an instant later the connecting door between their offices opened and she appeared with the familiar cup, her blonde hair radiant and her child big in her and pushing harder than ever at her stretched maternity dress. She put the coffee down. 'This morning we no longer walk,' she said. 'We waddle.' She laughed and went on. 'Mr Jedder is not in. He had an eight-thirty appointment here and missed it. He's expected at the Ministry of the Interior at nine-thirty with both Mr Ender and Mr Collins.'

'What about his home?'

'We called at eight-thirty. He wasn't there. Mr Ender's secretary is going to phone the Ministry in a few minutes in case he went to it directly.'

Aaron pretended to think. He'd asked about Jedder simply to go on record. Later, it would help substantiate his own innocence. He hated the lie where she was concerned but it was necessary. 'Let's try Mr Ender,' he said casually.

'I think he's with Mr Collins.' Jacqueline reached for his telephone.

Aaron concentrated on her while she dialled, drawing strength from her presence and the close, unified world that was their relationship. He heard Collins's secretary reply.

175

'Marguerite?' Jacqueline asked. 'Is Mr Ender there? It's Mr Zeismann. Thank you.' She handed the phone to Aaron. 'He's coming.'

There wasn't time to think further. Ender was on the line. 'Aaron?' He sounded off guard.

Aaron put vague alarm into his voice. 'Good morning. Listen, I can't find Henry. Jacqueline tells me you can't either.'

There was a moment's hesitation, then Ender said, 'That's right.'

'She said you tried him at home half an hour ago.'

'Yes, I did.'

Aaron said, 'Jesus . . .' as worriedly as he could. 'Well, maybe he's still on his way.' And nothing more. He waited for Ender to rise to the bait, certain he would.

He was right. Ender came back, 'Is there something wrong, Aaron?'

Aaron smiled thinly to himself. Ender was suddenly less confident. 'I don't know,' he answered. 'I hope not. I saw him last night. When I returned from Lyon. He was pretty upset about Reymond.'

'You went to Lyon?' Ender's pretence was weak.

Aaron played along with it. He said matter-of-factly, 'Of course. The moment I heard. I flew straight there and when I got back went straight to Henry. I thought he might be seriously upset. He was, but I was certain I had him calmed down. I had to take him out to his favourite bar, among other things. I never should have left him there.'

'Hold on a second, Aaron.'

He heard the phone cupped as Ender spoke to Collins, voice muffled. Then Ender came back. 'Can you come down to Banjo's office?'

'I'll be right there.'

He hung up, palms sweating, but certain of two things: he was under serious suspicion, but unless they were deliberately playing with him they'd heard nothing from Margita, nor had they learned anything from Bejerec if they had him.

'I'll be in the conference room,' he said to Jacqueline.

'Okay.' She nodded at his desk diary. 'Did you see that?'

She'd paper-clipped a newspaper cutting to it. One quick look was enough. She'd never know what she'd done for him. He met her level blue eyes. 'Thank you,' he said. 'You just earned yourself a five-franc-a-month rise.'

She laughed and returned to her own office. He'd prayed for some sort of break. Miraculously, there it was, an excuse to be away for a couple of days. It was notice of an address by the head of the French Communist Party to the National Student League at the University of Grenoble. It was important to Dallas to be constantly informed of party-student thinking. Both groups could cause serious trouble if Tricolor ever leaked out. With Louis Tattel's help he would 'attend'. It was the very sort of routine thing he did all the time.

He pencilled 'Grenoble' across two pages of his diary. As he went down the hall towards Collins's office he remembered that Ender hadn't once mentioned Reymond. But if you were Ender and a coward, you weren't likely to speak voluntarily of a man whose murder you probably condoned.

Chapter Twenty-seven

Ender was by the window, hands in his pockets, looking down on the courtyard, a favourite stance when under stress; Collins sat dry and stiff in his deep swivel chair, eyes behind his rimless glasses small and hard. 'Come in, come in,' he said. The whining tones of his accent were deliberately emphasized. 'Y'all want coffee?'

It was a stall. Aaron knew at once, and for all the reasons he'd thought of, that Collins was indeed out for his head and that Ender was close to surrender.

Ender didn't wait for any formalities. He was truculent. 'Let's start from the beginning, Aaron.'

Aaron made his reply aggressive. 'That would put us in Amsterdam,' he said and smiled. 'For personal reasons I didn't go to London.'

Ender looked surprised. He hadn't counted on candour. 'You might have told me. I called everywhere yesterday looking for you.'

Aaron knew Ender had probably been apprised of his going to Amsterdam as early as Friday evening. He laughed. 'What I do on weekends, Richard, is my business.' He took them both in. It was in some ways a ludicrous situation. They had to pretend innocence in order not to expose that they had him under surveillance through Margita. He, on his part, had to go along with their pretence in order to keep up his own. Meanwhile, the whole clownish game was in the name of a power struggle which really had nothing to do with him, but with himself the pawn and actually guilty as hell, and with them trying to prove it while not totally believing he was.

Ender asked, 'How did you hear about Reymond?'

'The early-morning press,' replied Aaron. 'My hotel called me. I've had messages from Reymond occasionally and the *concierge* thought I might want to know. But I

178

didn't actually go to Lyon about him. I went about Henry. You know how he was all week. When I heard the news I thought, Christ, Jedder's blown it. Reymond has to be connected with him somehow. We'd better know the details and not just what Jedder might tell us. Besides, the police might have run on to something we didn't want noised around.'

He waited. Ender glanced quickly at Collins. Collins said, 'And what did you find, Mr Zeismann?' There was real hatred in the softness of his voice. Sick, bullying bastard, Aaron thought, the kind who got others to do their dirty work for them while they went to church with their wives on Sunday after Saturday night whoring with 'good ole boy' buddies. A fleeting picture came to him of Madame Reymond out at the mill. She'd be putting on black and shortly she'd be burying what was left of her husband and her life. Collins and Ender were responsible.

He said, 'Not much. Unless we can get Henry to tell us we can only guess. Reymond's kids were playing a tennis tournament and his wife was off some place. That left the gardener and the maid. They heard raised voices and their boss doing a lot of shouting but they didn't know what it was all about. They're hardly corporate financiers. Then Henry slunk off and Reymond made a couple of phone-calls and went to his office.' Aaron looked straight at Collins. 'The important thing is, apparently nothing leaked. We're okay in Lyon. Henry Jedder is, I'm afraid, another question.'

'Maybe we're panicking,' Ender said. 'Maybe he's just sleeping off a big head in some girl's apartment.'

It was a loaded statement. Ender knew better. Aaron decided he might as well stop fencing and say what was needed. He sensed that Ender was close to being won over. Putting all his own cards down was the only way to complete the job.

'I wish I thought so,' he said. 'But I don't. I think he's hiding.'

'Hiding? What the hell for?' Ender's tone continued false.

'Well,' Aaron said, 'I might as well be frank. Down in Lyon I had to come to a basic conclusion. You probably can guess what it was. Achille Reymond was hardly the kind to kill himself. And certainly not because he thought some Americans were playing dirty. On the contrary, he was the kind who fights back. His personal life was happy so the conclusion I had come to was that Jedder may have thought the same and then gone on to realize Reymond was eliminated and we might be planning the same for him.'

There was the complaining sound of a chair-swivel. Collins had abruptly leaned back. His expression hadn't changed, just the position of his body.

Ender reacted differently. He turned fast on Aaron. He'd gone white. From shock, or because he'd been caught? 'Wait a minute. Do you realize what you just said?'

Collins spoke. 'Oh, he realized all right. He just said we pushed Achille Reymond out of a window.' His smile was deadly.

Ender said, 'Aaron, you're wrong. If we ever started that sort of thing, there'd be no end to it.' He'd gained a little control and some of the colour had come back to his face.

Collins put on a show. He laughed and shook his head and then said, again with lethal softness, 'Now, Mr Zeismann, Ah'd like you to tell me something. Ah'd like you to tell me y'all didn't really intend what you said because Ah'm sure now you didn't.'

Aaron pretended surprise. 'No offence meant, Banjo,' he said. 'What you people do is your business; you make the decisions. I don't question either morality or ethics. I only advise.'

It was all it took. 'No offence meant,' Collins repeated. And then it came. He lost control; the Elder Statesman mask dropped and the red-neck country-and-western banjo-player surfaced. 'Well, y'all listen to me, you bright-assed Jew-boy, you just keep your bright-assed ideas to yourself, hear?'

Aaron enjoyed his triumph. Collins had risen to the bait, and the fact that he had, revealed that he'd lost his advantage and given up. He was in the clear. Ender, too.

Ender also saw it. 'My apologies, Aaron,' he said. He sounded authoritative and confident for the first time.

Aaron was gracious. 'It's all right,' he said. 'We're in a

180

nervous situation. Let's just say, right or wrong, that we ought to think "elimination" could be Jedder's worry. As a motivation, I mean, if he actually has disappeared.'

He smiled and went on to both men, 'You have a tap on Jedder's phone, don't you? Haven't you picked up anything? Last night he started babbling about joining Rosemary in Portugal. I didn't pay much attention to it. This morning I wish I had.'

'I'm afraid not,' Ender answered. 'But as you may have gathered we also have had him under surveillance. Unfortunately, they lost him at Elsie's last night so they went to his house. He wasn't there either, so they looked around. We have a nasty feeling he took home some eyes-only stuff he should have consigned to his shredder. His secretary said there was almost never anything in the shredder disposal-bag. But they found nothing. They've staked out his house now. He still hasn't returned.'

Aaron put real fear in his voice. 'That's bad. Have you tried the airlines? All that?'

'Yes,' Ender answered. 'And no luck.'

For the first time Aaron noticed a look of complete exhaustion about Ender. He guessed that besides coping with Collins he'd been up all night organizing the search for Jedder and was acutely aware that if Tricolor became jeopardized because the French could not find him, then ultimately the full responsibility would be his. Aaron didn't envy him.

'You've got to find him, Richard,' he said.

'We will. We have every cop in France looking for him. I called the Minister at two o'clock this morning.'

Collins had begun to put things in his briefcase. He had to have a last word to save face. 'He outsmarted you, Zeismann, how about that? That big fat pervert. He acted you into thinking you'd calmed him down when all the time he'd decided to clear out. I'm recommending you for serious disciplinary action.'

'That's your privilege, sir,' Aaron conceded.

Later, when Collins had gone, Ender said, 'Look, Aaron, you may be right about the elimination. It's horrifying and I

181

see Collins in it all the way. But we'll never know for certain so we might as well forget it.'

Aaron had been expecting Ender to try to cover himself and had decided to let him think he could. Disputing with him would be dangerous and gain nothing.

'You're right,' he said. 'It stops right here.'

Ender's relief was betrayed by sudden warmth. He grinned and said, almost pleading, 'And, Aaron, in the future could you please let me know your moves?'

'No time like the present,' replied Aaron. 'For the next couple of days I'll be at the Hotel Sofitel in Grenoble.'

At first Ender didn't believe him. Fear came back to his eyes. Then he managed a weak smile. 'What's happening there?'

'The Reds meet with the Students' League. I'll be back Wednesday, maybe Thursday.' Aaron took a chance, 'That is unless you need me here.'

Ender relaxed a little. 'If Henry shows up I can manage him. If not . . .' he shrugged. 'Can you leave the number with your secretary?'

'Of course. Maybe you could let me know from day to day about Henry. No matter what turns up.'

Ender brightened even more. 'You can count on it.'

He was suddenly almost like the old Ender again, having it both ways for his own benefit. Aaron went back down the hall. He'd guessed Margita right. It meant he was half way safe and home. He only had to avoid the French police and, difficult as that might be, it was something far easier to do than cope with treachery.

It was nine-forty. It wouldn't pay to bolt immediately. He'd keep up appearances, sweat out necessary phone-calls and finish up his quarterly report. It was going to be the longest morning ever, but it had to be that way.

Jacqueline was typing a dictation tape and nearly missed him as he passed through her office. 'Oh, there you are. I stepped out a minute and when I came back this was on my desk.' She held out a sealed eight-by-ten manila envelope with his name on it and stamped 'Eyes Only'. 'Do you want me to find out who left it?'

'It won't be necessary,' answered Aaron. 'I know about it.' He paused in his doorway. 'I'm incommunicado for the next ten minutes. To anybody.'

'*D'accord*,' she said. And went back to work.

Aaron closed his door softly behind him. He felt sick. He took the envelope to the shredder, switched the shredder on and prepared to feed the envelope into it unopened. Then he switched the machine off again. He had to look. Not because he wanted to but because he owed it to Bejerec to have the courage to do so. If you'd been part of a man's life and at least partially responsible for his death, you couldn't not face it.

He took out the photographs. There were three of them, big, detailed blow-ups in vivid colour.

It was hard to recognize Bejerec, not so much for the revolting things they had done to the poor, soft, overweight body as for the darkness that rushed behind his own eyes. He forced himself to concentrate and to look carefully.

Because he did, he found he could think almost objectively and see in Bejerec's remains something which made his death slightly easier to bear. The torn flesh and shredded skin tissues were oozing but showed no sign of acute bleeding or of bright oxygenated blood. The skin areas which were burned, the upper thighs, the underarms, the abdomen and genitals, showed little blistering. That and the lack of blood showed he'd been dead perhaps an hour before the psychotic mutilation of his insensitive corpse.

Aaron quickly studied the face, hideously distorted in death. The lips were blue and there were small bleedings into skin spots which looked like chicken-pox. Bejerec had died of cyanide poisoning and thus unquestionably by his own hand. He had defeated Larsen. The post-mortem was for Aaron Zeismann.

Aaron shredded the photographs and the envelope.

He sat down at his desk and composed himself and began to work. At ten-thirty, he had finished the quarterly report and a suggestions memo on what to do about COPIC and the Swiss holding company. He took them both to Jacqueline and, as she hurriedly looked up Grenoble flights for him, said a silent good-bye to her bowed blonde head and a wish of good luck to her and her baby. Then using a basement fire-stair door which took him directly out on to Avenue Kléber, he soon lost himself on foot in a maze of small office buildings and stores across the neighbouring Champs-Elysées.

He made one call to Louis Tattel from a public pay phone, and at twelve o'clock he was in an anonymous car rented under an assumed name, free of Paris and any conceivable tail and on the Auto-route d'Orléans headed south-west for Bordeaux.

Chapter Twenty-eight

It was six in the evening. The desk clerk at the Relais Maritime thumped frantically on the brass call-bell adorning the old mahogany reception counter, while simultaneously trying to cope with the antique switchboard which buzzed incessantly. Guests, newly arrived from New York, had just signed in and needed to be escorted to their rooms; someone else had appeared from a taxi outside with a small mountain of luggage; a woman wanted her theatre tickets.

'*Bagagiste!*'

The *bagagiste* was nowhere to be seen.

And to the telephone, '*Oui, Monsieur,*' and '*De suite, Madame.*'

And, 'But your tickets were sent to your room, Madame. *Bagagiste!!*'

Finally the balding, hunched old *bagagiste* appeared on the run to add to the bedlam, carpet slippers shuffling, and wiping crumbs from his bent hands on to his flapping denim apron.

It was that busy time of day when Louis Tattel himself usually supervised his desk and lobby, and in spite of everything maintained disciplined calm. But Tattel wasn't there. He was cloistered in his private room, sitting on the edge of his bed in his vest like some peasant patriarch, the receiver of his private telephone jammed between his shoulder and his ear and a perpetual, yellowed *cigarette au balayeur* dangling from the corner of his mouth. He was jotting down things on the back of an envelope with a ballpoint, the shaft of which was lost in his big fist.

'All right,' he demanded. 'What else?'

Aaron's voice was very far away and came on a wave of sound like the moan of wind. 'What's my room number?'

'At the Hôtel Sofitel? Six-eighty-three.'

'Anybody call?'

'Your secretary at four-thirty, Richard Ender at five-fifteen. Your secretary said it wasn't urgent, your wife had phoned from the US and you could call her back any time. She said she sounded lonely, that's all. You should call Ender at home this evening, but only if it's convenient.'

'How much does the check-in look like me?'

'Close enough to be a brother. Dark-haired, same age, same height. We had him dress like you and gave him a phoney American passport in your name.'

'Where did they pick him up?'

'We took a chance. We got him into your office building, had him come out to the courtyard and take your car with a master-key. If anyone decided he wasn't you and challenged him, he was to say he was taking the car to a garage for a service. He left it at Orly West and took Air-Inter to Grenoble. He's pretty sure he was followed right from Avenue Kléber. Then a guy got on the plane with him and the same guy checked into the Sofitel right after he did.'

There was a pause, the line moaned. Aaron's voice came again on distant waves. 'What about my plane?'

Where the hell was he? Tattel wondered. Not Bordeaux itself, he was just planning to use the airport at Bordeaux. And why? The hotel-owner fought down nagging unease. He didn't like any of it, especially the phoney hotel set-up in Grenoble. He drew in a lungful of smoke and shouted back, 'We're still working on it.'

'When will you know?'

'Don't push me. I did miracles already.'

'I'm running out of time, Louis.'

'I'll have something for tomorrow.'

'*When* tomorrow?'

'Noon-time, maybe!'

'Can't you make it sooner?'

Louis Tattel stamped out the pulped butt of his cigarette. 'Can't help it, Aaron. The pilot's on a flight to Geneva. He's not due back until midnight and it always takes me a while to close with him.' He saw the greying pilot, an embittered failure, needing money badly enough to fly anywhere and keep his mouth shut and always slyly holding out on principle for a little more, no matter what you offered him and no matter what the urgency. But better that than some wise-guy youngster you couldn't trust to do what you bargained for.

Aaron's voice came again. A curse. Grudging agreement. 'Okay, I'll call you at seven-thirty.' And then, 'What about the money?'

'You haven't given me enough time, this end. You'll have to wait for London.' He shouted an address. 'It's in Hatton Garden, the diamond market. I pay the pilot from here. I'll let you know later how much you'll owe me.'

He waited while Aaron repeated the address and then said, 'And listen. It's not all mine. When you pay it back, you could throw in a few hundred for my friends, understand?'

'Okay.'

'All right, you have twenty-four hours' cover. If we leave the guy in Grenoble past tomorrow night, they'll see through him.'

They said good-bye and Tattel hung up. The room was foggy with smoke. He was sweating. He poured an *eau-de-vie* and lit another cigarette. Presently he reached for the telephone and made a call. It was to a friend who worked at the central exchange. In ten minutes his private number would cease to exist. When he had finished, he rose and struggled into his shirt and black tie and *concierge*'s jacket. He wished he knew what Aaron was doing and why. He hated being in the dark this way; it was stooge's work and he couldn't use his own judgement. That's the way mistakes were made, when a man had to depend on another man's decisions and couldn't think for himself. These days, too, his old friend didn't have the same sort of detached sang-froid which had seen him through so many bad situations in the old times. He'd changed somehow, become vulnerable. Louis Tattel had a dull feeling things weren't going to turn out well. It was that goddamned woman, he thought. How could Aaron have been so careless? Women, good God, were for going to bed with occasionally because a man needed that to stay sane. But they weren't for anything else, at least not when you played the games he had an idea Aaron Zeismann must be playing. Any man who ever trusted any woman for anything else was a fool.

Then Louis Tattel turned off the light and went out to the front desk and made himself forget about it. He still had a hotel to run and there was nothing he could do anyway until midnight. Aaron's business would have to wait until then.

In five minutes order reigned in the crowded lobby.

Chapter Twenty-nine

The telephone was on a veneered cabinet, the sort of place people kept liquor. Aaron opened a door and felt bottles. He pulled one out and removed the top. It was vodka. He sat on the floor with his back against the cabinet, drank two deep swallows and forced himself to relax. It had been a very long day; he was exhausted and cold. Gisèle's house, far down the dunes, was a dark shape in the opaque light of a thin moon partially veiled by high overcast. It looked empty and forsaken but Margita was there and he had to go back and pretend to love her, and cope with Henry Jedder and Jedder had been drinking too much. What he wanted to do instead was crawl into the warm safety of a bed someplace, alone, and surrender to the total escape of sleep.

It would be early afternoon in America. It was a national holiday there and Juliet must be in Oxford. She would have spent the morning putting the garden to bed for the winter and she would be in the kitchen now, the knees of her jeans dark from damp peat moss, her face dirty and her hair a tangle and stuck with leaf and shreds of garden flotsam. She would have washed her hands at the kitchen sink and perhaps made herself a sandwich and opened a can of beer, and Esther might have come over to help shell late peas for the deep freeze or just to be company because she understood loneliness. Wanting to be there with them came over him in waves and wanting to tell Juliet he loved her and that everything was going to be all right.

Presently, he put the bottle back. He rose stiffly to grope through the unfamiliar living-room to the pitch-dark hall. He'd left the door to the cellar stairs open and he felt a draught of air coming up from the window he'd jemmied open below. He descended slowly.

As soon as he'd repaired Gisèle's broken pane, he'd gone to work to get in. It had taken an hour. There was always the possibility the house was wired with an anti-burglar device, keyed into the *gendarmerie* at Vensac. The power transformer was on a pole fifty yards down the road and he'd had to climb to it without spikes, using a pair of sneakers he'd found and a makeshift belt. He'd cut the power, prayed that if there was indeed an alarm it didn't have a back-up battery system, and had gone to work on the cellar window.

From within, the window was head-height. He pulled himself up and through, and on to the cold sand outside. He closed it carefully to make it appear as though its shattered catch were holding and brushed the sand to obliterate footprints.

He had taken his first step back towards Gisèle's when he felt, rather than heard, someone very close by. He froze. There was a faint cloth sound of clothes in movement, the whispered weight of footsteps in soft sand. A large bulk loomed. It was Jedder. Aaron could smell the Scotch on his breath and it occurred to him immediately that either because of drink or because he'd been watching him all along, Jedder wasn't surprised to see him.

When he didn't speak, Aaron took him by the arm. 'Anything wrong?'

In answer Jedder heaved around and without a word lumbered back towards Gisèle's. Aaron followed, worrying. Drink and strain were rapidly making the man irrational. Earlier, he had locked and bolted the kitchen door, deciding to use instead the living-room doors which led to the beach and which could not be seen from the road or the garage. He slid the doors shut behind him, grateful for the warmth beginning to build up inside. To his surprise a faint light came from the kitchen. Margita had lit a candle, waxed it into the neck of a bottle and was cooking.

'I stuffed a blanket against the shutters,' she explained. 'You can't see any light at all from the roadside.'

Aaron thought briefly of food smell. The wind had risen strongly and would almost certainly tear away any odour, and if possible they had to eat a hot meal, especially Jedder.

'Corned beef hash,' she said. 'And look what I found.' She held up a bottle. It was Mouton Rothschild '67, half-covered with dust. She put it down and smiled and reached her arms around his neck. 'Hello.' She brushed her mouth softly against his. He forced himself to respond.

'Any luck?' she asked.

'The phone works.' He sat at the table. She'd set three places. She had on an apron and looked like a housewife. He'd never seen her like that.

'When do we leave?' she asked.

'Tomorrow.' He remembered Jedder. 'Where the hell's he gone to? He was right in front of me when I came in.'

She glanced at the dark doorway and lowered her voice. 'Probably looking for Scotch.' She began to serve out the hash. 'I hid it.'

'How much has he had?'

'Nearly a bottle.'

Then Jedder suddenly appeared, a great black shadow materializing in the doorway from the dark hall.

'Come and eat,' said Aaron.

Jedder stared and sat down heavily.

Aaron poured wine.

'We'd all better turn in early,' he said. And then to Jedder, 'I have a plane laid on for tomorrow. Sometime in the early afternoon. The local airport.'

Jedder looked up, 'If we have the police after us, how are we going to manage it?' There was unexpected hostility in his tone.

Aaron heard it and was cautious. 'There won't be any problems.'

'But how?' Insistent.

'I have friends in the police,' Aaron said. He forced a smile.

Jedder gulped his wine, put down his glass and said suddenly, 'I'm not going. Not until I hear it from Strachey himself.'

Aaron was aware of two things, his own surprise and Margita. Without fully understanding the implications of what Jedder had said, she knew it was bad. Her hand went unconsciously to her throat.

He tried to think how to handle it. Jedder might have been drinking heavily but he wasn't drunk. 'I take it you want him to come to France,' he said.

'Any reason why he can't?'

'He has a pretty heavy schedule. It might not be easy for him. What brought you to this decision?'

'I want guarantees from Strachey himself,' Jedder said belligerently. 'Personally. Not just from you. If he doesn't and I'm in England, I'm in worse trouble than here.'

'How so?'

Jedder poured himself more wine. His reply was petulant. 'I know France. I know people here who would help me. I don't know anyone in England.'

'You could meet him at the airport in England,' ventured Aaron. 'You'd never have to get off the plane until you were satisfied. If you weren't, I'd fly you right back.'

There was a heavy silence. Jedder finally said, 'If he wants us badly enough to guarantee our future, then he'll want us enough to come over here. It's not the Atlantic. It's just the English Channel.'

There was a devastating reasonableness about it. And yet at the same time, it wasn't right. It was the sort of twisted logic Aaron knew Henry Jedder would apply to a financial deal, and he also knew there was no way around it.

Jedder turned abruptly to Margita. 'Where did you put the Scotch?'

'The Scotch?'

'You hid it.' And to Aaron, 'I don't like being treated like a child.'

Margita said quickly, 'I am sorry, Henry. Honestly. I thought if Aaron had made arrangements to leave tonight and you went to sleep, you'd feel awful if you had to wake quickly after a lot to drink.'

'I'll have it back,' Jedder said. 'Right now.'

It was cold and it was unpleasant. It was an order. The big man was running the show. Suddenly Aaron wanted to rise up and smash his fist into the heavy face, grab the tangled mass of hair and snap the head sharply back and smash again and again. He hated him and his whole world of selfishness and quick-dealing. He hated his sick, little-girl sexual weakness and his fear of his *nouveau riche* snob wife. He hated him because he was weak and because a weak man was someone you couldn't trust.

The hate rose behind his eyes and the room blurred. Margita was on her knees by the sink. She pulled a Scotch bottle from behind cleaning things and silently took it to Jedder.

He rose cumbersomely and clutched at it. The pitch-darkness of the hall flowed in after him and he disappeared. They heard his heavy tread on the stairs, the door to the guest-room slammed. They heard the creak of bed-springs and then there was silence.

Aaron filled his own wine-glass and resumed eating. Margita came back to her chair and presently he heard her speak his name. He looked up.

'Will this Strachey come?'

'I think so. I'll find out tomorrow.'

'You can't call him tonight?'

'He's gone to Chequers for dinner. I can't call him there.'

'Chequers is the home of the British Prime Minister?'

'His country home, yes,' he answered.

She cleared the table. 'If we're going tomorrow, I'll leave the dishes for Gisèle in the spring.' She laughed and put an arm across his shoulder and held her face close to his. 'I've made up the bed in her room and turned on the electric heater. Are you coming?'

'In a minute.'

She hesitated in the door. 'Aaron, if I'm one too many for this trip, say so. I can join you later.'

'Would you rather?' The response was automatic, un-thinking. The moment the words were out, he regretted them. It would be far safer to take her. She'd burn all her bridges by going and would not be able to come back to talk. Left behind, she could only cause trouble. Who knew what she might already have learned from Jedder? She'd been alone with him for eighteen hours now.

'Of course not,' she said earnestly. 'I want to go with you. But I don't want to louse things up for you either.'

He took her in with a sidelong glance. Her grey eyes were steady and without guile. Had she been testing to see whether he still really wanted her or to gain a hint of his reaction if she decided to back out? Or had she actually made up her mind to stick with him no matter what? There was no way he could tell.

'Don't worry about it,' he said.

'I promise I'll try not to have two left feet.' She smiled and then looked concerned. 'You look exhausted, Aaron. You need sleep. Don't stay down here too long.'

She disappeared. He sat for a long time hardly hearing the moan of wind and the muffled lonely thunder of surf. What had Jedder been doing wandering about in the dunes when he'd emerged from the cellar of the neighbouring house? Looking for him or for some way to listen to his telephone conversation with Louis Tattel?

There were too many questions, too few answers. The kitchen began to get cold and the wine tasted stale. Upstairs Margita would have arranged another candle and would wait patiently for him in its soft light. And no matter how he would loathe himself for it and loathe her too, he would give her the love she asked for because he had to keep up the farce no matter what the cost. It was bitter.

He tried to think of what to say to Strachey. He could hardly tell him Jedder was hunted and on the run. It sounded too dangerous. Strachey would almost certainly and quite justifiably refuse to come over. He'd confine himself to the assurances Jedder wanted and nothing else and would caution Jedder to do the same.

He snuffed out the candle and went upstairs.

In the guest-room Henry Jedder was awake and heard him. He was still fully dressed and he sat on the edge of the bed with the Scotch bottle in his hand. The door to Gisèle's room was closed. After a few minutes, Jedder put down the bottle and went very quietly out on to the landing and stood in the dark, listening.

He heard the murmuring of voices through the door and the thin wall of the room and then in a little while he heard a rhythmical sound that rose quickly to be furiously hard and long-drawn. With it he heard the faint whimpering protests of a woman half-exulting, half-distressed by unexpected harshness in her lover.

He used the sound and what it meant to slip quietly down the stairs and out into the wind-swept night.

Chapter Thirty

At eleven o'clock at night the opulent, crowded bar of the Hôtel George V had quieted considerably. Beneath twinkling overhead spotlights, which bathed each table in a soft island of white, there remained only a handful of couples too engrossed in each other to leave, or the occasional late starter buying a drink for one of those very expensive women about town who have not yet found anyone to pay for their evening.

Richard Ender had discovered just such a girl. She was very blonde and very beautiful. Even more important, there was about her that exquisitely provocative air of the forbidden. She had been sitting in a darkish corner for some time. He had caught her eye and joined her, bought her a Daiquiri, then another. Before long he had discovered that for late dinner at Maxim's or the Tour d'Argent and five hundred francs she would more than willingly spend the night with him and fulfil any conceivable fantasy he might have. His blood raced with expectation. There was an excitement for him about such a woman that exceeded anything he could find with an ordinary girl. He had just called for the check when a bell-boy came from the lobby striking a gong and holding a small blackboard with 'Richard Ender' printed on it. A phone-call. Because of Henry Jedder he had telephoned his whereabouts for the evening to the Dallas Switchboard.

He excused himself. She softly smiled her promise of patience. He left the bar inwardly cursing. He was never to see her again.

'Mr Ender?' The *concierge* on duty waved at lobby phone-booths. Ender went into one and closed the door.

'Hello?'

The voice that replied spoke in the nasal twang of Ambassador Ryan 'Banjo' Collins. What he told Ender was hands-down the worst thing Ender had ever heard. Henry Jedder had called half-an-hour ago and reached Arnheimer Larsen. He said he'd been kidnapped by Aaron Zeismann and a girl friend and was holed up in a beach-house some place. The girl sounded like Roche-Corbon's mistress, and a check showed her as missing since last night.

Not more than ten minutes later, Ender had signed in with the night guard at 37 Avenue Kléber and had gone upstairs and down the silent office corridor to the conference room.

He was past embarrassment or even rage at Aaron Zeismann's betrayal. His very existence was in total jeopardy. Everything he'd worked for, his career, his social life, was about to turn to ashes. Unexpectedly, he found he had almost never been so clear-headed. He hardly noticed Larsen who sat in his usual silence, one well-groomed ankle resting on the knee of his other tailored leg, the fingers of his perfectly manicured hands interlaced and his pale, almost albino eyes totally without expression.

'You haven't heard a thing yet,' Collins said. He was icily stiff behind the mask of his rimless glasses, but what came from him nevertheless was fear, and Ender realized that Collins right now was in as much of a mess as he was himself. Collins could never clear himself of blame by saying he'd always suspected Aaron. He would be asked why, if so, he hadn't acted on such a suspicion.

He heard Collins tell him Strachey would probably be coming over to meet Jedder and Zeismann and he realized Strachey might have been briefed for some time and been unable to act only because he didn't have a major witness. The reason for Jedder's empty shredder-bag suddenly fitted. He felt physically ill. He tried to concentrate. There had to be a way to stem disaster. He sensed something in the back of his mind but couldn't formulate it yet. He needed more information.

'You said a beach-cottage. Where?'

'He wasn't sure. A flat beach, a lot of surf and wind.'

'But surely his phone-number would tell us?'

'We couldn't get it.' Collins glanced at Larsen, then back.

'It was asked for. He said it was dark, he was in a strange house, he'd have to find a light. Then suddenly he said someone was coming and he hung up. There wasn't time to trace it.'

Ender swore softly. A large wall-map of France dominated one side of the room. The northern beaches of Brittany and about half of Normandy, as well as those of the Côte d'Azur far to the south, were for the most part small and steep and often rocky. That left the rest of northern France along the Channel right to Belgium. It also left the Mediterranean west of Marseilles and curving south-westward all the way to Spain. Finally there was the awesome Atlantic coast which began north of Bordeaux and stretched south for three-hundred kilometres to Biarritz at the foot of the Spanish Pyrenees.

It was virtually looking for a needle in a haystack. Until Zeismann moved on. Then, if they did find him, what next? Strachey wouldn't take two missing key-witnesses lying down. A lot would depend on finding out just how much Strachey knew.

Collins was saying, 'The French have put a computer on the call. They have to check out every single phone in France on the billing-register of their local exchanges and find which one called our number. This time of night it could take a while.'

Ender ignored it and asked Larsen, 'Did you manage to talk to him at all before he hung up?'

Collins answered it, 'He told Jedder to sit tight and play innocent until we decided how best to handle it. He wouldn't need to contact us again. If Zeismann moves him, go along with him. He said Zeismann wasn't going anywhere until morning.'

Something didn't ring right, Ender thought. 'If he's free to telephone,' he asked, 'how come he doesn't just walk the hell out of it, wherever he is?'

'He said he was miles off in the boonies,' Collins replied impatiently. 'He was scared Zeismann might find him missing and come after him and he'd be a sitting duck.'

'I don't believe it,' Ender declared. 'And I don't believe he was kidnapped, either.'

Collins was annoyed. He leaned back in his chair.

'Maybe you'd like to tell us, then, just what the son-of-a-bitch is doing with Zeismann?'

'Trying to have it both ways,' Ender answered. 'Look here, let's remember something. Henry Jedder knows France like you know Pickens County, and my guess is he knows damn well what beach he's on. It just doesn't suit him to tell you. Here's why. First, he thinks just the way Zeismann told us he would. He figures he'll follow Reymond. Zeismann probably used that. You're next, Henry, but play ball with Strachey and you'll be all right. Henry probably panicked enough to buy it. He also probably wondered what Zeismann would do to him if he refused. After all, if Zeismann told him he had contacted Strachey, how did he count on keeping Henry quiet if Henry didn't go along with him? But now Henry's having second thoughts. Defecting isn't as easy as it first seemed. He's holed up in a cold beach-house. Zeismann would have had to tell him the police were after him. If Zeismann gets him away, okay. But suppose we catch up to him before he does? Why not tip us off, half way at least, and get credit, if ever necessary, for saving our necks? What would he know about our finding him overnight with a phone-company computer? So either way he wins. Does that sound like our Henry?'

Collins stared from behind his glasses, taking it in. He seemed about to speak when his telephone rang, jarring the silence. He picked it up, listened, made a couple of notes. Ender glanced again at Larsen. Larsen still hadn't moved. He felt once more the physical revulsion Larsen always produced in him. The security chief sat there, an isolated, invulnerable power and unquestionably he'd been right from the very beginning. Aaron Zeismann had to be the legendary de Gaulle mole, effectively blocked by his own superiors in France, and turning in desperation to Julian Strachey.

Collins suddenly said thank you quite abruptly and hung up. Then he smiled and it was vindictive and ugly. He obviously didn't need an ally any more. 'I'm sure you're right,

Richard,' he said rudely, 'but I'm not really interested.' He swung to face Larsen. 'The telephone Jedder used is the last unit on a single line coming out of a place called Vensac, north-west of Bordeaux. It's a beach-house belonging to some optician. There were two other calls. One to Paris to a number the telephone-exchange says doesn't exist, probably a misdial. The other was to the Connaught Hotel in London. That's where Strachey is staying. Make arrangements to pick them both up.'

'What about the woman?' It was the first time Larsen had spoken.

Collins shrugged. 'It depends on how much she knows. We don't need her any more and I shouldn't think her banker would want her back.'

Larsen smiled faintly and rose.

Ender said, 'Just a minute.'

It was sharply authoritative. Collins stared.

'Wait down the hall, please,' Ender said to Larsen. 'The Ambassador and I need to talk. Privately.'

Larsen waited for Collins.

Collins reddened and leaned forward to protest. Ender bore down hard. 'Sorry, Banjo. Jedder will keep five minutes. So will Zeismann.' A coldness he had never felt before got across to Collins. The Ambassador nodded at Larsen. Larsen shrugged imperceptibly and silently headed out. Before he closed the door behind him, Ender said, 'You don't do a thing or pick up anyone until we're through. Is that absolutely clear?'

The pale, unblinking eyes remained expressionless. The door closed with the order unacknowledged.

Collins said impatiently, 'All right, Richard. What the hell is it?'

Ender let him wait. He went to the liquor cabinet and took out two glasses and a bottle of Jack Daniels. For the first time ever he had Collins exactly where he wanted him. The initiative was his. It made no difference whether Collins agreed or not. What he was going to say would regain him complete authority.

He poured two straight shots, pushed one at Collins and

said, 'Listen carefully, Banjo, because like it or not we're in this one together. Laying hands on Jedder and Zeismann hardly gets us out of the woods all the way, does it? What about Strachey? And I don't mean his banking committee either. Without him it means nothing.'

'What about him?' Collins demanded. 'He has no witnesses any more.'

'That's correct. But do you want to take the chance he might know enough already to subpoena us to testify why they both suddenly went missing or died or whatever likely story we come up with to silence their families?'

Collins's eyes suddenly showed fear. 'Go on,' he said.

Ender continued. 'Julian Strachey is such a notorious womanizer, I should think a girl friend in France would keep his family from getting over-curious as to what he'd been doing here if he met with an unfortunate fatal accident.'

It gave him no small amount of pleasure to see Collins register it, to know Collins hadn't yet thought of it himself. He'd taken far too much from Collins.

'Well?' he asked.

The Ambassador to France agreed.

Chapter Thirty-one

In the morning there was an ominous sky and a bitter cold wind off the sea. The tide was high, the surf pounded and foamed close to the steep, rolling dunes.

Margita awoke. The bed next to her was cold and Aaron not there. She had no idea of the time. She used Gisèle's toothbrush and dressed quickly, pulling on an extra pair of socks and a heavy sweater she found in Gisèle's closet. They were damp from the sea air. She felt exhausted and depressed. Last night there had been a sort of hostility in Aaron as though he were punishing her for some inner torment of his own. She'd been rawly vulnerable because inexplicably and in spite of everything she was in love with him again. Almost overnight the intervening years had suddenly fallen away. Where were they? Roche-Corbon no longer existed, nor anyone else, nor any dark times of compulsive debasement. She was once again a young refugee from the Russian rape of Prague. As she went downstairs, she remembered she'd given Aaron two days to get her out of France. Had that really been her? Today, as years ago, love stripped her of all resources of her own. Aaron was everything. Today she would hide in a dank cellar and for a lifetime if necessary just to be with him. And whereas in Paris she'd thought a lot about his wife, in the last twenty-four hours she'd hardly remembered her once, if at all. People outgrew each other. Juliet had had eight years, more than fair time to hold him. No woman had the right to expect more.

Then, at the foot of the stairs, Margita stopped short, all thoughts instantly driven from her head by what she saw through the living-room's sliding glass doors.

Henry Jedder was out on the beach watching the surf. From time to time he bent to pick up a shell. What on earth could he be thinking of? Aaron had warned him. A man in a business suit, seen on the beach this time of year, would surely provoke questions. It was terrifying. She hesitated, feeling it wasn't even safe to call out to him.

To her relief Aaron suddenly appeared on the top of a dune. He too saw Jedder and went down to join him, and it struck Margita with complete irrelevancy that of the three she was the only one dressed for the beach. She nearly laughed. She watched as Aaron seemed to remonstrate with Jedder, and when they headed back for the house she went into the kitchen to light the gas-stove and put some water on to boil.

Presently they appeared. Jedder, to her surprise, seemed quite a different person from last night. 'Aaron's been chastising me,' he said, good humouredly. 'He was afraid some airborne *flic* might drop out of the sky and whisk me away.' He put a handful of small shells on the kitchen table and poked them about. 'Your choice,' he said. 'A lasting memory of the French seaside.'

He laughed and coughed and Margita could smell the Scotch he had drunk yesterday and last evening. She turned to Aaron. He was very quiet, she thought. Unnaturally so. She smiled and said good morning and behind Jedder's back touched his hand. It was ice-cold and he didn't respond. She hadn't imagined his hostility last night, then. It was still there somehow. But why? She served out coffee, feeling suddenly close to tears.

'When do you want to leave?' Jedder asked Aaron.

'Right away.'

Margita said, 'Don't you want something to eat?'

'I'd rather not take the time,' he replied.

'Where are we going?'

'The north-east coast,' Aaron told her. 'Montreuil-sur-Mer.'

'Oh.' She remembered Montreuil. It was not far from the Channel port of Boulogne, a shabby old Picardy market-town perched on a high bluff a few miles back from the sea and with a half-ruined château and an old country inn frequented mostly by Englishmen just landed from a Channel crossing or spending a last night in France before embarking for home.

She didn't question further. But Jedder, continuing his good humour, volunteered the reason. 'We're meeting our friend Strachey there,' he said. 'He's decided an evening out in France won't kill him. If he and I get along, we'll all fly on to England. If not, you and Aaron will have to manage the Channel crossing somehow without me.' He grinned at Aaron and waved his coffee-cup. 'Have we time for a small dividend?'

Aaron nodded at Margita and she poured Henry Jedder what was left. He drained his cup again, pushed back his chair noisily, wiped his mouth on the back of his hand and lumbered to his feet.

'I want to speak to you a moment,' Aaron said abruptly.

Jedder looked first surprised, then vaguely irritated. 'Go ahead.'

Aaron spoke instead to Margita, 'Maybe you could wait in the car. Mine. Keep the garage doors shut until we come out.'

'All right.'

She glanced around the kitchen and frowned. It was against her instincts to leave a mess.

Aaron followed her to the hall and looked out. The long, tar ribbon of beach road was empty. Here and there sand drifted across it.

He unlocked the front door. She went out without a word. He watched her as she walked to the garage, her slender figure bowed into the wind. Last night, this morning, she was more beautiful than ever. But seeing her was like seeing a photograph of someone remembered from long ago. Last night he'd been angry. Now, instead, he had a feeling of all-embracing sadness. What had happened to what once was? Where had it gone, leaving a hollow coldness in its place?

He kept watching until the side door of the garage closed behind her. Then he turned back to Jedder. When he had telephoned Louis Tattel last night, he'd left the phone, without thinking about it, on the veneered cabinet beween a stack of magazines lying flat and some books standing on end. This morning it was on top of the magazines and the books had fallen across the empty gap where they had been. The awful moment of discovering someone else had been using the phone came back to him. The sheer terror of it. He had completed his call to Strachey before he remembered last night at all and realized the phone had been moved. He'd stood stock-still in the ice-cold dawn and stared at the sideboard. All his mind would do was ask the question, Who? Who had been there and why? Were they being tailed? A couple of silent men holed up for the night and upstairs right now, waiting? Seconds ticked by without his moving and the only sounds the beating of his own blood, the outside moan of wind, the rumble of heavy surf. Eventually he had searched the house and then he'd thought of Jedder. He had to know whether it was he or not. But a misplaced phone wasn't enough to trap him. He needed something more specific, something guaranteed to produce an unguarded reaction.

On the way from the beach he'd pulled a package of cigarettes from a carton found in a drawer by Jedder. He'd ripped a pack open, dumped half the contents into a wastebasket and shoved the pack into his pocket.

Now he took it out. 'You left these by the telephone last night, Henry. I have to know whom you called.'

It worked. It caught Jedder completely off guard. All the good cheer drained instantly from his heavy face, leaving him soft-jowled and grey. He ogled the cigarettes and avoided Aaron's eyes. 'Why?' he demanded.

'Because certain calls could be monitored,' answered Aaron. 'Out of the country ones. We don't know how hard they might be looking for us. A watch on Strachey, for example. Or on your wife. Whom did they receive calls from?'

Jedder stared at the floor, silent. Then he said anxiously, 'Of course. I never thought. I'm sorry.' His tone was genuinely contrite. 'I called Paris to check with my answering service. I wanted to know if Rosemary had been trying to reach me. I'm afraid if she doesn't hear from me regularly, she gets upset. I didn't think we'd want her telephoning around. To the office, say. Just on the odd chance they hadn't missed me.'

If it was a lie, Aaron thought, it was so utterly guileless as to be nearly perfect. 'It might be better in the future if you asked me,' he said.

Jedder smiled. 'I didn't because I had the impression you didn't want me to know you had a telephone over there.' Some of the good cheer was back, and that was guileless, too. Aaron tried to think whom else he might have phoned. There was no point in asking. He'd learned all Jedder was going to let him learn without risking rebellion. If it was a lie, let him think he'd got away with it.

He forced a pleasantness he didn't feel. He still had to call Louis Tattel and he couldn't take the chance now. Not from the same phone. 'Hiding on the run can be very tricky,' he explained. 'You'd be amazed at what can give you away without your ever realizing it.'

He'd found a small carryall in Gisèle's room and had stuffed into it the two files taken from Jedder's desk. The black book remained in his pocket. They went out by the front door. The wind bit deep, the sand stung. They hurried to the garage and drove out the rented car and left Margita's Maserati locked up. Gisèle would find it, along with the dirty dishes, when she came to open her house next summer.

They pulled away and drifting sand at once began to fill their tracks in the parking area. In twenty minutes there was virtually no trace of them left.

Chapter Thirty-two

It was all like that, Aaron was to reflect later, the whole drawn-out, frightening trip to the north-east coast of France. It was like the swirling, drifting sand, it had an unreal quality. And was far too easy.

The French police take chauvinistic delight in road-block efficiency. Expecting to run into trouble at any minute Aaron headed south from the beach-house and along the coast. They passed through Lacanau, a resort where wind swept the empty streets and where bleak new high-rise condominiums vied for an ocean view with old Victorian hotels shuttered for the winter. They saw no one. Soon their road joined a main highway leading directly east to Bordeaux's Mérignac airport just a few kilometres out of Bordeaux itself.

Some of Aaron's tension began to diminish. Rationally, he thought, it would be difficult for *Sûreté* as well as the *Gendarmerie Nationale* to spare the forces to block all of France. They would concentrate on the international airports at Paris: Orly, Le Bourget, Charles de Gaulle; on major Channel ports and on the frontier entries to Spain, Switzerland and Germany, Luxembourg and Belgium. It was unlikely they would be looking for Henry Jedder in Bordeaux, or in Amiens where they would fly to. If not totally out of trouble, he was certain they were at least for the moment half safe.

Minutes later, an uncomfortable incident jarred that feeling. Just before Mérignac, they stopped for a red light. A highway-patrol *gendarme* who had come up behind, eased his motor cycle alongside and bent his helmeted head down to stare intently into the car.

Henry Jedder's shambling size and appearance made him someone difficult to forget even from a vague radio description. Aaron poised his right foot on the accelerator ready to smash into the bike and bolt. But whatever the *gendarme*'s motives, he gunned away as soon as the light changed, hunched bulkily in his winter leather coat.

Gnawing anxiety returned. Margita who had also seemed to relax now became silent again. Only Jedder himself appeared cheerfully unmoved. Perhaps, thought Aaron, he was a fatalist; or perhaps finally away from the nagging supervision of Banjo Collins he had regained confidence.

When they reached the airport, he left Margita and Jedder to wait in the car while he went to a post office sub-station to call Louis Tattel. He took an empty booth and dialled. There was no answer. He tried again. After six rings there was a musical signal and then a scratchy, recorded voice told him the number was no longer valid and to verify it.

He hung up, shaken. Louis Tattel had pulled the plug. Some time during the night the special circuit-connector in the central exchange had been eliminated, a job of seconds. There could be a half-dozen reasons why. He had to protect himself and think of the worst: that his Grenoble cover had somehow been blown and that they'd checked out the Relais Maritime to see if he'd left evidence of his intentions. Nobody knew of his personal connection with Tattel and the old para would have moved at once to protect first himself and second the man they searched for, from being caught on his telephone.

Had Louis had time to arrange the flight?

Aaron went back to the car. They drove past service hangars to the private sector and a shabby little one-storey building belonging to France-Europe. Inside there was a small waiting area and a counter with a display poster saying they would fly you anywhere you wanted to go. Beyond the counter was the office, three or four desks, some filing-cabinets, photographs of European capitals.

Aaron asked for Paul Ruchet and said he was from the Relais Maritime.

The receptionist put down a magazine, pressed an intercom button, and relayed the information.

The intercom crackled. '*Ah bon? Quelques instants, alors.*'

From the accent Aaron knew immediately that Ruchet was a Swiss. The receptionist without further word went back to her magazine. Presently a tall, greying man with prominent teeth appeared from a back room. The disapproving and humourless set of his face confirmed his nationality. He wore a heavy cardigan and cavalry-twill trousers and also looked as though he'd been up all night. He came at once to the point.

'I have filed a flight plan for take-off at twelve-thirty.'

Aaron's relief was intense. One way or the other Louis Tattel had managed to complete arrangements before he cut out. 'There's been a slight change of plans,' he said. 'We're not going to England direct. We have to stop off at Amiens first.'

Ruchet's expression betrayed no reaction. He simply said, 'I'm sorry, that won't be possible.'

'Why not?'

'Those weren't my instructions.'

'Tattel's instructions came from me. He just passed them on.'

'I would have to have his verification. I don't accept changes in plan. Ever. Or a change in who gives the orders. That's the way you get into trouble.'

The Swiss pushed a counter telephone at Aaron. Aaron ignored it. 'He's out of town this morning. I don't know where to reach him.'

Ruchet shrugged.

'You made a deal,' Aaron said. He was beginning to feel real anger.

'If you're worried about the money, we won't accept it when it comes through.'

Ruchet started to turn away. Aaron's hand shot across the counter and pinned his wrist to it.

'Listen,' he said. 'Dirty Swiss bastard! You don't do this to me. And you don't do it to Louis Tattel. Not if you know what's good for you.'

The older man ignored the insult and met Aaron's eyes unflinchingly. 'Someone who has to use me to leave the country,' he replied, 'doesn't tell me what I do and don't do.'

Aaron knew when he was beaten. Still holding Ruchet's wrist, he tried to think. Unless he could find another pilot he was in for the nightmare choice between flying with the public carrier, France-Inter, or driving.

'*Touché*,' he said. He forced a smile, withdrew his hand and turned for the door.

Ruchet said. 'Of course, there's nothing to stop you making a new deal of your own.'

Aaron came back slowly. So that was it. He remembered what Louis Tattel had said about the pilot being a hard one to deal with. He wanted to tell Ruchet to go to hell but a drowning man doesn't reject rescue because he dislikes his rescuer.

'It would have to be a personal cheque,' he said, and added, not without a certain pleasure, 'on a Swiss bank.'

'What's my guarantee?'

'As you implied yourself, someone who has to use you to leave the country also needs you not to say where he's gone.' He waited. It was weak but the best he could think of.

After a moment Ruchet said, 'It's that plane out there. Twelve thousand francs.' He'd upped the ante by two thousand. He read Aaron's mind and smiled his superior, Swiss smile. 'We charge additional for non-reserved flights,' he said.

Par for the course, Aaron thought. He smiled coldly back and took out his cheque-book. The cheque would bounce, but by the time it did, he hopefully would be out of the country and it wouldn't make any difference. Ruchet would take Louis Tattel's ten thousand and be glad of it and shrug off the fact that his hold-up hadn't worked, and Tattel would go right on using him because nobody dumped a good pilot because he'd tried for a mere two thousand francs extra when scrounging a little extra was part of the game.

Half-an-hour later they took off in a six-passenger twin-engined Sud-Aviation *Gazelle*. Two hours after that they landed at Amiens, eighty kilometres south of Montreuil and the English Channel, a provincial market-centre for the rolling farm plains around it.

'What's the latest you can hold?' Aaron asked Ruchet.

'Twenty-three thirty,' replied the Swiss.

'We'll be here.' Aaron had his eye on a strolling airport guard.

If indeed his cover was blown, Aaron knew they would be looking for him and Jedder together and Margita, too, because they would have quickly checked on her, discovered her gone and presumed her story to her banker to be a lie. One person could pass unnoticed. Three could not, especially when one was big and shambling and another so beautiful as to constantly turn heads. They waited in the plane until the guard disappeared into the France-Inter building, then carefully skirted around a parking-lot and flagged a waiting taxi. It took them to the motel which served the airport and a nearby autoroute. It was a modern place which had a large daily turnover. They could leave it that evening without checking out and nobody would know they had gone.

Using his police identity card, Aaron checked them in, putting himself and Margita in a room next to Jedder. He didn't relish being alone with her again. It made him uncomfortable with Jedder, and how long, too, could he disguise his feelings towards her? At the same time, however, not to be with her might have sent her running right back to Paris.

There was also the question of her clothes. He would have to take her along to dinner. She could sit at another table in the restaurant, Strachey did not have to know she was with them, but she had only blue jeans and Gisèle's old oversized sweater. He cautioned Jedder to stay in his room no matter what and took Margita to an adjacent shopping centre. The risk was minimal, he'd decided. It was vast and garish and crowded, and the last place anyone would ever pick on to look for either of them.

There was a boutique. He let her choose a smart tweed skirt and a blouse and a cashmere cardigan which was very French and suitable for a country inn especially during the winter. She was excited, like a young girl, and kissed him hard, eyes shining. 'Do you realize, Aaron, you've never bought me clothes before. This is the first time. It makes me feel I really belong to you. Does that seem odd?'

He said it didn't. He picked up some shaving gear for himself and let her choose the after-shave and then they went next door to an Avis office and, using a false Visa card and a French driving licence, he rented a Peugeot 504.

When they returned to the motel they brought sandwiches and coffee from the cafeteria. They delivered Jedder his and went to their own room. Margita at once tried on her new clothes again and when she was finished folded them neatly on a chair. Aaron knew she wanted to make love. He found it unthinkable. As every moment went by, she filled him with a greater revulsion. He could hardly bear her to touch him and had to force himself to respond to her embrace. 'Not with him that close,' he said. He nodded at the wall which separated them from Henry Jedder, acutely aware that Jedder's presence hadn't stopped him last night. But she seemed to accept it and turned on the TV. Soon, she was curled up like a child, immersed in it.

Aaron took a shower, trying to think. He had a growing sense he'd somehow and somewhere made some sort of serious mistake. Something was wrong, very wrong. Had Jedder really telephoned his own home or somewhere else? And why was he so different today from yesterday? What went on in the mind of a free-wheeling international financier? What made the Henry Jedders and the Bob Vescos of the world happy? Or for that matter many a less-glamorized banker? The harder Aaron thought the less progress he made. His anxiety increased to a razor's edge.

There was a sudden explosive sound. The steamed-up glass door of the shower flew open. He leapt convulsively back against the shower wall. His heart nearly stopped.

It was only Margita, holding out a Scotch-and-water she'd ordered for him.

She smiled and nodded in Jedder's direction. 'He hasn't left the room,' she said. He accepted the glass, she disappeared. His heart, thudding against his ribs, slowly diminished its speed. Who had he expected to burst in on him? What nameless face behind the ultimate black-holed muzzle of a hand-gun and a last realization of life? Or had he expected Arnheimer Larsen himself and a promise of a far worse obscenity?

He got out and dried off. It was six o'clock.

'We have to go now,' he said to Margita. He picked up the phone and called Jedder and told him the same thing. There was an exit down the hall which led to a parking-area. They would go out that way, leaving Gisèle's clothes and his shaving gear behind to maintain an impression of occupancy for the maids in the morning.

Margita began to dress before a long mirror, pulling on her new skirt and smoothing it over her slender hips.

She said suddenly, 'Will you tell me some day what it's all about? I mean why he is running away? And you?'

Aaron realized that up to now she'd never once asked. And that the total innocence of the question probably meant she actually didn't know.

'When we get to England I'll tell you,' he said.

She smiled gratefully and hurried to finish dressing.

Chapter Thirty-three

The country inn known as the Château de Montreuil was tucked away on the outskirts of Montreuil-sur-Mer. It faced a small and quiet park at the edge of which the ramparts of an ancient citadel fell steeply down to the river Canche and to the flat Picardy coastal plain leading to the sea. At eight o'clock the park was as winter-deserted as the beamy, candle-lit dining-room where the only other guests were two middle-class English couples who had crossed the Channel that afternoon and were innocently trying out their school French on a waiter who spoke excellent English.

Julian Strachey had taken a taxi down from the beach and gambling resort of Le Touquet eight miles away. He'd landed there after a short thirty-minute British Airways flight from London's Gatwick airport. He arrived at the Château only five minutes late for the rendezvous and only moments after Aaron had seated Margita at a table by herself. He had left his perpetual bodyguard at the hotel in Le Touquet where he planned to spend the night. 'They didn't like it, but too damn bad. This is France, after all. Who knows I'm here?' He laughed. 'You caught me just in time, Aaron. We're wrapping up the conference quickly now and I'm due back in Washington this weekend. I presume you drove up from Paris. Where are you staying?'

'At Amiens.'

'Ah, yes. South of here. My father was in a big tank battle there during the war. How soon will you be coming over?'

Aaron said, 'Depends on you two.' He nodded at Jedder. 'I hope tomorrow at the latest.'

Strachey laughed and graced Jedder with a politician's slap on the shoulder. 'If you're half as good as Aaron claims,' he said, 'I'll give you the world and IIC to boot.' He was dressed for country dining, flannels and a tweed jacket with cavalry-style slash pockets, and chukka boots. His thick silvery mane was held down by a cloth cap with a smart leather strap across the back of it. He radiated a special sort of American vitality and a charisma which nearly hid a certain vaguely disturbing weakness around his mouth.

They settled at a corner table out of earshot of the English couples and Margita, who played her part well, gave no hint by glance or expression that she was in any way involved. Aaron put the carryall with Jedder's files under his chair.

They began talking as soon as they had ordered and Henry Jedder was very specific in what he wanted in return for testifying before the Strachey Committee. He emphasized his demands by scrawling them boldly out on the white tablecloth with a felt pen, heedless of the raised eyebrows of the silently watchful *maître d'hôtel*.

First and foremost he wanted protection. He wrote the number 1 and the word 'protect!' Strachey agreed at once. 'We have our own force,' he explained. 'Most of them are ex-Secret Service. I should think several could be assigned to you the moment you reach Washington. Say in a day or so?' He said to Aaron, 'You can't fly to the States directly from here?'

Aaron replied he was afraid they couldn't. Strachey looked for a moment as though he wanted to question why not but seemed to think better of it and turned again to Jedder. 'Once you've testified,' he said 'I should think you'd probably be safe as rain. Going for you then would be a little post-facto and not worth the risk.'

'I also want immunity from prosecution for my part so far in Tricolor,' said Jedder. A heavy number 2 darkened the tablecloth.

'You shall have that also, of course.'

'By any court, Federal or State. Or French,' Jedder specified. 'And I want it in writing. Now.'

Strachey was slightly taken back. 'I can't guarantee the French, of course.'

'I realize that. But you can guarantee sufficient diplomatic pressure on them to perhaps bring them in line. It shouldn't be difficult. After all I'm saving their necks.'

Strachey looked vaguely annoyed, but swallowed it gracefully. He opened a dispatch-case he'd brought and produced several sheets of his Senate Committee notepaper.

While he wrote, Jedder said, 'I also want help in getting re-established.'

Strachey looked up and afforded him an indulgent smile. 'Want that in writing, too?'

'Yes.'

'By re-established do you mean in business?'

'I closed my consultancy when I went with Dallas,' Jedder explained. 'I'll need new office space and a small staff and capitalization to see me into my first deals. I'll accept it on a two-year no-interest basis.'

After some minor bickering, Strachey agreed to recommend a special Senate appropriation of three hundred-thousand dollars and to personally undertake to see it was pushed through. 'Any place in mind?' he asked.

'I'm not sure if I'll move to Switzerland or stay in France,' Jedder answered. 'That will depend on what happens.'

Strachey smiled wryly. 'When Tricolor becomes public,' he said, 'France is likely to go at least Socialist, but I shouldn't think they would bother you. They might even regard you as a hero.'

'I wasn't worried about the Left,' Jedder said. 'I was thinking more of the Right. If your committee were unsuccessful and the Right stayed in power, they'd want revenge.'

'I suppose that's true,' admitted Strachey. He turned to Aaron. 'Well, you said you could deliver and you did. We'll talk about your future later. He finished the letter in silence, signed his name and handed it to Jedder to read. Jedder, meanwhile, had scrawled several more demands on the tablecloth but Aaron knew they were minor. They were over the hump and with any luck would sleep that night in London. He glanced at Margita. She caught his eye and smiled faintly. That was all. Across the room, the English couples were ordering more wine.

Strachey did likewise. Aaron decided the time had come

216

to unburden himself of the files. He pulled the carryall bag from under his chair and unzipped it.

'With your permission, Henry.'

Jedder shrugged assent. Aaron put the files on the table. He kept Jedder's small black notebook in his pocket, however. Jedder wasn't going to know he had it, he'd decided. Nobody else was either until he'd had every page xeroxed and put in a safe-deposit vault. The names, the numbers of the secret Swiss bank accounts, the step-by-step procedures of transferring huge sums of money from Dallas to private individuals; it all added up to what might some day prove crucial leverage on Henry Jedder in case he should have any last-minute change of heart.

Strachey scanned the files and whistled softly. 'With your testimony to back it up,' he said, 'this will certainly do it. And, I might add, the other way around, also. It will solidly verify you as a witness.'

Jedder was folding the letter Strachey had written. 'I trust you find that satisfactory,' added the Senator. Jedder assented. Strachey put the files in his dispatch-case. The wine came, and then Henry Jedder began to talk, at first only the occasional remark, then more and more expansively, and finally, certain of his audience, compulsively. By nine-thirty there was little about Tricolor or Dallas or even Ender and Collins that Aaron could have added to. Jedder had given an overwhelming preview of himself as a witness. He had completely exposed the French Government's complicity in selling out a vital part of their nationalized oil-reserves, thus exposing themselves to total economic coercion. He had virtually destroyed IIC and its parent bankers and had pointed a damning finger at both Houston and Washington.

Strachey was nearly spellbound. 'We'll be avalanched with testimony,' he declared, 'Everyone trying to save his skin before it's too late.'

Jedder went on, but Aaron suddenly wasn't listening. His instinct that something was wrong had begun to nag, again unidentifiable but there just the same, and then with a sort of blinding clarity, it had revealed itself. Jedder was a man who had tried for a deal and had pulled it off. But if you were a

Jedder you always had a fall-back if your deal didn't work. It was never all or nothing at all. Men like Jedder hedged, and it was always all or something nearly as good.

Unidentifiable anxiety turned instantly to identifiable horror. Aaron's hand remained motionless, poised reaching for his glass. Strachey's silver head, Henry Jedder, the English couples with their atrocious French, Margita quietly sipping her coffee, her beauty framed in the soft aureole of the candle on her table; none of it was real. Everything seen or heard was a photographed still life enclosed in a nightmare.

Was Jedder's phone-call from Bordeaux not Jedder somehow covering himself with Collins and Ender in case the Strachey meeting didn't work out? Getting reassurance not to worry, come back when he could, all would be forgiven? And, in spite of Achille Reymond, his own overwhelming ego deceiving him into believing them?

Aaron glanced at his watch. It was ten o'clock. They were due soon at the Amiens airport. If it was true, why hadn't they been picked up long ago? This morning at Bordeaux or even before then at the beach-house? The call from Bordeaux could have been computer-traced in a matter of hours.

The answer to that was equally clear. The horror gripped Aaron even harder. He focused fixedly on Strachey. It was madness. It couldn't happen. Perhaps to the unwanted head of a small Third World nation, to a poor devil like Allende in Chile or a Cuban Castro, but not to one of their own, a United States Senator. If you started with that, there was no end to it. Ever.

But it could happen. And was going to happen. Just the same. Desperate men lost their heads and did desperate things. They would presume Strachey had been briefed long ago. Now he was in France, unprotected. There was too much at stake to allow him now to return to Washington, with or without a witness.

Aaron rose from the table. If what he thought was true, then he himself had made it possible.

Out in the hall he gained control over a wave of nausea and asked for a telephone. He had to know for certain. He was shown to a booth near the desk and the elderly woman receptionist put his call through to the pilots' lounge at Le Touquet.

'I want to speak to Paul Ruchet.'

'He's not here.'

'What time did he say he'd be back?'

'Back? *Mais, alors!* He's not coming back. He took off for Bordeaux an hour ago. *Allô? Allô?*'

He hung up. There was no point at all in asking why Ruchet had left. Ruchet would not have told anyone. There was no point either in pretending Ruchet might have decided to cheat him. Just as there was no point in telling himself Jedder had indeed really phoned his home as he said he had. Or that what he thought might be only seeing terror in shadows where there was none. A life of playing a double game had long ago taught Aaron better. The one thing that kept you alive was to presume the worst and avoid the seductive luxury of hope. Ruchet had left because he'd suddenly sensed or even learned he was involved in something too big for him to handle. He'd cleared out because his passengers were never going to be allowed to leave France.

It tied it all up. They would know Strachey had landed at Le Touquet. That was easy to check out. They knew he and Jedder and Margita were due to show up at Amiens.

Where were they? Waiting at the airport? Combing the countryside? Just outside? The back of Aaron's neck tingled. The only thing they didn't know was that he knew. But if they were intelligent, and they were, they must be working on the supposition that he might.

The little park between the Château Montreuil and the ramparts of the Citadel was silent and empty. Only a small dog wandered it, nose to the half-frozen grass.

Aaron made a quick mental picture of a road map he'd studied before he left the motel. The road to Le Touquet from Montreuil-sur-Mer ran due north to the Channel. The road to Amiens ran in precisely the opposite direction, due south and for fifty miles. Both roads were well surfaced. This time of night at this time of year both would also be empty. An overtaking car, a sudden scream of tyres, the shriek of shredding metal, and you were off the road and into the trees; or someone coming from the opposite direction, and from behind blinding headlights a burst of machine-gun fire. The police would hardly investigate their own terrorism.

The alternative was the closest small harbour on the Channel. There were several just a few miles down the coast. If a fisherman wouldn't take them, the sleeping harbours had moorings for dozens of boats awaiting their choice.

But in the event that he discovered their net, wouldn't his choosing just that alternative have been foreseen? Alone he could have made it. He could have braved the cold and struck off across the country, if necessary hiding with some small farmer. He was French. But Strachey wasn't, and to give Strachey even one hint of what was happening might double the nightmare. He hadn't forgotten the moment of blind panic back at Oxford when the old Admiral had unexpectedly turned on the landing-light.

A gust of wind blew a lonely rustle of brown leaves across the brick terrace outside. Aaron shivered. And at the same time felt the first trickle of sweat beneath his shirt.

He turned back through the lobby. There was one other possibility left to him, something that couldn't be ignored for the very reason that it was so blatantly unthinkable. Between Montreuil-sur-Mer and the Belgium-to-Paris autoroute which ran a hundred kilometres inland across the wind-swept Picardy plain, there lay an intricate network of small country back-roads, here and there crossing small rivers and lazy barge canals and disappearing in and out of tiny, clustered, farm villages where bordering farmyards and farm machinery hazarded the road's edge.

At the Paris end of the autoroute was the Charles de Gaulle airport at Roissy with twenty-four flights a day to London. There was an even-odds chance it was the last place anybody would ever expect Strachey to be. Nor perhaps himself and Jedder now they had run him to ground three hours to the north. He had his *Sous-Préfet* identity and that would certainly help. They didn't know about it.

It was his only option. He went back into the dining-room, asking for the check on the way.

Chapter Thirty-four

He noticed at once that Strachey had drunk too much wine. The Senator's movements had become deliberate, his voice a little thick. But it could be helpful. Strachey wouldn't realize for some time where they were going. He might even sleep all the way to Roissy. There, if handled firmly, he would more than likely accept the unexpected and pull his own weight.

'We can't raise a taxi,' Aaron said. 'I'm afraid you'll have to let us run you back.'

The *maître d'hôtel* hovered, expressionless. Aaron had silenced him with an extra hundred francs when he paid.

Strachey registered it slowly. 'You're sure that's all right?'

'No trouble at all.'

'Fine.'

On the way out the Senator slowed to take in Margita and to make a verbal pass. *'Bonsoir.'*

She ignored him.

He chuckled and continued on to the hall where he said, 'I'm staying at the wrong place. God, I bet some of these French girls could make an old man of you in a week.' He laughed and slapped Jedder on the back. 'How do you live here and stay married?'

Jedder's smile was weak and bored and gratuitous, all at the same time. He was no longer the centre of the stage.

The *maître d'hôtel* helped Strachey to struggle into his duffel coat. Aaron said, 'Why don't you two go on to the car? I'll be right there.'

He watched them exit then returned to the dining-room. Margita was just leaving her table, hurriedly stubbing out a cigarette. The English couples were engrossed in their waiter, the women's laughter shrill.

He hadn't really thought what to tell her. He only knew he

had enough on his hands without explaining her to Strachey or having Strachey come wide awake because of her presence. Or for that matter, having her at Roissy as one more highly identifiable person to call attention to them. He said quickly, 'I've had to make an urgent change in plans. I want you to spend the night here.' He ignored her unguarded surprise and pulled what was left of his cash from his pocket, keeping only enough for petrol. If they made it, his chequebook or credit card would work for the plane fare.

'Here. Take this.' He put the money in her hand. 'It's all I can give you.'

The colour slowly drained from her face.

'You're not taking me?' Her voice was flat with incredulity. And with shock.

He made it as gentle as he could. 'I can't. Not tonight. You must understand. It's not possible.'

'But what's happened?'

'Margita, I haven't time to explain. I have to get Strachey out of here. Immediately. Alone. I'll try to contact you tomorrow.'

'Are you still flying to England?'

'I'm going to try to.'

'But you can't leave me. If you are in that much trouble, so am I.'

She was right. It was too late for her to steal back to her banker. She'd reached the point of no return.

'I'm sorry. If by any chance you're picked up, claim I forced you against your will.'

'Aaron.'

'There's no choice, Margita.'

He forced himself to kiss her, a hard brief kiss that said he cared. She didn't respond and he left her standing by the table, face white and eyes unnaturally large.

He went outside quickly. It could all come back on him. If she thought he'd just used her, she might still somehow turn dangerous. Although he didn't see how. There was nothing he could do anyway. Strachey was in the front seat, Jedder just getting in the rear. He slid behind the wheel and started the motor.

Strachey leaned back. 'Will you have time for a drink at the hotel?'

'I don't see why not,' replied Aaron.

As he drove the car out of the square, he looked in his rear-view mirror. Margita had come to the door and was standing there. She seemed strangely small and vulnerable and for a fraction of a second everything he'd once felt for her returned. He wanted to stop, to tell her to come on and quickly. Then he turned a corner and she was gone.

He kept his headlights off. Instead of driving down the escarpment to the Le Touquet road below, he cut south directly across the main square of the town and then took a side street to the railway station. It was the back way out of town.

Strachey waved at passing slate roof-tops and the worn stone of centuries-old buildings, textured soft in the diffused light of a street lamp. 'They actually thought they could buy this,' he said. 'France. All of this. Centuries of history. Another whole nation of people. For a few billion dollars.' He laughed and leaned his head back again and closed his eyes. 'In California we make wine in steel and glass vats,' he said, 'And claim we're just as civilized. Oh, my God, what we haven't yet learned.' Then he was silent.

At Montreuil-sur-Mer the railway station is by the River Canche. It's primitive, a ticket-office and waiting-room, a baggage depot, an outside platform.

Aaron swung down to the pot-holed dirt parking-area and then between two long corrugated sheds which served for off-loading freight. He had remembered from years ago a narrow dirt road which began just the other side of the tracks and which led along the banks of the river for ten kilometres before it rejoined a hard-topped secondary road leading south-east. Once, years ago, he had whiled away some time there, rowing up the sluggish river and getting a tow back from an amiable barge captain bringing a load of scrap-iron up from Paris. Some local gravel trucks had swirled clouds of dust over a deck-line of drying laundry, reducing the captain's wife to inarticulate rage.

As he crossed the tracks, his rear-view mirror filled with a bright flare of headlights. A car was coming down out of town behind him. He turned on to the dirt road and slowed. If he was being followed already, he had to know.

The headlights seemed to hesitate, then headed into the station parking-area, their beams swinging up and down as the vehicle behind them bounced heavily. Aaron realized he'd left a tell-tale haze of dust behind him. He tried to think what to do. He had waistbanded the little .25 Beretta Louis Tattel had forced on him. It had pressed, a hard and lethal lump, against his abdomen all the way from Paris to Bordeaux and from Bordeaux to Montreuil. Now that he might have to use it, it seemed ridiculously ineffectual.

The lights headed for the tracks. He swung his wheel all the way over, getting ready for a fast reverse of direction, and then in the station light caught sight of the vehicle itself. It was the Ford Cortina belonging to the two English couples back at the Château. He could plainly see its square silver-on-black British number plate. He knew at once who must be driving it. If Margita hadn't found the keys in the vehicle itself, then she'd quickly rifled the pockets of the British trench-coats hanging in the Château hallway and found success there.

He was swept by helpless anger. He let her pull alongside. He wanted suddenly to get out, to end the charade, to tell her he knew why she had come back to him after all the years and what she had done. He wanted to smash his fist through the driver's window and tell her she was a whore and a liar and that because of her Bejerec had died and he was underground, cover blown, and a Senator's life hung in the balance.

He didn't do anything. He saw her face in the glow of the Cortina instrument-panel, her wide eyes on him and filled with a sort of animal desperation. He knew his own eyes must look the same; he was equally guilty for ever having trusted her.

He switched on his own headlights and drove on along the dirt road and she followed.

Strachey stirred. 'What's happening?'

'Just taking a short cut.'

'Are we lost?'

'No.'

Strachey said, 'I keep forgetting this French stuff is right up your alley. Bloody old frog.' He laughed good-naturedly. 'Tell me when we get there if we don't drive off the road first.' Then he was a dark shadow, slouched and head rolling to one side.

Aaron picked up speed. The Peugeot's wheels rumbled on the dirt surface like a steady drum-roll. The Cortina's headlights distanced as Margita fell back before the dust. But then steadily kept that distance.

Jedder said in a low voice, 'He's asleep.'

Aaron didn't answer.

'What's happened?' Jedder insisted. His bulk pressed against the back of the seat as he leaned forward, voice anxious. 'This isn't the road to Le Touquet. Where are we going? Amiens?'

'Amiens is blown. The pilot's gone back to Bordeaux.'

'I don't understand.'

'I think you do, Henry.'

'I don't.' Truculent. 'I want to know where we're going.' A board-room order.

Aaron's reply was through his teeth. He'd had enough of Jedder and if Jedder didn't like it, there was the Beretta. He said, 'Where I hope your friends Collins and Ender don't expect us to go.'

A dead silence. Jedder hesitating before asking, 'What do you mean?' There was fear in his voice, the same fear Aaron had heard back in the marble town house in Paris.

Aaron said, 'You damn well know what I mean, you filthy Judas bastard. I'm talking about your idiot phone-call from Bordeaux. Trying to have your cake and eat it, too. Well, it didn't work. Collins and Ender aren't going to play. They've taken all the chances with you that they want to, and you're in for the same as Achille Reymond if I can't get you out of it. You can count on that. And you can count on something else.' He jerked a thumb at Strachey. 'If it weren't for him, I'd stop this car right now and kick you the hell out of it. With pleasure.'

Another silence. Then Jedder said, 'Can't you slow down a little?' There were tears in his voice. The bluffing financier had disappeared. And he'd denied nothing. What better proof that it was all true, Aaron thought dully.

He glanced at his speedometer. The pale needle-tip touched the luminous kilometre number 120. That meant seventy-two miles an hour. It was too fast for the road. He eased off a little and worked to take the next corner smoothly. The headlights of the Cortina were still there, behind. He knew there was little chance of losing Margita; the Cortina was a hot car.

A minute later the dirt gave way to asphalt as they re-joined the main south-east road. The headlights of the Cortina were clear of the dust and piercing sharp in their whiteness. They seemed out of place. All French headlights were yellow and after a while the white lights of cars from other countries jarred.

There was a fork in the road and signs. He bore off right and on to a local road that would by-pass several towns. It was narrower, nothing more than a country lane, the surface serrated by tractor cleats or here and there lumped with dirt dragged on to it from surrounding fields. But it was straight and would run a long, fast line under the nearly touching branches of an endless avenue of European elms, perhaps twenty kilometres or so, and through half-a-dozen nameless villages before it joined with another even lesser road which in turn would take him directly to the autoroute.

He put his foot down. For five miles. The Cortina dogged his wake. There was no sign of any other vehicle and they owned the night.

A red-bordered yellow sign with a bent blue arrow loomed, warning of an approaching curve. And almost immediately another sign saying that the road narrowed and to reduce speed to forty kilometres an hour.

That meant there probably would be a bridge and canal. He slowed going down a slight hill and saw first the dark surface of the water snaking away between banks thickly lined with alders and brush and tall Lombardy poplars, and next, directly ahead, the low, rusty iron railings of the narrow spanning bridge which arched high in the middle to allow barges passage beneath it.

And then it all happened. And very quickly. And even as it did, he realized if they had a spotter aircraft aloft, which would be automatic with the French police, that Margita's dogging white headlights were what had told them where to pull the net tight. Not his. His could have been any local farmer's.

One moment the bridge was confined to the soft, narrow tunnel of pale yellow thrown out by his Peugeot; the next everything flared brilliant bright and blinding. A car had swung abruptly out of the darkness beyond to block his path. With the terrible speed with which the mind sometimes understands, he knew immediately that he'd out-guessed nobody: he had failed. If not from Margita's headlights, they would have had him some other way. Tricolor wasn't to be defended by half-way measures.

His tyres screamed. His brakes locked, pulling him into the bridge kerb. The Peugeot wiped out its left side on the low bridge-rail in a shrill of tearing metal, then slewed to a stop just half-way across.

Strachey and Jedder piled shouting into the dashboard and seat. Aaron hardly heard them. His mind said, one chance in a thousand and he could back off and U-turn and maybe reach darkness before he hit the road-block they would surely have run up behind him. In the darkness they could get out and run.

He jammed the gear-lever into reverse. It was too late. Before he could lift his foot off the clutch he felt the jarring shock on his rear bumper. And simultaneously knew what it was and what would happen. They'd run a heavy vehicle without lights up behind him.

He'd hardly thought it when its motor roared. The Peugeot was lifted violently towards the bridge-rail. There was the crunch of steel into steel. Tyres screamed again. The rail held a fraction of a second then buckled in the nightmarish slow motion. The glare of lights twisted dizzily and turned grey-silver with impact spray. And then pitch-black with a shuddering boom as the canal water smashed in and around them.

Aaron felt himself falling, falling, turning upside down. He was slammed against the roof as the car stopped abruptly and sighed slowly into something soft. Mud, ran through his mind, deep, filthy mud and weeds.

Everything was upside-down, steering-wheel and seats overhead. There was a deafening rush of water. It poured in ice-cold from everywhere and in high-pressure streams that stabbed. A body thrashed, clawing, kicking, and an unintelligible human scream burst forth.

It was Strachey. He heaved him away. He tried to feel a window or door handle. Something struck hard at his face, the gear-lever. Water reached his waist, howling, squeezing out the air. It rushed up higher and higher. He could hardly breathe. And the human scream went on and on.

He found a handle. A window? He took a deep breath and began to turn it as fast as he could. An instant wall of water embraced him, became everything except for something else that clutched and held him back. Weeds. He kicked and tore at their wrapping tendrils. His lungs spasmed, stopping thought.

Suddenly there was a greyness, next a blaze of light.

He heard a distant shout, a man's. And from much closer his own name.

'Aaron.'

Somebody dived. A heavy smash of water beside him and Margita's face appeared, white in the headlights.

'Aaron. Take my hand.'

He screamed back, 'Get out of here! Get out!'

She had him by his sleeve and was swimming and trying to pull him to the bank a few yards away. She was very strong. 'Aaron.'

'They'll kill you.' He tore loose and pushed her away. 'Get out!'

He kicked her off a second time.

'Aaron. Leave them.'

He gulped air and went back down.

He felt the weeds almost immediately, endlessly long and

thick and grasping, alive. His hand struck something sharp.
Metal. It cut and tore at him. He felt with his other hand,
kicking to stay down. There was terrible pain in his ears and
head. He couldn't stand it.

There was glass, then a void. He reached through and
pulled himself down and in, shoulders and head first. And
suddenly water was air, a thin black layer of it up over his
head and against the Peugeot's floor carpeting.

The screaming burst out again. Mindless, shattering. He
aimed for it, shoving past something big and blocking that
floated inertly. He felt flesh and hair, backed away pulling.
The hair came with him, stuck, came again as he went
through the window. The weeds tangled and held him and
what he pulled. He couldn't breathe any longer and the pain
became a soundless scream. Then there were hands on his
body, swimming feet flailed next to him. The weeds vanished. His chest heaved and he thought I don't care I have to
breathe and he opened his mouth and miraculously air came
in.

The headlights of the car on the bridge still flooded the
canal. He had Julian Strachey by the hair and held his head
up into the glare, Strachey choking and Margita pulling
them both towards the bank.

There was undergrowth.

'Here.' She pulled a branch down. He grasped it with a
free hand, felt the bank, nearly vertical. His feet groped for a
toe-hold. He held on to Strachey.

Margita flopped up and out and turned and knelt to help
him. He could see her face bent down.

'Margita, run for it. For Christ's sake.'

Where were they? What the hell were they waiting for?

She didn't answer. She kept pulling and then Strachey was
up on the low bank, his clothes caught in branches holding
him. Margita bent again, white face close, her hand clench-
ing his.

'Aaron!'

Two things happened suddenly, simultaneously.

The right side of her face disintegrated explosively, her
nose and cheek-bones an instant tangle of blue-white splin-

ters spattered with crimson and flying amidst bushes and grass.

And the sharp report of a high-velocity rifle.

Next the side of her head heaved out, brains sprayed like vomit and eyes with them but still connected to part of her skull.

And two more simultaneous reports.

What was left, the neck and lower jaw and teeth, stiffened, pumping great spurts of dark red blood. The slim body quivered, bursts of air bubbled through the blood, it pitched forward, hands outstretched, on to Aaron, driving him off the bank and back down into the water and blackness.

Chapter Thirty-five

When he came back up, he was a dozen yards down the canal beyond Strachey. He ducked under again, moving further, fingers just touching the bank, hand over hand. There was a heavy tuft of grass out over the water. And shadow. He slid behind it, found another foot-hold, forced a last effort and heaved upwards. He fainted, then, lying in the dry winter grass until their search for him became an audible warning. He felt for Louis Tattel's .25. It was gone.

There was a clump of trees between him and them. They were talking in French, almost casually, and crashing around in the brush. A flashlight flared.

'Here's the grey-haired one.' A kicking sound. And the ugly metallic noise of an automatic pistol being charged.

'Hey! Don't shoot him, for God's sake, you dumb bastard. He's supposed to drown. If he comes up, hold him under, remember? No wounds.'

'What about her then?'

'Not the same thing. Nobody gives a shit for her.'

'OK, OK. Then lend me a hand. He's all tangled up in branches.'

'Leave him. He's not going anywhere. We'll come back.'

They moved closer, one trailing a dozen yards behind the other and stumbling in the dark to keep up.

Aaron lay very still, feeding his strength.

'Will you slow down, for Christ's sake? He's probably at the bottom anyway.'

'You want to chance it and go home and have him show up?'

It was time. He stood slowly, a tree between him and them, back braced against it, legs at an angle.

He brought his right arm up, forearm across his face, parallel to the ground, his palm flat, fingers extended and held

232

stiffly together. He had to find more strength somewhere or he was dead.

The flashlight had a wide beam and threw an opaque light on the ground close by. And then it was right next to him and behind it and above it was the darkness of the man who held it.

He lurched straight up on to his toes, judged, and back-handed with everything he had.

The shock went deep into his own ribs. But it wasn't bone he'd hit. He'd hit something that crushed in, gristle and cartilage, the man's unguarded throat. A low, gagging choke, the light filtered aimless through deep grass where it had fallen.

The man behind said, 'What are you doing?'

Aaron muttered hoarsely, 'I dropped the light.' He bent and felt the body at his feet, face down. Its hands were to its throat, it couldn't breathe and it burrowed blindly into the grass and dirt. He rolled it over.

'Hurry up. Christ, what's the matter with you?'

'Shut up!'

Time was running out.

He did what he had to do, very quickly and surely. He felt for the face with one hand and swung the straight knife-edge of the other down on to the unprotected bridge of the nose. The bone splintered like a matchbox into the face.

The larynx below it gargled. The body arched its whole length off the ground in a giant paroxysm of agony. He measured again, slammed the butt of his hand forward, driving the mess of bones up between the eyes and into the brain.

His numb fingers found the flashlight, closed on its roundness. He turned it off.

The indignant protest was a whine. 'Now what?' The other hadn't counted on all this, he'd counted only on quickly shoving a car into a canal. That was all there would be to it. That and waiting around five minutes while he smoked a cigarette with his pals and made certain no one came up. And then driving back to Paris for a drink and the comfortable, dry sheets of his bed and maybe to empty himself into the warm body of his woman. But it hadn't worked

233

out that way and woods and brush and floundering around in the cold dark were something he hadn't reckoned on.

His voice rose, 'Will you for Christ's sake turn the damned thing on again?'

It was the last thing he ever said. He sensed movement. The flashlight suddenly flared right in his eyes. A blow, hard like a heavy hammer, smashed his groin.

The pain delayed long enough for his mind to register stupefaction. Then it hit and he tried to scream and had no breath to. An iron force propelled his head violently downward and everything exploded in fire.

Aaron jerked up the man's face and smashed it a second time on to his upraised knee, making sure. He caught the sagging body, heaved it into a sitting position, threw his right arm across the chin, locked his right hand on his left forearm and with his left hand grabbed the hair at the back of the head. He shoved his knee very hard into the small of the man's spine and exerting all the strength he had left pushed forwards his left hand and heaved back his right forearm at the same time.

There was a sharp audible crack as the neck broke. Aaron let the body drop and fell back against a shelf of rock, remembering only to switch off the light.

The persistence of a voice calling brought him to his senses. He was numb with cold.

'Alors, les gars. Qu'est-ce qu'il y a là bas? Pierre-André? Denny? Qu'est-ce que vous foûtez, les deux?' It was a third man on the bridge. What the devil was going on?

Aaron flicked on the light and fumbled beside the dead man and found the automatic pistol. It was a Mauser.

The man on the bridge had the rifle. He'd killed Margita with it, exploded her incredibly beautiful face into eternity and her with it. Where was she now, lonely and cold in death and far, far from home? Everything she was, the bitter and the beautiful, was meaningless, torn flesh drifting away in the slow-moving current of a French barge canal towards the icy, alien grey of the English Channel.

Aaron could see him in the headlights of the car which still blazed out over the dark water and he could see the other vehicle, too, the one that had pushed them in. It was a small wrecker.

Had there been more than three men?

The man shouted again, 'Denny?' He moved about restlessly to peer beyond the canal-bank. His shadow swept long across the water.

Aaron found Strachey. He had disentangled himself from the branches and was curled up in the grass, embryo-like and whimpering softly. If he tried to move him, he might cry out and that would make getting to the man on the bridge doubly difficult. At the same time, in the darkness, Strachey might roll into the canal. He couldn't be left alone.

'Denny!? Pierre-André?' The car headlights switched off and on impatiently.

Aaron gauged the distance to the bridge. Fifty yards at least. It was a very long pistol shot. He couldn't think of any other way. He took a chance and shouted back, in French, 'Shut up! We're here!'

'*Mais, qu'est-ce qu'il y a?*' There was confusion as well as relief in the man's voice.

'*Toujours ce charogne d'Americain a foûter dans le canal. Viens pour nous donner un coup de main.*'

'*Merde! J'arrive.*'

The man on the bridge left the semi-darkness beside the headlights, cursing that his two friends couldn't handle Strachey without his help. He moved into the brilliance of the car's headlights and came down off the bridge on to the canal bank.

But Julian Strachey wasn't to be thrown in the canal and drowned. Julian Strachey had to live. Somehow. Aaron flicked the automatic off safety, hand slippery with his own blood from gashing himself on the car, and from theirs, the two men he'd just killed. He used the fork of a low sapling to steady the automatic. He took very careful aim, holding his breath. He was shaking from head to foot.

He shouted, '*Mais, alors! Dépêches-toi.*'

Thirty yards, no more.

Now,

He carefully squeezed the trigger. Harder, harder. The Mauser bucked and roared. The man with the rifle jerked straight up in the air, seemed to hang on his toes, suspended.

Aaron squeezed a second shot.

The man flipped backwards and sat down heavily, head lolling. The rifle fell from his hand.

A third shot. He slowly stretched out and rolled once, twice, three times, arms and legs loose, and faster and faster down the gathering steepness of the canal-bank. He hit the water, floated a moment in the foam of the splash, then sank like a stone.

Aaron waited. The bridge was silent. How long had it all taken? Five minutes? Seven? Someone had to come. And very soon. He dragged the two dead men into the canal and went to Strachey.

'Senator. On your feet. Quick.' He shook Strachey and pulled him to his knees. 'It's OK. Come on. Get yourself together.'

Strachey shrieked and convulsed and clawed. Aaron slapped him hard and he stopped and began to cry.

'Come on,' Aaron urged. 'Help me.' He shoved the Mauser into his belt and lowered his shoulder under Strachey's armpit and tried to heave him up in a fireman's carry. On the third attempt he made it and didn't drop the flashlight.

It took time to reach the bridge. He fell twice and had to go through the whole business again of lifting Strachey, of heaving him up. By the time he made it, he knew that if there had been anybody else, he'd have been dead a dozen times and Strachey, too. He'd been that helplessly exposed.

The car with the headlights was the one which had blocked the bridge. It was a black Citroen DS 21. He dumped Strachey into the front passenger seat and went around to the driver's side and reached in and switched on the interior lights. A police radio crackled but said nothing except, by its very existence, that the man with the rifle must certainly have broadcast a report. Not three-hundred yards away, lights had come on in a farm-house. A dog was barking wildly and voices carried through the night. They had heard the crash and shots. Probably they had called the local *gendarmes*.

The nose of the wrecker was pointed at the canal, motor running. He couldn't leave it there as evidence that something had gone wrong. He released the hand-brake, slipped the gear-lever into first and watched it grind through the smashed rail and into the water and disappear. Then he got in the DS 21.

He started it up, put on the heater to warm Strachey and pulled away, turning off his headlights and driving half by night-sight and half by instinct, leaving the lights off until he was well away from the farm and had reached an intersection a mile beyond.

The radio spoke suddenly, impersonally, asking him what was happening. He answered. He said the hit was successful, the car was at the canal bottom and nobody had come up. He said some farmers had probably called the locals, and was told to leave the site and check in with Paris *Sûreté*. Others would take over now. He acknowledged, said he'd be about two hours at least; they had to drop off the wrecker and they needed coffee. He switched off and put his accelerator foot to the floor.

In a little more than thirty minutes he had joined the autoroute. It started to rain. He drove fast against the reflected glitter of oncoming headlights, concentrating on as high a speed as possible without arousing the autoroute police.

He thought about Margita Majerová. She was dead and he had once loved her and she had died loving him and had saved his life. Henry Jedder was dead, too, buried in a metal coffin in mud and weeds at the bottom of a French barge canal, and with him the dispatch-case of records damning Tricolor and Dallas Research, and the black notebook he'd taken from the desk which criminally indicted half the French Government.

He had failed. He had deluded himself in ever thinking he could succeed, and he had done so because over the years he had become an American and had lost the hardness of his youth and had found, in part with Juliet, a certain American

237

innocence that produced optimism and hope. It was good, that side of America, but it was threatened more and more by that other side, the dark side emerging in recent years, the terrible abuse of liberty in the name of liberty.

But Bejerec hadn't deluded himself. Not for an instant. Bejerec was French and as old and tired and cynical as Europe itself. He had known all along that they couldn't do it but was willing to try because he wanted above all to stick by his own to the very last. And had died because of it, probably knowing he would. That's what life had come to mean to him and that was another kind of love.

The windshield wipers played a rhythmical tattoo, the rain hissed up from the road. Oncoming headlights blazed, were engulfed by darkness, more endlessly followed.

Next to him Strachey stopped weeping and retched up water again. He'd be dry in an hour, Aaron thought. And before daylight would be in London and safe and he with him. Nobody would be looking for them now in Roissy; the forces there would be called off.

He explained what had happened and what they had to do. Strachey didn't answer. He just stared out at the darkness and rain and oncoming lights.

But shortly before they reached Charles de Gaulle airport, when the red approach beacons of its north runway became visible through the wet night, he finally spoke. Calmly and matter-of-factly.

'You realize, of course, that I can't go on with it. Even if we did have any evidence or witnesses. They killed my father, there's no one to look after my mother but me. Or my own family. You don't know what it was like, the way they killed him. Nobody could. Nobody could ever know.'

They were the first words he'd uttered since they left the bridge.

Aaron parked the car.

'As soon as I get back I shall resign my chairmanship of the Banking Committee,' Strachey said. 'That will clearly demonstrate to them my intent to be silent.'

Aaron realized dully that for a long time he hadn't really expected anything else.

238

Chapter Thirty-six

Spring the following year, as so often in Europe, was slow in arriving. April dragged by in bitter winds, snow flurries and icy downpours, but it was late May now and Louis Tattel stood bareheaded before the Relais Maritime enjoying the blessed warmth which had finally swept up from the south, bringing with it leaves to the chestnut trees of Paris and flowers to its beautiful parks and gardens.

It was a relief, also, to see the 'stake-out' gone. *Sûreté* had badgered him incessantly all winter; they'd twice had him down to the *Préfecture* for questioning, they'd tailed him night and day, they'd hounded his employees, they'd even threatened his hotel suppliers. They had decided he must know of Aaron Zeismann's whereabouts, and it was clear to Louis Tattel that whatever Aaron had been up to it was enough to make him wanted almost beyond reason. The old para often thanked God Aaron had never told him. It was also clear that the only thing protecting him from arrest, beating and probably torture was the blackmail he had on numerous police officials as well as the political strength he still enjoyed with fellow veterans of Algeria. Someone high up had finally decided he was less dangerous left well-enough alone.

What they had succeeded in doing, however, was to make it excessively difficult for him to provide Aaron, now that he had returned from America, with a new police identity, even though overnight Aaron had changed so shockingly as to be unrecognizeable, his hair turned white, his body nearly that of an old man.

Louis Tattel came back inside. It was nine in the morning; there were guests in the lobby going out for the day. He answered a question about Notre-Dame Cathedral, promised to arrange tickets for that evening's ballet at the Opéra, booked a table for the late show at the Lido and

239

gave the devil to a maid for forgetting a guest's breakfast.

Then he went into his inner sanctuary to change from his uniform into ordinary clothes. An hour later he had passed through the Porte de Bercy in south-east Paris and was on Route Nationale 5 amidst the heavy exodus of the great, lumbering trailer-trucks which had come to Paris in the pre-dawn to discharge their daily provincial cargo.

He was certain he wasn't followed. Even if he was, he reflected, they couldn't round up and interrogate an entire Arab shanty-town in the hopes of finding the one person he was visiting.

Perhaps, too, he thought, they would be busy with the students who, along with a few radical intellectuals who always caused trouble, were almost alone in protesting that the Americans were these days apparently able to dictate France's politics as well as control the nation's economy. It was ridiculous. No country, not even America, had that sort of power over another. Last week the students had rioted in Grenoble. This week they were once again pouring out of the Sorbonne and the Université de Paris to tear up paving-blocks the whole length of Boulevard St Michel. The Government had been obliged to reinforce the dread CRS riot police with a battalion of *gendarmerie* urgently rec-ruited from the provinces. The hospitals were full of chil-dren with cracked heads and lungs burning from tear-gas. It had to be what the papers claimed, Marxist-inspired. People said that's the way students always were; they were young and easily persuaded and always listened to the worst coun-sel. Life would quiet them down eventually, the unrelent-ing need to give up foolish ideals for daily bread. Life, after all, was the great leveller. It put every hot-head in his place.

The homes and shops by the roadside had become shabby, the scurf which clung to a big city's skirts, and then suddenly off to the right there was a choked-together mass of lean-to shacks mixed with scores of rusting old wartime corrugated-metal huts, a derelict protection against rain and snow put together by refugees with no money and no hope of ever having any. France had many such *bidonvilles* for those Arabs who had been loyal in Algeria.

Louis Tattel turned in and up a dirt street until it became impassable with rubble. He locked his car, and tucked a large heavily wrapped package under his arm. The air stank of human waste. A crowd of dirty, dark-skinned children came running. He pushed through them and went on foot another hundred yards to where the street ended at a crumbling wall which had once surrounded someone's country estate. Crushed against the wall was a one-room shack. It was ironic, Louis Tattel thought, that Aaron Zeismann had sought final refuge in the squalid roots of his childhood, as though denying that anything else had ever existed, that twenty years of prosperous and privileged American life had ever happened.

The children had disappeared, finding nothing of interest in a balding Frenchman. He rapped on the door of the shack. '*Alors, c'est moi.*'

There was a movement inside. The door, askew in its frame, was pushed open, splintered boards protesting. Aaron Zeismann appeared. Louis Tattel tried not to stare. If anything his friend's colour in the last week had become even more grey, his hair more white, the old scar across his cheek more pronounced and the gash in the corner of his eye now something that made you look away. Worse were his eyes themselves. They were without any expression, as though their owner lived somewhere deep in an untouchable world of his own.

The hotel-keeper held out the package. 'It's what you asked for.'

The other, with barely a glance, dropped it on to a bare wooden table in the small space behind him. It made a heavy, metallic sound.

'Do you have a cigarette?'

Tattel silently produced a yellowed *cigarette au balayeur*. His lighter flared. Acrid smoke drifted up.

'There's also a carton of Gauloise in the package,' the old para said. There was no answer. 'Look, it's not too late to get out,' he added. 'It never is. I can still arrange anything.'

Again there was no reply. Tattel wondered if Aaron had even heard. His mind was gone, he knew. It was what had happened to his wife. The story had come out, little by little, during his last several visits. It started, from what Tattel could gather, when Aaron had returned home to find her not there. Some black woman who worked for them said she had driven off only the day before with three men, apparently government officials of some sort. One was a tall, almost albino, executive-looking person.

They had told her, apparently, that her husband had been in a serious accident and that she was to be flown to Paris by the Air Force. She had quickly packed an overnight bag.

Aaron had looked desperately for her. It was not easy because he had had to keep under cover. His very life depended on it. Everyone else had looked for her, too. Her father had influence in Washington and her disappearance, while not headlines, was certainly news.

Then a week later they had found her, torn to pieces and nearly incinerated in a car-crash. She was identified by dental work. The official story was that she had skidded and smashed at high speed into the rebutment of a concrete underpass cutting beneath a north-south interstate in West Virginia. It was surmised that she had been escaping her kidnappers. Unofficially, everyone knew she'd been made an example of to help keep the Intelligence community on their toes.

One night, Louis Tattel remembered, Aaron had drunk a great deal and in his ravings had talked about some photographs mailed to him care of her father. He had broken completely and had tried to kill himself and only failed because he was too drunk and not alone. Tattel had never seen such black despair in any man.

'It's never too late,' he now said again. And when there was no reply he said, 'Aaron, we've been good friends for years. You won't prove anything by it.'

Aaron ignored it. 'Did you burr the identification?' he asked abruptly.

Tattel stared resignedly at the package on the table. 'Of course, and we found a manufacturer's part number on the trigger mechanism. We burred that, too.'

'Who made up the identity cards?'

Tattel mentioned a name. 'They are untraceable,' he added. Then he tried a last time. 'Aaron, you finish them and there are more where they came from. It's not "them" anyway. It's the system. Look at the students, getting their brains beaten out. And for what?' He took a breath and went on. 'I can still slip you out to Brazil. Or any place you might want to try.' He added with a wry smile. 'Even the US.'

It was a waste of breath and he knew it. It was just a formality he felt he had to go through. Let Aaron do what he wanted. Let the cocksuckers pay. Didn't the Bible say 'whatsoever a man soweth, that shall he also reap'? Those who would die weren't important. But his friend was, and what his friend might feel and need.

The man in the doorway took a final drag on the cigarette and crushed it out in the dirt. 'Have you heard of any change in official plans?'

The answer stuck in Louis Tattel's throat, perhaps because it underlined total inevitability. But if he lied Aaron would surely find out and he didn't want to add that betrayal, no matter how small, to everything else. 'No change,' he said.

He offered another cigarette. It was refused. It was time to go.

'*Alors, bonne chance*,' he said. His mouth felt dry and his chest tight and there was an unaccustomed sting behind his eyes. He'd felt that way once in Algeria when he knew he'd never see some of his men again.

They shook hands. Louis Tattel turned abruptly and walked off. Oh God, oh God, he thought, the years go by and the tree becomes more and more bare.

He only glanced back once, just before he got into his car.

Aaron Zeismann was still standing in the doorway of the shack. For a flickering moment when they'd said farewell his eyes had come to life and he had smiled faintly. There was

still that much contact between them. And between him and
reality.

But Tattel knew it would do no good to go back. He
started up his motor and drove down the littered dirt street
towards the highway to Paris.

Epilogue

Even after the most exhaustive investigation, the joint Assassination Committee, appointed by both governments and composed of an equal number of French and American experts, could find no conclusive indication of how security had been so effectively breached. They could only presume and indulge in conjecture.

The visit to France by the Chairman and several members of the Senate Foreign Relations Committee, along with the National Security Adviser, was to bolster solidarity between the two oldest allies in the West and to try to help quell the vicious rumours circulating Paris of unwarranted American interference in French economic affairs. It had been urgently arranged because in recent elections the Communists, taking advantage of the rumours and in spite of open rupture with the Socialists, had made sweeping gains all across the nation. A presidential visit was to follow at a later date.

Air Force Two arrived at Charles de Gaulle International Airport at Roissy on schedule at 1630 hours European Standard Time. The French First Minister as well as the Foreign Minister was on hand to greet the visitors. There was more than the usual welcoming ceremony. The French Government was anxious to impress. There was a Guard of Honour to inspect, television cameras and microphones to address and then the fast drive to Paris in a convoy of black limousines, escorted by a siren-screaming phalanx of smartly uniformed motorcycle *gendarmes*.

The Chairman and the First Minister rode in the lead car, the National Security Adviser and the French Foreign Minister in the second. The other American Senators, accompanied by the President of the French Senate, came next, followed by the Minister of the Interior with the American Ambassador. Lesser officials, some selected journalists and two cars of French and American Secret Service personnel, brought up the rear.

The Paris-Lille autoroute, serving the Charles de Gaulle airport, enters Paris proper at Porte de la Chapelle, a sprawling warehouse area of urban redevelopment. From there, the convoy swooped rapidly down past Montmartre and the Madeleine to Faubourg St Honòré and the presidential residence, the Palais de l'Elysée where, in keeping with the importance placed on the visit, the French President himself waited to give welcome.

In view of the political unrest in France, a force of nearly ten thousand had worked for weeks at security and the route had been thoroughly cleared. Armed police were stationed at every overpass, and on scores of roof-tops all along. Buildings had been inspected for snipers; police informers had been rigorously ordered to bring in any information no matter how insignificant which might give the remotest hint of trouble.

As with any foreign visit, one of the more difficult aspects was meshing the activities of the foreign security forces with those of the host nation. The Americans with their frightening history of political assassination were insistent on having near-veto power on virtually all French preparations. They were arrogant and showed little respect for French capabilities which were often in advance of their own. The French, on their part, were jealous and often deliberately obstructionist. Along the road, for example, they frequently refused to recognize American identification or to understand English which most of them knew reasonably well.

At the airport, and at the Palais de l'Elysée itself, things were at their most awkward. As officials got in and out of cars, both forces of protection came into actual close contact. Barely able to disguise their mutual hostility, French plain-clothesmen from the SDECE and from the *Deuxième Bureau* mingled with CIA agents attached to the American Embassy and with Secret Servicemen direct from Washington.

It was precisely this area of divisive weakness that the

assassin shrewdly chose to exploit. Using both CIA and Secret Service credentials which later were found impeccable, and with a clearly profound knowledge of the whole American security system, he easily persuaded the French of his American authenticity. Then, and with astonishing audacity, he made himself equally acceptable to the Americans as a Frenchman by showing equally *bona fide* French identification and equal knowledge of French security. The fact that he was fluently bilingual of course helped him immeasurably.

Thus, the investigating committee deduced, he was able actually to be standing and armed in the cobbled courtyard of the Palais de l'Elysée itself and not twenty-five feet from the front door where waited the President of France, flanked by two lines of ceremonial *Gardes Républicains* resplendent in their full-dress uniforms, their sabres raised to their epauletted shoulders in rigid attention. Ice-cool, he had been there the better part of an hour when the motor vehicle procession arrived and the first four cars pulled up.

As with many brilliant and carefully thought-out schemes, however, there was a specific weakness inherent in its very strength. Although at such a close range he could not miss he would, nevertheless, have very little time in which to act. Restaging the assassination later, the French determined that it required six seconds to pull the weapon, a Swiss machine-pistol, from beneath a light gabardine coat and to effectively aim and theoretically kill the people who had died.

Those six seconds were the precise time it took in the actual massacre for both French and American security agents to react, to draw aim that would not kill others and to destroy the assassin himself. The shots that first felled him came from a uniformed corporal of the *Gendarmerie Nationale*.

The assassin obviously had realized the time factor was the plan's weakness. There was great risk: not to himself, for his own death was, of course, the very suicidal core of his whole scheme. The risk was that he might not be able to achieve what he wanted to achieve, which was clearly the elimination of as many members of both governments as possible. As it turned out, his fears were not unfounded. Something occurred to cost him two precious seconds and to save several lives. It was something apparently quite unexpected by him, and his reaction to it was beyond the comprehension of the investigating Assassination Committee.

It happened as follows. The Chairman of the Senate Foreign Relations Committee was first out of the lead car, followed immediately by the French First Minister. They stood briefly getting their bearings and then walked up the three wide steps leading to the front door to shake hands with the President and to wait for the French Foreign Minister and the American National Security Adviser, already out of their car and about to follow. Meanwhile, the third and fourth cars bearing the other Senators, the French Minister of the Interior and the American Ambassador, had pulled up directly by the assassin and the occupants were also getting out. All three groups were thus for a few moments completely exposed and within virtually point-blank range. Outside of weapon failure nothing short of a miracle could have prevented the instant death of almost everyone.

But it was precisely then, just seconds before the hail of bullets would begin, that such a miracle happened. Because of it, a number of lives were spared.

The fifth car in the convoy had pulled up. Two men had come out of it. One was the French Minister of Finance. The other was later revealed as a former FBI counter-intelligence agent and currently a personal aide to the American Ambassador. He was a tall, well-tailored man whose very pale blondness bordered on albino and he had urgently insisted on entering the fifth car at the airport at the very last minute, although not originally scheduled even to go to the Palais de l'Elysée.

The assassin was in the very act of unmasking his machine-pistol when he spotted him. Whether he saw him as an instant threat to his plan, or was governed by some other more obscure motivation, was not subsequently determined. But he hesitated. And, according to testimony, for an estimated two precious seconds.

Two seconds when the entire scene seemed frozen in ghastly detail. Two seconds when the aide apparently recognized the assassin in spite of what later testimony revealed as the assassin's totally changed appearance since six months previously.

And two seconds when those uniformed police and plainclothesmen who had seen the machine-pistol appear finally realized that cold-blooded terrorism was in the very act of happening.

The Ambassador's aide died before he could utter a word or think to defend himself. Fire from the machine-pistol cut him nearly in half.

Then, still before anyone else could move, the assassin fired again, first one, short, impatient burst at the Minister of the Interior and the US Ambassador, and then, in the last two seconds left, at those gathered at the head of the steps with the President including the Adviser and the Foreign Minister.

It was too late.

The *gendarme* corporal's weapon saved five. The French President was to live with only a shattered shoulder and one finger blown away; the Adviser was to survive minus his lower jaw and with a bullet in his thigh which destroyed the femur and eventually cost him the leg; the American Ambassador with a bullet in the neck which was to make him a quadriplegic for life; the Minister of the Interior miraculously with only a grazed left arm; and the Chairman with nothing worse than the loss of one eye.

Three met death. The First Minister fell with a bullet in the brain, the Foreign Minister was to succumb three days later from stomach and chest wounds and an American Senator was struck twice in the heart.

The assassin died instantly. And then was nearly torn to shreds by subsequent fire from a score of weapons. In all he received eighty-seven hits, nine in the head, seventeen in his limbs, the remaining sixty-one in his torso.

Within hours he was identified by his finger-prints. The investigating committee, however, in probing his background, could find nothing, either in his impeccable Establishment life in Washington or in his apparently being a double-agent, that would give them hard evidence as to what had led him to mass murder. A psychiatrist appointed by the committee could only deduce that his wife's tragic death in a recent car accident had caused the total imbalance of his mind. Official statements, of course, insinuated that he was linked to the Communists.

When sealed records and the testimony of an obscure computer technician employed by the French SDECE revealed his identity as Aaron Zeismann to be false, it was impossible to determine his real name or origins or to know even the country of his birth. Thus, as a final postscript to the deception which for so many years had clearly been his very existence, the governments of both France and the United States refused to claim his remains.

After lying for six months at municipal expense in the refrigeration section of a Paris morgue this diplomatic impasse was resolved. The body was accepted by neutral Switzerland which, embarrassed by the Swiss manufacture of the assassination weapon and with professed shame as an excuse, sought, as it did on frequent occasions, to add a little lustre to its self-perpetuating image of magnanimity.

A memorial service and subsequent cremation were paid for by a dissident Left-wing youth group who saw an opportunity to protest against American imperialist designs abroad. The ashes were scattered in the River Rhône, perhaps, eventually, to find their way to that mother of all seas, the Mediterranean.

Except for a very brief notice in the *International Herald Tribune*, published daily in Paris, these observances went unnoticed by the rest of the world.

THE WORLD'S GREATEST THRILLER WRITERS
NOW AVAILABLE IN GRANADA PAPERBACKS

Gerald A Brown

11 Harrowhouse	£1.25	☐
Green Ice	£1.50	☐

Trevanian

The Loo Sanction	£1.50	☐
The Eiger Sanction	£1.50	☐
The Main	95p	☐
Shibumi	£1.95	☐

Alan Williams

The Widows War	95p	☐
Shah-Mak	95p	☐
Gentleman Traitor	£1.25	☐
The Beria Papers	75p	☐
Barbouze	£1.25	☐
Long Run South	85p	☐
Snake Water	£1.25	☐
The Purity League	85p	☐
The Tale of the Lazy Dog	85p	☐

THE WORLD'S GREATEST THRILLER WRITERS
NOW AVAILABLE IN GRANADA PAPERBACKS

Len Deighton

Twinkle, Twinkle, Little Spy	£1.50	☐
Yesterday's Spy	£1.50	☐
Spy Story	£1.50	☐
Horse Under Water	£1.50	☐
Billion Dollar Brain	£1.50	☐
The Ipcress File	£1.50	☐
An Expensive Place to Die	£1.50	☐
Declarations of War	£1.25	☐
Close-Up	£1.50	☐
SS-GB	£1.50	☐
XPD	£1.95	☐

Ted Allbeury

The Only Good German	85p	☐
Moscow Quadrille	75p	☐
The Man With the President's Mind	85p	☐
The Lantern Network	85p	☐
The Reaper	£1.25	☐
Consequence of Fear	£1.25	☐
The Twentieth Day of January	£1.25	☐

GF1681

THE BEST OF JAMES BOND NOW AVAILABLE IN TRIAD/GRANADA PAPERBACKS

Ian Fleming

Casino Royale	£1.25	☐
Live and Let Die	£1.25	☐
Diamonds are Forever	£1.25	☐
From Russia, With Love	£1.25	☐
Dr No	£1.25	☐
Goldfinger	£1.25	☐
For Your Eyes Only	£1.25	☐
Thunderball*	£1.25	☐
The Spy Who Loved Me	95p	☐
On Her Majesty's Secret Service	£1.25	☐
You Only Live Twice	95p	☐
The Man with the Golden Gun	£1.25	☐
Octopussy and the Living Daylights	£1.25	☐

Based on a screen treatment by Kevin McClory, Jack Whittingham and Ian Fleming

Christopher Wood (Film Tie-ins)

James Bond, The Spy Who Loved Me	85p	☐
James Bond and Moonraker	85p	☐

TF581

THE WORLD'S GREATEST THRILLER WRITERS
NOW AVAILABLE IN GRANADA PAPERBACKS

Robert Ludlum

The Chancellor Manuscript	£1.95	☐
The Gemini Contenders	£1.95	☐
The Rhinemann Exchange	£1.95	☐
The Matlock Paper	£1.50	☐
The Osterman Weekend	£1.50	☐
The Scarlatti Inheritance	£1.50	☐
The Holcroft Covenant	£1.95	☐
The Matarese Circle	£1.95	☐
The Bourne Identity	£1.95	☐

Lawrence Sanders

The Second Deadly Sin	£1.25	☐
The Sixth Commandment	£1.95	☐
The Anderson Tapes	95p	☐
The Tangent Objective	80p	☐
The Tangent Factor	£1.25	☐

GF1881

BESTSELLERS AVAILABLE IN GRANADA PAPERBACKS

Leslie Waller

Trocadero	£1.25	☐
The Swiss Account	£1.95	☐
Number One	85p	☐
A Change in the Wind	40p	☐
The American	75p	☐
The Family	£1.25	☐
The Banker	£2.25	☐
The Brave and the Free	£1.95	☐

Peter Lear

Golden Girl	£1.50	☐

Calder Willingham

Natural Child	95p	☐
The Big Nickel	£1.25	☐
End as a Man	£1.25	☐
Eternal Fire	£1.50	☐
Providence Island	£1.50	☐

All these books are available at your local bookshop or newsagent, or can be ordered direct from the publisher. Just tick the titles you want and fill in the form below.

Name _____

Address _____

_____

Write to Granada Cash Sales
PO Box 11, Falmouth, Cornwall TR10 9EN.

Please enclose remittance to the value of the cover price plus:

UK 45p for the first book, 20p for the second book plus 14p per copy for each additional book ordered to a maximum charge of £1.63.

BFPO and Eire 45p for the first book, 20p for the second book plus 14p per copy for the next 7 books, thereafter 8p per book.

Overseas 75p for the first book and 21p for each additional book.

Granada Publishing reserve the right to show new retail prices on covers, which may differ from those previously advertised in the text or elsewhere.

GF1581